PIGEON

pigeon

A novel.

PRES MAXSON

© 2017 Pres Maxson. All rights reserved.
ISBN: 9781522058595

For Mollie, Cece, Josie, and George

"Pigeons have no purpose."

-Napoleon Bonaparte, June, 1805, famously (and incorrectly) to the sister-in-law of the Prussian Ambassador to France, for whom he had a well-documented affection despite her rabies of the brain and on-again, off-again inability to pronounce the letter "o," just before the two locked horns in a game of Yahtzee, in which Nancy (her nickname) would be unjustly accused of cheating, and would ultimately but unrelatedly end with her death at the hands of God, a sacrilegiously named and recently escaped walrus from a nearby marine-life circus.

Chapter I.

The pigeon stared back at the busboy. Raindrops scurried their way down the awning above and hurled themselves onto the sidewalks of Montmartre. Wet footprints freckled the café table around the bird.

Luc Martin always placed the salt and pepper shakers side by side. He stacked exactly six cubes of sugar in their tiny bowl, which he left off center on the table. And following almost every table he bussed, Luc washed his hands.

And this pigeon didn't care about any of it. Luc could tell from the look in the creature's eye that it was an agent of chaos. And it was Luc's fear of that entity—chaos—that would keep the young man working in his parents' café every morning, seemingly for the rest of his life.

Luc Martin adjusted his black-rimmed glasses. "Shoo." He leaned in and swatted. The pigeon didn't flinch. The busboy got a little closer. "Shoo!"

The bird flew off. Luc felt the mist from the flapping wings. Bird wing germ mist. His apron took the worst of it, but he felt the cool wetness on his face, hands, and arms.

Luc re-entered the café, very aware of the viruses that surely covered him. He wiped his glasses on the underside of his apron as he walked. The room was almost empty. The busboy passed the only patron at a table as he headed to the kitchen to clean up.

"Bet you weren't counting on the bird to be part of this," the man said.

2

"Um…" Luc answered. "I'm sorry?"

"The pigeon. Chasing him away. I bet that wasn't what you were expecting when you agreed to meet me here to talk about the job." The man's teeth clenched between sentences, and Luc could see his jaw muscles flex. The man inched his fedora on the table with an index finger as he reached for his drink.

"I'm sorry. I have no idea what you're talking about," Luc said.

The older man made his eyes thin. "The baker makes three."

"I'm sorry, what?"

The man cleared his throat and stroked the lapels on his grey suit. "The baker makes three."

"What are you talking about? This… this is a café."

"Thank you. That's the response I was looking for," the man answered, sitting back. "Please. Have a seat. Join me."

"Wait…what?" Luc answered.

"It's our organization's secret identification haiku."

"I must have missed something. What haiku?"

"The ba-ker makes three/what are you talk-ing a-bout?/This is a ca-fé. It's our call-and-response code. It's okay. You can drop the act now. You got it right. I know it's you." The man loosened his tie.

"Um…" Luc counted the words on his fingers as rain sounds outside intensified.

"I have to hand it to you," the man said. "Posing as a busboy just to remain anonymous for our meeting? That's genius."

Luc looked around. They were still alone. "I really am the busboy."

"They told me you'd say that. You come highly recommended. President Cravenmoore believes you're the only man for the job."

"You really must have me mistaken for someone else," Luc stuttered. "I... I do just work here."

The man scrutinized Luc's face. "You are good. No one would know that you're the greatest detective of all time."

Luc's eyes widened. "I'm not."

The man looked from the small hexagonal floor tiles to the wooden ceiling fans. "Nice place you've picked here, detective. The fact that you'd choose this particular café, on this day, at this precise time—is very telling about your character. The irony is palpable."

"Irony?"

"At least it demonstrates a sense of humor—and a razor-sharp intellect, I imagine."

"Um... okay?"

"You need a drink? I ordered two in case you wanted one."

Luc saw an untouched whiskey sour sitting on the table across from the man. "I'm sorry. I'm pretty sure you're looking for someone else."

"Please. You are a little younger than I imagined, but there's no mistaking someone with your gifts."

"My gifts?"

"I was told that you don't show up for meetings half

4

the time. I feel lucky that you're even here."

Luc looked around. No one else sat in the café—let alone anyone who looked like he or she could be the greatest detective of all time. Through the small window on the kitchen door, the busboy noticed his father in his cook's uniform, using his reflection in a spoon to check his teeth. Luc did not suspect that his father might have been leading a double life as a detective.

"Tell me something," the stranger continued. "Is it true that you are the one who solved the Trujillo case?"

"No. I don't even know what that is," Luc answered.

"Hmm." The man nodded. "Client confidentiality. My boss will love that."

"Look, I don't know anything about—"

"I bet you're also the type of person that will do anything to get a witness to talk."

"I am *not* that type of person," Luc laughed.

"You seem like the kind of man who would jump up and down on someone's heart just to get them to talk."

"That's a rather specific idea."

"And I bet you're incredible at it," the man said, folding his napkin repeatedly.

"Oh no, I could never—"

"You are so obviously ruthless."

Luc shook his head. "Is there anything I can get for you? Maybe I can go get your server?" Luc asked.

"No timid man would do the kind of work that you do," the man continued. "Tell me about your last investigation. Was it a head of state? A celebrity maybe? A footballer in over his head with a gambling ring?"

Luc wondered why his parents let crazy people into the café. The busboy took a step toward the kitchen. "I just remembered that I have to go to this thing right now."

"Never mind. On to business," the man stated.

"Listen, I really think—"

"Sit down. I'm sorry if I was forward."

The man pushed an empty chair toward Luc with his foot. The busboy didn't move.

"Sometimes I get caught up with the past. I realize you are probably not able to discuss prior jobs. I'm sorry. Anyway, Here's the address." The man pulled a business card from the inside of his suit coat. "Please come at your earliest convenience." He extended the card to Luc between two fingers.

With a look of skepticism, Luc took it. "Maurice de Mouton," he read aloud. "That's you?"

"Yes, but the address on the card. That's the important part."

"171 Rue des Bananes, Paris," Luc read. "Is this your house?"

"Of course not. It's our headquarters."

"Headquarters for what?"

"I would never speak of it around all these plebeians."

Luc looked around. The café still sat empty.

"We'll fill you in on all the details of the case when you arrive," Maurice de Mouton continued.

"The case?"

"Of course. I know you've been informed at least a little. But, there's more to the story. And don't forget your white pants."

"White pants? Why?" Luc asked.

The man straightened. His nose twitched. "There's a strict 'white pants only' policy."

"I don't own any white pants."

De Mouton exhaled and place both hands on the table. "It's the most closely-held tradition of our organization. White pants are worn and celebrated at all times."

"Celebrated?" Luc asked.

"What's your rate?" the man continued.

"My rate?"

"Two million? Two million-five?" De Mouton guessed.

Luc choked on his own breath. His adrenaline surged. This man must be *really* crazy. The busboy knew he would have to play along to be left alone.

"Uh yes," he stammered, rolling his eyes. "I'll do it. I'm definitely the greatest detective of all time. Two million will be fine."

"Great!" Maurice de Mouton pulled a few euros from his suit pocket and threw them on the table. He put on his hat as he stood. "Remember—white pants, please."

"Definitely. White pants, all the way," Luc lied.

"Excellent. Thank you. Please come as soon as you can."

"You got it," Luc answered, watching the man go.

Before he reached the sidewalk, Maurice de Mouton

turned toward Luc. "I know you prefer to remain anonymous, so I will simply say, 'farewell sir.'"

"See you later," Luc lied before tucking the man's card into his apron pocket. The busboy couldn't take him seriously, but the encounter made Luc forget that he was covered in bird wing germ mist.

* * *

Luc's small attic apartment sat in the same block as his parent's café. The space was much wider than it was deep and would have seemed a lot larger if the ceiling opposite the door didn't slice through the room, angled with the rooftop.

A familiar and revolting smell greeted him upon arrival. Wet fowl. Luc placed his keys and wallet in a neat pile on the small table by the door. He hung his apron in its spot on a hook next to an umbrella and a windbreaker. Then, the busboy made his way to the kitchen—only to find another pigeon. It stood on his table in front of an open window.

"I hate pigeons," Luc whispered to himself.

The bird picked at the morning's bread. Luc reached for a can of disinfectant spray and some paper towels.

"You know, you don't have to do that," Charlie said from the doorway. Luc's roommate was a lanky young black man. He held a beer in one hand and cradled two identical open boxes of crackers in the crux of his other arm. His t-shirt read, "MERDE!"

"Do what?" Luc asked.

"Clean."

"Why not?"

"The pigeon would eat it all if you'd let him."

The bird seemed to nod in agreement.

"Why would we let a pigeon stay in our kitchen and eat the bread?" Luc asked. He noticed some of Charlie's cracker crumbs fall to the tiled floor.

"Because the bread is stale," Charlie answered with crackers in his mouth.

"But he's making a mess," Luc stated. "Think of the disease he carries."

"He's fine," Charlie answered without care.

"But we'll wind up with pigeon spit all over our table."

"I think we already have pigeon spit all over our table."

"Yeah, I guess. Shoo!" Luc swatted at the bird. The pigeon flapped its way to the top of the refrigerator. Luc cowered. Several feathers hung in the grey light, defying gravity.

Charlie turned on the kitchen light. As soon as he did, the space looked warmer on the rainy afternoon. The table took up most of the space despite the fact it was only large enough to sit three people—two comfortably.

"How was work today?" Charlie asked.

"Fine. Some crazy guy offered me 2 million euros," Luc said as he started cleaning the table.

"Whoa. Like as a tip?"

"No, it was more like a job offer."

"To do what?" Charlie asked.

"Don't worry. He was crazy. It wasn't real."

"I imagine you'll get a few of those every now and then, huh?"

"I guess."

"How's it going with Janet?" Charlie asked. The young man shuffled the cracker crumbs on the floor with his foot.

"We broke up. Why is the window open?" Luc said without looking up. The busboy squatted to get a low look across the kitchen table.

"You did? That's great!"

"You knew it was coming," Luc said.

"But still, cheers to you. This is big news!" Charlie exclaimed.

"Why?"

"She was your first girlfriend."

Luc grimaced. "Don't put it like that."

"Why? It's true, right?"

"I guess." Luc corralled crumbs from the table.

"Good for you, then," Charlie said. "Why are you upset? You didn't even like her."

"I know. And I'm not upset. But when you put it like that, you're just reminding me that I'm 26 and have never had a girlfriend before."

"I'm proud of you." Charlie sipped his drink. "Of course, as you know, I have had many."

"Right. I know. So why is the window open?" Luc asked again.

"You didn't want her as something long-term,

anyway. She was pretty bossy. Even bossed me around and I was just your roommate."

"Well, I told you, she has 17 little brothers."

"Oh, right. She's used to just bossing people around then, huh?"

"Must be. Now, answer me." Luc stopped scrubbing and looked at his roommate. "Why is the window open?"

"I left it open. Sorry."

"How long was it in here?"

"What?"

"The pigeon."

"I don't know," Charlie shrugged. "I saw him near the sink after lunch."

Luc furled his brow. "The pigeon was in here all afternoon?"

"I don't know, maybe he came and left a few times. I'm not his babysitter."

The soft tapping of the bird's toe on the refrigerator sounded like the slow ticking of a bomb in Luc's brain. "But you knew about it, and you didn't close the window?"

"I like the breeze."

"You have to be kidding me," Luc sighed. He began scrubbing again.

Charlie fell into a kitchen chair. "You want to go out tonight and meet some girls?"

"No. Not yet."

"But, this is so great. You have experience now. They'll all like you."

"I have to work the breakfast shift tomorrow

morning."

"Girls are always more attracted to guys with experience," Charlie said as he crammed several crackers into his mouth at once.

"You keep saying that."

"Well, I should know," Charlie answered as he tried to chew the mass.

"I told you I have the early shift tomorrow," Luc said.

"Call in sick. I'm sure your folks will understand."

"That's not how it works."

"Why not?" Charlie swallowed without thoroughly chewing the crackers. Many crumbs lingered on his shirt.

"If you had a job, you'd get it," Luc answered. The busboy threw away a handful of paper towels he'd been using to clean up after the bird. It dawned on him that he disliked bussing café tables for a living, and there he was bussing his own kitchen table. He opted against complaining to Charlie about it. Luc reached for more paper towels.

"But you work for your parents," Charlie said. "They don't let you call in sick?"

"They do when I'm actually sick."

"I bet they would let you off work if they knew you'd just had your first breakup."

Luc chuckled as he sprayed disinfectant on the table. "They'd probably have a heart attack if they even knew I had a girlfriend in the first place, let alone broke up with one."

"Well," Charlie said, "let me get you a beer now to celebrate anyway." He placed his two cracker boxes on the table. One fell over, spilling more crumbs on the table as he moved towards the fridge.

"Wait! The bird!" Luc warned.

"Relax, he's fine."

"Don't go too close to it."

"Calm down, I'm just getting a beer." Charlie swung the refrigerator door open. The bottles clinked against one another as he pulled one out. Luc's roommate pulled out a second and waved it in his direction.

"I said I don't need one. I'm going to find a way to chase the bird out first. Then I want to relax for a bit," Luc answered.

"Richard wants you to have a beer," Charlie coaxed.

"Who's Richard?"

"The pigeon."

Luc's shoulders dropped. "You named him?"

Charlie popped his beer, smiling.

"Why did you name the pigeon?" Luc continued.

"I don't know. He was in the living room earlier. We became friends. It just happened."

"He was in the living room?!" Luc pictured all the pigeon germs in the apartment. The couch cushions. His own pillow. Every coffee mug on the shelf. His toothbrush. Was anything safe?

"You've got to relax about this stuff, my friend," Charlie urged with a deep swig.

Luc thought he heard the bird make a laughing sound.

"How'd she take it?" Charlie continued.

"Who? Janet?"

"Obviously."

"She seemed fine," Luc answered with a sigh. *Just try and forget about the bird*, the busboy thought.

"Oh no," Charlie sighed.

"What?"

"I see what happened." Luc's roommate took another drink as he slumped back into his kitchen chair.

"What happened?"

"I bet she doesn't know you dumped her."

"What do you mean?" Luc asked.

"I bet you were same old, nice guy Luc."

The busboy shrugged. "I didn't want to be a jerk."

"I bet she didn't even realize that you broke up with her. Am I right?"

Luc paused, trying to remember the exact tone of the conversation. "I'm sure she did."

"I knew it." Charlie shook his head. "You know, one of these days, you are going to have to hurt someone's feelings."

"Why would I want to hurt someone's feelings?" Luc asked as he continued cleaning.

"I mean, you're going to have to do something for yourself. Not get pushed around. Say something that is good for you, even if it's something that someone else doesn't want to hear."

Luc didn't answer.

"Look, I get it. You're not a risk taker," Charlie said as he peeled the label off his beer bottle. "You do what's comfortable. Well, one of these days, you're going to have to do something that's not comfortable. Like breaking up with someone."

"I did break up with someone. I broke up with Janet."

"It doesn't count if she doesn't know."

"I'm sure she knows."

Charlie raised his eyebrows. His forehead wrinkled. "Really? Because the Janet *I know* wouldn't have been cool with it. She probably would have thrown something. She is crazy, man."

Luc ignored him and tried to focus on his scrubbing.

"That's what I thought," Charlie continued. "I'm just saying, you're going to have to get uncomfortable someday."

"I'm cleaning the kitchen right now. That's not comfortable."

"You know what I mean. Are you ready for that beer?"

"Why is that bird still in here?" Luc nodded toward the top of the fridge. "Can you get him out, please?"

"You know how you could start?" Charlie was ignoring his roommate. "Take a small risk on something, my friend. Anything."

Luc huffed as hard as he could. "This speech is getting old."

"I'm just saying. Working in that damp little café would kill me."

"Working at all might kill you."

"I'm just saying that you're wasting this moment by cleaning up after Richard," Charlie said.

"Stop calling him that."

Luc thought he heard the pigeon grunt.

"You're a free man," Charlie said. "Do something crazy. Take a weekend. Get on a train and just go. Have no plan. Get off in some town that you've never been to, and get really drunk."

"I usually have to work the weekends."

"Stop it. You're thinking too practically," Charlie said.

"Where would I stay?" Luc asked without looking up.

"Doesn't matter. You'll figure it out."

"I'm not doing that."

"Of course not," Charlie said, sitting back in his chair. Luc thought his roommate was finally resigning from the conversation, before Charlie shot upright again. "Wait. Better yet. Take that 2-million-euro job from the crazy guy. Just see where it goes."

Luc laughed. "I did take his card. He told me to go to an address." He wasn't seriously considering the idea.

"Yes! That's what I'm talking about. You should do it."

"He was a crazy person. I'm not doing it."

"Who cares if he was crazy?" Charlie said. "You aren't getting the two million. That's obvious. But that's not what this is about. It's about having an adventure."

"Look," Luc sighed as he threw away another handful of paper towels. "I like things the way I like them. Stop making me feel bad about it. I'm not you."

"That's true. We're different. I have one more pigeon friend than you," Charlie answered.

Chapter II.

The next morning, Luc's toes pressed against the inside of the front of his shoes with every step as he carried dirty dishes to the kitchen. Hot water reddened his hands with every return trip to the washbasin. The inside upper corners of his glasses turned steamy as his forehead got hotter with every step. The place was crowded.

His parents' café was wedged into its block in Montmartre. Its sides were smashed together by thin buildings on a slanted street. Tiny cars rested bumper to bumper along the curb, tilting down, stressing their parking brakes.

"You're dragging, Luc."

"Sorry."

"Don't forget, our customers like smiles," Luc's mother reminded him between breaths. She was a small, plump woman about her son's height. Wiry dark hair twisted into a bun like a tornado with nowhere to go.

"It's like I always say," she continued, "a smile goes a mile."

Luc carried a half-eaten crepe to the kitchen. Part of it touched his finger. The busboy's stomach turned.

"Remember, Luc. Smiles!"

"Right." Luc forced one.

The busboy unloaded the dishes. He turned to walk back to the front of house, but his mother blocked his path.

"My baby. What's wrong?"

"Nothing, why?" Luc answered.

His mother grabbed his apron and pulled it tight. She ran her hand across the crease, trying to flatten it. "Something's on your mind."

"It's fine, Mom," Luc answered, glancing at his watch. It was only 8:50 a.m.

"Luc. I hate to see my baby boy in pain."

"What? I'm not in pain. Why would you think I'm in pain?"

Luc's mother wrung her hands as if she was worried about something. Luc recognized her tell. It was his mother's subconscious way of indicating she had a secret—and she just had to tell it. "Charlie dropped in last night," she said.

"Oh no."

"And he said, you have a little girlfriend."

Hearing his mother say the word 'girlfriend' sounded strange to Luc. She never talked to him about girls.

"No, Mom," Luc said, shaking his head.

"And he said maybe things weren't going so well." The woman bit her lip as if she were dreading Luc's reaction to the idea.

"God, no. Please Mom. I just want to go bus a table."

"Did she break your heart?"

Luc avoided eye contact with his mother. "This is so embarrassing."

"Come here. You need a hug."

"No, mom. I'm really fine. I *had* a girlfriend—"

"Yes, Janet," Madame Martin interjected as she reached for her son's shoulders.

Luc tilted away from the approaching woman and rolled his eyes. He couldn't believe Charlie told his parents. "Yes. Janet. That is her name."

"Yes. I know, honey."

"Anyway, we broke up. Rather, I broke up with her."

"Are you sure?" The busboy's mother asked.

"God! Yes Mom! Whatever Charlie said… just don't listen to him, okay?"

"Okay, as long as you're happy, dear."

"I'm happy." Luc took a step, but his foot stopped short on the ceramic kitchen floor tile. His mother still blocked his path.

"Good. Because I'm always here for you," she said.

"I know."

"Good."

"May I go now?" Luc asked, finally looking the woman in the eye.

"Are you sure you don't need a break, Luc?" his mother asked.

"No, why?"

"It's just that Charlie said you might need a weekend off to get on a train or something? I'm not sure. He wasn't clear about it. He may have had a few beers."

"I promise you he did, and no, don't worry about it."

"Okay. If you had something planned, just let us know. We rely on you around here."

"Yes, I know."

"Good." Luc's mother tried one last time to smooth out the crease on her son's apron. Her face brightened with another thought.

"Also," she continued. "Charlie introduced me to your new pet."

"What?"

"The pigeon."

Luc threw his head back in disbelief. "Oh no. He's not a pet."

"It was sitting on his shoulder."

"It was?" Luc asked, shaking his head. "Of course, it was."

"C'mon, Luc. I think it's nice. Just don't bring any of those bird germs in here."

"This whole conversation is my nightmare. May I go?" Luc felt the sudden urge to go wash his hands again.

"Hey," Luc's father said as he passed. "Could you give me a hand with a table out here?"

"Go help your father."

Luc shuffled after his dad, into the noise and urgency of the dining room. The busboy felt Maurice de Mouton's card, still in his apron pocket.

*   *   *

Thick ivy made 171 Rue des Bananes in Montmartre look like the building was one big square bush. Each dark window peered through the plant life. Luc wondered if the crazy man from the café had led him to an abandoned building. *Did he invite me here to kill me?* Luc wondered. His palms started to feel clammy.

For a moment, another reality occurred to the busboy. What if the offer had been legitimate? The busboy was struck by fear that he might actually have to pretend to be a detective. He knew he wanted adventure, but was this the right way to do it? Pretending to be someone else is always a bad idea—let alone someone like the greatest detective of all time, which Luc was very far from being.

Luc was about to turn around when he thought of Charlie. He had nothing to prove to his roommate, but he also didn't want to be accused of not being a risk taker. The busboy envied his roommate's ability to try exciting new things.

The callbox chirped to life. Luc hadn't even decided to knock.

"May I help you?" it crackled.

"Uh... yes...no...I don't know. I'm sorry, I was just passing..."

"Please identify yourself, visitor," the voice said.

"I'm...well...funny story... I was in a café yesterday, and someone started talking to me. He gave me this address. I...I..." Luc's voice cracked. "I...I'm the greatest detective of all time." It sounded stupid when he said it out loud.

Silence.

What a mistake, he thought. *Who would open the door for an introduction like that?*

"Hello?" Luc asked. "I'm going to go ahead and go..."

"Please come in."

The door opened, and a scowling elderly man stood hunched before the busboy. He scrutinized Luc before saying, "The President has been expecting you."

Luc walked by the heavy, slow wooden door. The man put all his weight into closing it. Low light from ancient-looking sconces kept the small foyer mostly dark. The busboy needed a moment for his eyes to adjust. Another ornate door stood opposite Luc.

"What is this place?" Luc asked the man.

"You're not wearing white pants," the little man grunted as he shuffled by Luc.

"I'm sorry. I forgot."

"The President isn't going to like this."

"I'm sorry," Luc apologized again.

"I don't really like it either."

"Okay, sorry."

The man turned to face him. "Do you have a coat to check?"

"I don't." Luc thought that was obvious.

"Follow me." The little man opened the other door and led the busboy into a bright hallway. Luc squinted.

Floor-to-ceiling windows stood tall before him. On the other side of them, a large courtyard with a greener-than-green lawn glowed. Luc would never have guessed it was there based on the building's exterior.

The illusion was staggering for Luc, who observed several figures—all wearing white pants—milling about on the lawn, some leaning on large mallets as they conversed. Balls of all sizes were strewn on the short grass across the entire space like a model solar system. One majestic white horse stood grazing in the middle of it all.

"The President's office is right over here," the small

old man said.

The hallway itself was adorned with paintings, some of historic wars and some of nudes, but mostly historic wars being fought entirely by nudes. Luc's feet sank into the red plush carpet with every step.

"Right this way," the little man said as he opened a door a few feet from the entrance. Luc's heart pounded so hard that his shirt moved a little bit. He put his hand on his chest, hoping to calm it.

The President's office was almost as dark as the entryway had been. Luc needed another moment to let his eyes adjust. Each wall of the narrow room was lined with books. He recognized Maurice de Mouton lurking in a corner. A tall man in his sixties with bright white hair rose from a desk at the far end of the room.

"Oh! Welcome! I'm so glad you came, detective! Please have a seat."

"Thank you."

The President looked at the little elderly man. "Thank you, Coat-check Carl."

"He's not wearing white pants," the little man grunted as he backed out of the room and shut the door. The President ignored him.

"You are a little younger than I pictured," the President said. "De Mouton was correct."

"Okay." Luc answered, his voice almost shaking with nerves.

The look on the President's face turned grim, almost dire. "I see that you aren't wearing white pants." For the first time, Luc was worried about his brown corduroys.

"No, I'm sorry."

"So be it. In the future, please respect our tradition. It is sacred."

"I will, sorry."

The President's tone and look eased again as he fell into a big leather chair behind the desk. "Please, have a seat!"

Luc lowered himself into a small chair opposite the President, but he had trouble resting all his weight on the seat.

"Let me begin by introducing myself. I'm Keveen Cravenmoore, and I'm the President of the Paris Publique Plouquette Pitch, Grounds, Gardens, Grass Court, and Lawn Club."

"I'm sorry, the what?"

"I know it's a mouthful. You may just call it the PPPPGGGCLC for short."

"I'm sorry?"

"The Paris Publique Plouquette Pitch, Grounds, Garden, Grass Court, and Lawn Club. We call it the PPPPGGGCLC."

Luc was sure his palms would start to drip sweat at any moment. He tried to swallow, but his dry mouth and tight throat wouldn't let him.

"What is plouquette?" The busboy managed.

"Right. Good question. Plouquette is the sport of elite society. Our club members are the most wealthy and powerful citizens of Paris. Kings have played it. Movie stars. Business tycoons. Unfortunately, my ex-wife." Cravenmoore winked at Maurice and they laughed. "Just a small joke around here."

"Oh, okay."

"It was a long time ago. I'm only kidding. Where was I?"

"You were talking about plouquette. I've never heard of it."

"Well, it's so elite, most people have not." Cravenmoore leaned back in his chair.

"Oh, okay," Luc answered.

"And this club is one of the oldest in the city to play."

"There are others?" Luc scratched his knee.

"Of course. But we don't have to talk about those jackals."

"Sure," Luc agreed, trying to breath normally.

"And you've already met our Sergeant-at-Arms, Maurice de Mouton. He's my right-hand man."

"Yes," Luc said.

De Mouton stepped out of the shadows long enough to nod.

"Before we continue," Cravenmoore added, "I must fill you in on a little history. I've been the President of this club ever since my grandfather abdicated the position due to an unhealthy number of open sores on his body, mostly due to complications with the flu and a series of crow attacks. As President, it's my job to keep everyone happy around here, which is why all those years ago, my first act in office was to put moon pies in all the vending machines. It was a popular move that still defines my legacy." Cravenmoore ran his fingers along the hair behind his ears and picked at the edge of one nostril. He took a deep, satisfied breath. "Anyway, enough about me. I must thank you for taking the time to meet with us."

"Sure."

"You come highly recommended. Your credentials are impeccable, and your reputation precedes you."

Luc shifted and winced.

"The case we have for you," Cravenmoore continued, "begins 22 years ago with the tournament for the Waterford Cup."

"What's the Waterford Cup?" Luc asked.

"The Sir Larabee Waterford Cup is the most celebrated trophy in all of plouquette. At least, it was, until 22 years ago."

"Who was Sir Larabee Waterford? Was he a great player? Or the founder of the club?"

"No, he was the President and Founder of Sir Larabee Waterford Fountain Pens and Ashtrays. Back in the 1880s, they made the finest pens available. Their ashtrays were pedestrian at best, though."

"I've never heard of them."

"Well, they have a very elite clientele, and they were our sponsor for the Waterford Cup—that is, until 22 years ago."

"What happened 22 years ago?" Luc asked.

"Well, you've already heard most of the story, or you wouldn't be sitting here. Let me pick up with this week—"

"No," Luc interrupted in his best greatest-detective-of-all-time voice. "Go ahead and tell me everything. Don't leave anything out." The busboy felt a rush of adrenaline as he spoke. He couldn't believe he was actually doing it.

"I like your style. Thorough," the President said.

De Mouton interjected, "He's the kind of man who would probably stand on someone's heart with both feet and jump up and down just to get them to talk."

"Good for him." The President nodded with approval. "Anyway, 22 years ago, we had a club member named Dorian Thibault. He was young, about your age. And he was truly the best plouquette player we'd ever seen—or so we thought."

"He never lost even the most casual of matches," de Mouton added.

"Maurice! I'm telling it!" Cravenmoore snapped.

De Mouton sank back into the dim shadows near the President's bookcase. President Cravenmoore smoothed his lapels as he regained his composure.

"Did you know, that this desk was built from the oldest known tree on the planet?" Cravenmoore said as he rapped on the wood.

"No," Luc answered.

"It was cut down in 1910 just to construct this beauty. A former President had it commissioned, demonstrating this club's dedication to killing beautiful things as long as it leads to something even more beautiful."

"Someone cut down the oldest tree in the world just to make a desk?" Luc asked.

"Correct," Cravenmoore confirmed with a satisfied smile.

"That's horrible."

"Anyway, Dorian Thibault had never lost a plouquette match. He was simply the best we'd ever seen."

Although he was appalled by the President's anecdote about the desk, Luc decided to forget about it for now.

"What's the idea behind plouquette? How do you play?" The busboy asked.

Cravenmoore laughed. "Never mind the details there. Anyway, Thibault was on top of the world. Everyone around here loved him. Especially the girls. Only one problem: he was a cheater."

The President dropped his head in disappointment as if he were hearing his own story for the first time.

"He'd had us fooled," Cravenmoore continued. "He knew everything. He knew trick shots. He never missed a long ball. His stroke was unbelievable. The Waterford Cup tournament 22 years ago was his first big event, and he waltzed his way to the championship round."

"It wasn't even a contest," de Mouton added.

"Once on the big stage," Cravenmoore continued, grimacing at the interruption," he recorded the final points with such precision and authority, that we didn't believe anyone would ever be able to beat him as long as he was alive."

"But he was a crook," de Mouton interjected.

"He sure was. A dirty thief. And we caught him red-handed."

"What happened?" Luc asked.

"He'd won the Sir Larabee Waterford Cup, but only a

day or so later, our equipment manager at the time discovered he'd been greasing his balls."

De Mouton shook his head in disgust.

"Is that bad?" Luc asked.

"It's heinous," Cravenmoore said.

"So, greasing balls gives you an advantage in plouquette?" Luc asked.

"Obviously, yes."

"I don't think I have a clear idea for how greasy balls would help someone win at plouquette." Luc paused as he thought for a moment. "I guess my problem is that I don't really understand at all how to play plouquette in the first place."

"Don't worry about that," the President assured him again.

"I saw people with mallets out in the courtyard," Luc offered. "Does greasing the ball change how it moves through the grass? Or how the mallet hits the ball? Puts a spin on it or something?"

The President grinned at his sergeant-at-arms.

"He thinks the mallet is for hitting the ball," de Mouton mumbled between quiet giggles.

"Well, to be fair," the President answered, "the mallet *can* be used for hitting the ball. Technically speaking."

"I'm sorry," Luc interrupted. "I still don't understand."

"My dear friend," Cravenmoore said. "You're getting mired in the smallest of details. Where was I?"

"I have no idea," Luc gave up on plouquette for the

moment.

"Ah yes. I remember. So, after the great ball-greasing discovery, we knew we needed to take action. We immediately banned Dorian Thibault. We took his front-door keys, and told him never to return. Then, we retroactively awarded the second-place player with the trophy. That was Yelly Reardon."

"Ah, poor Yelly," de Mouton whispered, shaking his head.

"That's right," President Cravenmoore nodded. "Poor Yelly."

"Why 'poor Yelly'?" Luc asked.

"Yelly has been more devoted to plouquette than anyone I know," the President answered. "He is out there day in and day out. I've seen him trying to perfect the impossibly-majestic-high-arc-rainbow-hammer-mallet throw. He's been working on it for years."

"What's the impossibly-high... whatever-you-just-called-it?"

"The impossibly-majestic-high-arc-rainbow-hammer-mallet throw," the President clarified. "It's the most difficult maneuver in all of plouquette. I've never seen it done perfectly. Still, he works at it tirelessly."

"So, why 'poor Yelly' then?" Luc asked again.

"Well, it didn't take more than a week, but we had a break-in here at the club. It was the only robbery we've ever had in more than three centuries of plouquette. And the Waterford Cup, Yelly's prize, was stolen. The police went to question Dorian, but he'd gone into hiding."

"Everyone around here knew it was he," de Mouton

added.

"Definitely!"

"How did you know?" Luc asked.

"I had a hunch," Cravenmoore answered.

Just a hunch? Luc thought.

"...and there was a note from Dorian explaining why it was rightfully his and that we'd never find him."

"Oh," Luc answered.

"Arrogant little peon," de Mouton added.

"But if he didn't have keys, how did he get in?" Luc asked.

"My, my, my," the President said in genuine wonder. "You really are the greatest detective of all time. Clearly, you think with insight and critical problem-solving skills."

"Uh, okay."

"Anyway, we believe that Thibault had help. He was so popular around here that we knew he wouldn't have any trouble finding someone to aid him in his sick plans. In the end, we discovered that another member, Armande Marwane, and a busboy at our bar on the premises, Tag le Tier, helped him break in and steal the trophy."

Luc straightened when he heard the word "busboy."

"They had probably been helping him grease his balls up, too," de Mouton added.

"We should have known," Cravenmoore continued. "They were all three degenerates in their own way. Dorian was selfish and pretentious. Armande was brought up as one of our own, but he turned out to be a liar. A real con man, second only to Dorian maybe."

"Tag was a good-hearted guy who got in with the wrong crowd," de Mouton added.

"Maurice," the President interrupted, "I have tolerated your outbursts into my story, but as I said before, *I am telling it!*"

"Sorry."

"You simply don't have the storytelling skills to set this up for our guest."

"Sorry," de Mouton answered again.

The President sighed. "Thank you. You break up my flow. Anyway, Tag le Tier was a terrible busboy. Broke more dishes than he ever bussed. He was just looking for someone to look up to. Someone to follow. And he found Dorian Thibault."

"So, is that the case?" Luc asked. "Find the men and find the trophy?"

"Sort of," the President answered.

"22 years is a long time," Luc said. He knew he'd never be able to do it. His heartbeat reminded him that he wasn't a real detective. Cue more palm sweat.

"Well, there's more to it than that," Cravenmoore said. "The police were all over the case back then. They chased Dorian Thibault, Armande Marwane, and Tag le Tier all over town for a few days—always just a step or two behind. Finally, one morning after a standoff at a house in Montmartre, the three men perished in a fire. Thibault, Marwane, and le Tier were all gone, and the Waterford Cup went with them."

"That's horrible," Luc said.

"But coincidentally," Cravenmoore added, "that's one

of the reasons we're so impressed with you."

"What?" Luc was confused. "Why does that make you impressed with me?"

"Well, it's obvious. The way you insisted that Maurice meet you in the café that was built on the exact spot where that fire occurred, 22 years to the day after it happened, to the exact minute—that's the work of genius."

"Thank you." Luc felt his ears heat up every time he lied. His parents had only owned the café for the last 15 or so years. He wasn't familiar with the property's history.

"Anyway, we were able to dig what was left of the cup out of the ashes, but it couldn't be saved."

"Did you just get another trophy for the last 22 years?"

"Of course, but it didn't mean as much to anyone. There's still a tournament, but it's not what it was back before Dorian Thibault trashed the sport."

"I don't think I understand," Luc said. "What's the case? If those three guys died and the cup burned up, what do you need a detective for?"

"That's just it." Cravenmoore leaned towards Luc. "A man was arrested last week. He was caught trying to break into a pet store over on the left bank. 'Zoo La La' it's called, I think."

"I heard it was Giraffic Park," de Mouton added.

"No, that's out in the twentieth arrondissement."

"Are you sure?" de Mouton asked.

"We got my daughter's pigmy grizzly bear there. That wasn't it," Cravenmoore said.

"Ah, okay."

"I've never heard of those places," Luc answered.

"They're exotic animal shops, mainly for very elite clientele," Cravenmoore answered.

De Mouton added, "Can you imagine how the general public would react if they knew that a pigmy grizzly bear was just walking around in the shop next door?"

"Pure pandemonium," Cravenmoore said.

"No, 'Pure Panda-monium' is the shop in Nice," de Mouton added.

"I know that," Cravenmoore snapped. "You're as bad as my ex-wife. Anyway, the shop we're talking about was 'Zoo La La.' And they say a man was caught breaking in the back door there last week, trying to steal a re-venomized raccoon."

Luc made a face. "What do you mean re-venomized? Is that even a thing? Do raccoons have venom?"

"The man who was arrested is troubled. He could never afford that kind of thing, and frankly, was never very bright."

"I'm sorry, I've lost track of all this. What does Zoo La La, or whatever, have to do with anything?"

"Because, the man arrested," Cravenmoore answered, "had been presumed dead. It was Tag le Tier."

Luc paused, thinking back. "Was he the—"

"The busboy." Cravenmoore finished his thought for him. "He worked with Dorian Thibault and Armande Marwane to steal the trophy."

"But you said the police had a standoff with them, and they all wound up dying in a fire," Luc said.

"I know. We don't understand it either. That's why we called you. Tag le Tier is alive, apparently. Does that mean Dorian Thibault is still alive? What about Armande Marwane? And if they didn't die in a fire, is the Waterford Cup still out there?"

"But you said you recovered the cup from the fire."

"I know. But we need you to sort out the story. Where are Thibault and Marwane? Are they in their graves where they belong? Or are they running the streets, trying to steal re-venomized raccoons alongside the idiot of the bunch, Tag le Tier?"

Luc realized that he couldn't lie any longer. He wasn't a real detective, and they were asking for him to investigate something that happened 22 years ago. That sounded like a job for a professional, which Luc was not. Plus, damp and dark spots had formed on the plush chair around his palms.

"I know what you're thinking," the President said.

"I'm sorry, what?" Luc was lost in thought.

"You'll need help."

"Wait." Luc stopped him. "Actually, I was thinking that you should know—"

"Maurice, get the girl."

"Yes, monsieur," de Mouton answered.

"What girl?" Luc asked.

De Mouton moved to the door as Cravenmoore spoke. "You'll need a host, someone who knows the club. We're going to introduce you to one of our lawn girls, who can help you get around this place."

When de Mouton opened the door, Luc was blinded by the exterior light. Squinting, he saw the silhouette of a girl float into the room.

"Detective, this is Alaina Amandine."

She came into focus. The tips of her straight auburn hair danced just above her shoulders. Deep eyes managed skepticism and seduction at the same time.

"H...hello," Luc stammered as he stood.

"C'mon, Alaina," Cravenmoore said. "Would it kill you to smile every now and then? This is the greatest detective of all time. Show some decorum."

"Welcome," she answered with a casual, unenthusiastic wave.

"Alaina is one of our most veteran lawn girls. Her parents are some of our most esteemed members, and she's been a part of the culture around here since she was a little girl. She'll be happy to let you in each day if needed, introduce you to people around here, basically help you in any way that you need."

The busboy thought she was beautiful. Just a year or two younger than he, she looked like the type that would not ordinarily look in his direction. Instantly, he was ready to take this case no matter the cost.

"Detective, I don't think I caught your name," Alaina said.

"Please Alaina," Cravenmoore interrupted. "You are looking at the greatest detective in the world. He prefers to stay anonymous, so he doesn't get too close to any of his subjects, I imagine."

Luc was prepared to blurt out his name for this girl, though.

"But she has a point," Cravenmoore continued. "We should have a code name for you. Do you have any thoughts on that?"

"Like what kind of code name?" Luc asked.

"You're the pro here," Cravenmoore said.

Luc thought for a moment.

"How about 'The Eagle?'" de Mouton offered. "Or 'The Flying Tiger' or something? Something that inspires fear in his enemies?"

"I like those," Luc said.

"How about 'Pigeon'?" Cravenmoore answered. "Yes, that one is perfect."

"Wait," Luc protested. "Pigeon?! Why?"

Alaina smirked.

"That doesn't strike fear into anything," Luc said.

"Then it's settled. You shall be 'Pigeon.'" Cravenmoore looked satisfied with the decision.

"I think I prefer just 'detective'," Luc answered.

"I believe de Mouton settled on a fee with you as well when you met yesterday, no?" Cravenmoore asked.

It took a moment for Luc to process the whole code name conversation. "Uh... yes he did."

"And that's satisfactory to you?"

"Um, yes. Definitely. Two million euros. Thank you."

"No, it is we who should be thanking you!" Cravenmoore exclaimed as he stood. "Alaina, please take it from here. Give him the tour! I'm sure he'll have a packed schedule for the both of you."

"Great," Alaina answered. "Follow me."

Chapter III.

"Well, where would you like to start?" Alaina pushed a flop of hair behind her ear with the tips of her fingers.

"Uh… I don't know. I guess…" Luc couldn't talk. The busboy was too busy trying to learn how to swallow again. Plus, his conscience was in turmoil, swapping guilt for his lies with overwhelming, regret-erasing attraction to the girl.

Alaina leaned in, as if trying to pry the words out of him. She was taller than he, dressed in a white polo and a short, loose lawn skirt.

"How about a…" Luc tried.

"A tour maybe?"

"Yes, a tour. Yes. That would be perfect. Please. Show me around."

"Great." She dropped her voice. "Look. There's no way you want me to call you 'Monsieur Pigeon,' right?"

Luc finally exhaled. She sounded more human to him in that sentence than anyone he'd met so far at the club. His nervous energy started to subside. "No. Thank you."

"It's the worst code name ever, right?" Alaina asked.

"Yes. You're right. Thank you. I thought I was going crazy in there," Luc answered.

"Take it easy. You can relax now. Those guys are the worst. You'll see. You can have an entire conversation with them and they'll never listen."

"I got that feeling." Luc could only dream of speaking with the kind of coolness in Alaina's tone.

"Listen," she said. "I respect it if you want to stay anonymous or whatever, but you can give me a first name if you want. It doesn't even have to be your real one. Anything has to be better than 'Pigeon.'"

"Luc. It's my real one. My real name is Luc. And you can call me that."

"Luc. Great. Nice to meet you. I'm Alaina."

"Right, yes. Nice to meet you."

"Let's walk," she suggested.

The busboy exhaled.

Luc's marveled again at the immaculate carpet. His soles must have sunk an entire inch below the top of the fibers. Alaina saw him take a few tentative steps.

"Is something wrong?"

"I've never felt carpet like this before," Luc said.

"It's a high-fiber poly-synthetic lion hide," she said.

"Lion hide?"

"No. High-fiber poly-synthetic lion hide."

"I don't think I even understand what that means," Luc said.

"Me neither. It's in the tour guide manual though, so I say it. I do know that it gets replaced weekly so it never wears."

"Wow. That sounds like a lot of work."

"It's the burden of running a club for the elite," Alaina noted as they walked. "I'm told that these paintings are all lost treasures of the masters. Honestly though, I'm not really sure who painted which ones."

"That's not in the manual?" Luc asked.

"Yeah. But I didn't read the whole manual."

Luc stared out the windows at the courtyard.

"I don't go in rooms on this side of the hall very often," Alaina continued. "These last few doors have all led to the board room, where all important club decisions happen. We have a store up ahead on your left. It's a high-end farmer's market for some of the lodging upstairs that have kitchens—"

"I really don't understand this sport," Luc interrupted. "It doesn't look like they're doing anything out there."

Alaina stopped walking as she gazed out the windows. "I know it. I've been a club member here all my life, and I've only played plouquette once. No, twice. Maybe."

"Really?"

"Yeah. Maybe it's that I'm only a member plus."

"What's a 'member plus'?" Luc asked.

"There are different levels of membership. Basically, you start as an associate, then it goes member, associate member, member plus, executive council, senior associate, member-in-residence, executive member, gold level, master member, senior plus executive platinum member, executive first class, and then the highest level is grand emerald class rank. Unless you're the top level but too old to play plouquette, then you're a plus member bronze grand-level emeritus."

"That's a lot," Luc said. "What's the difference in levels?"

"I'm sure someone told me once. But half the time, I don't pay attention when people around here talk to me. I'm sure my parents know, though."

"Your parents are really into club life, huh?" Luc asked.

"Yes. They play all the time. It's a pretty social sport. They are always saying that they'll teach me when I'm old enough."

"When you're old enough?"

"I know. It's stupid. I'm 25."

"Huh."

Alaina nodded out towards the group playing. "A whole lot of nothing happens during a game, if you ask me."

"It doesn't look like those people are playing at all. That guy over there has been staring at the sun without blinking for over a minute, it looks like."

"No, they're playing. That's part of it. If you look closely, you'll see one make a play every now and then. In fact," Alaina went on, pointing outside, "there's someone about to make a move right now."

A bearded man hunched over his mallet as if the weight of his facial hair pulled him down. He wore the required white pants with a cream-colored sweater. Strands of brown hair hung in his face as he dropped his head to stare at the ball.

Luc watched him. The man didn't move.

"He is pretty interesting, "Alaina continued. "He's one of our best players. His name is Yelly Reardon."

"Yelly Reardon," Luc repeated. "The President was just talking about him."

"Poor Yelly."

Luc looked at Alaina. "That's exactly what the President said."

"It's what everyone around here says."

"Why?" Luc asked. "Because the cup was stolen when he won?"

"Well, I guess there's that. But he's devoted his whole life to the sport. I think it's pretty unhealthy. What a waste."

"The President said he won the tournament 22 years ago, after someone named Dorian Thibault won first—but got penalized."

"Sounds right."

Yelly tapped the ball with his mallet. It only went about two feet. Luc couldn't tell what the purpose of the shot was. Unlike other sports, there was no goal line, hole, or wicket. Still, Yelly yipped and pumped his fist. The big white horse looked up from its grazing. Its mane shook as the animal snorted. Luc wondered why it was out there and no one paid any attention to it.

Alaina added, "I do know that Yelly's come in second in the big tournament every single year since."

"Whoa," Luc answered. "Second every year for the last 22 years? Poor Yelly."

"Exactly. The real stinger is that no one has ever won more than once. He comes in second to a different person every year. It's almost like he's the second-best player here—to literally everyone else."

"Wow. That must be frustrating."

"Honestly," Alaina went on. "I always kind of

thought he was an idiot. He cares about the sport more than anyone else. He's out there practicing every day. I mean, get a life, you know?"

"Huh, yeah." In that moment, and almost by accident, Luc stopped looking *through* the window and more *at* it—at Alaina's reflection as the two gazed out at the courtyard. She stood close enough to the pane for Luc to become distracted by the illusion of two identical girls standing face to face. Her mirror opposite, a ghostly transparent likeness, was as beautiful as she was—but with the subtle differences that come with an image projected in reverse.

"C'mon," Alaina said, snapping Luc out of his thought. "Are you hungry?"

Luc hadn't thought about food. He just realized that he hadn't eaten at all for the day.

"Yes, I suppose I am."

"Great, I'll show you the bar and restaurant."

They resumed their walk down the hallway along the courtyard.

"What's on the other side?"

Alaina looked at him. "What do you mean?"

"Across the lawn. Are those windows into another hallway?"

"Oh, I see. Yes. On the first floor, there are more meeting rooms. The best stuff is upstairs: The librarium, the zarzuela theater, and the gallery for artwork created at the expense of someone else's freedom, health, or happiness."

"What's a librarium?" Luc asked.

"It's half library, half aquarium."

"That sounds pretty cool."

"It is."

"Can we see it?" The busboy asked.

"Sure. If there's not a zarzuela on in the theater, we can go in there too."

"What's a zarzuela?" Luc wondered aloud.

"It's a Spanish opera. Usually comic. Don't you own a word-of-the-day calendar?"

"No."

Alaina was unimpressed. "There's a big cigar and pipe shop up there too."

"Oh yeah? Is it just several rooms full of cigars?"

"No. It's a small shop—for big cigars. Not a big shop for small cigars."

"I see."

"Do you smoke?" Alaina asked.

"No. Do you?"

"Every now and then, when my parents aren't looking. But they don't allow cigarettes here without holders, so I never do it here. But if you want to smoke a pipe or a cigar or something, I can take you over there."

"No thanks. Smoke makes me sick."

The pair reached the end of the hallway and entered the restaurant. The wide room was mostly empty. Every table was set with perfect linens and shining glassware. Part of the space opened on to a veranda that spilled into the courtyard with some outdoor seating. One rowdy table of five or six dominated a far corner with noise enough for a crowded room, but no one was working the host stand.

"Follow me." Alaina didn't stop to wait for a staff member to seat them. "Let me introduce you to someone."

Luc followed her as she weaved between the empty chairs. A tall young man sliced limes on the bar. His blonde hair was spiked above his forehead. He looked up when he heard them coming.

"How's it going, my little puppet?" He asked Alaina.

"I'm not your puppet, Dolt." She turned to Luc. "Meet my boyfriend, Dolt D'Ormando."

Dolt tossed his head back and smirked.

"Hi," Luc said as his heart dropped. Boyfriend?

"This is a man that the club has hired," Alaina said. "He's a private detective."

"Cool." Dolt answered. "I don't think I've ever met a private detective before."

"I had a girlfriend," Luc said. "But we just broke up. So yeah, I've had a girlfriend."

"What are you up to?" Alaina asked the bartender.

"I'm slicing this lime."

"I see that."

"It's tricky," Dolt continued. "The thing is, the knife has to go through the... what's the word for the outside of the lime? The skin? The shell?"

"The rind," Luc answered.

"No, the green part." Dolt was annoyed. "The part you shouldn't eat. Anyway, the knife has to go through the green part, and then through the soft, less-greeny inside, all the way to the bottom until you feel it hit the cutting board—*without* cutting your fingers."

"Yeah, that really sounds tricky," Alaina rolled her brown eyes. "Anyway, everyone says that he's the greatest detective of all time."

"Really?" Dolt asked in amazement.

Luc nodded, ready to go back home immediately. It hadn't occurred to him that she would have a boyfriend.

"Yes. He's been given the code name of 'Pigeon,'" Alaina added.

"Okay, I can get on board with that." Dolt nodded. "Pigeon. Seems fitting,"

"No, it doesn't," Alaina protested. "Just call him 'detective,' okay?"

"I'll see if I can remember that," Dolt answered.

"Apparently, they're paying him millions to be here."

Luc had almost forgot about that, and Alaina having a boyfriend didn't feel so bad anymore.

"Whoa," Dolt muttered.

"Wait," Luc said to Alaina. "How do you know what they're paying me?"

"All people talk about is money around here."

"I see," Luc answered.

"Let's get some food," Alaina said.

"I'll get us a table," Dolt began. "I'm starving."

"Don't you have to work?" Alaina asked him.

"Uh, yes, but no one's here."

"It's almost 11, and people are going to come in here soon," she said. "If your boss catches you eating again, he'll put you on massage cleanup duty."

Dolt looked disgusted. "Ugh, you're right."

"Is that bad?" Luc asked. "Wouldn't that just be a lot of towels or something?"

Both Alaina and Dolt looked at each other, disgusted.

"Just towels?" Alaina asked. "I wish."

"I better stay behind the bar," Dolt said.

"Good plan," Alaina nodded. "Plus, I'm working here. Monsieur Detective needs to think, and I'm his host. So, unfortunately for you, you're not invited anyway."

"But baby!" Dolt protested.

"Sorry, puppet," Alaina said. "Let's go, detective."

Alaina and Luc chose a table in the middle of the empty room. Luc felt the pristine white linen as he took his seat in a thick leather dining chair. The table on the far side of the room was still loud and laughing.

No fewer than eight members of the wait staff appeared from nowhere, surrounded them, and began turning out their napkins, pouring water, and placing bread. One person even ran a lint roller over the front of Luc's shirt.

"Have you never been to a nine-star restaurant before?" Alaina asked.

"I thought they only rated restaurants on five stars?" Luc answered.

"The scale goes higher for the elite," Alaina noted. She lowered her voice. "But I prefer a two or a three star. I hate it when someone else puts my napkin in my lap for me."

"He's not wearing white pants," the lint-roller waiter whispered to one of his co-workers. Every server froze.

"What do we do?" one asked the other.

"I don't know. This is the first time this has ever

happened to me," another answered.

"Don't worry about it, guys. This is Detective Pigeon," Alaina clarified with authority. "He's here on the orders of President Cravenmoore himself. Verify it if you need to."

The waiters all looked to each other. One dashed away to the bar area. He picked up a phone and dialed a quick number.

The rest of the wait staff looked at each other. One shrugged and started, "Our special today is—"

Another waiter motioned for him to stop. "Wait for verification. No white pants."

"Sooooo…" another waiter asked. "Are you from Paris?"

"No small talk either," another interjected.

Luc looked to Alaina. "This white pants thing seems to really be an issue, huh?"

She nodded.

The waiter at the bar hung up. "We can proceed," he announced.

"Our special today is a limited-range male duck torso, prepared over a fire of bubinga wood and bamboo, marinated in a sugar, peach juice, and grain alcohol remoulade."

Alaina looked at Luc.

"That'll be fine, thank you," he answered, unaware of what to expect.

"Me too," Alaina said.

"Very good, mademoiselle. What may we offer you to drink, Detective?"

"Water. Will be fine."

"Excellent, sir," a waiter nodded. "Mademoiselle?"

"Vodka tonic with a lime."

"Excellent."

The men dispersed.

"Wait!" Luc exclaimed. "I'll have one of those too."

"Of course, sir," one man turned to say before dashing off to the bar.

"Good choice," Alaina commented.

"It's my favorite," Luc lied. He'd never had one before.

Luc stole a look at the loud table. An attractive woman in her forties held court. She was Victorian style meets modern beauty. Her hair climbed above her head, and her dress sparkled in spots from the light from the window.

"Who is she?" Luc asked, nodding in her direction.

"That's Marianne Merriweather. She's been around here forever. She's famous here," Alaina answered.

"Why?" Luc asked.

"She's the life of the party. Everyone loves her."

"The men at that table sure seem to."

"They are probably all in love with her," Alaina said. "She has a little bit of an entourage."

"Is she married?" Luc asked.

"No. I think she's been single her whole life. You can tell she loves the attention."

"I see."

"What happens next?" Alaina asked. "What would you like to do first, Detective?"

Suddenly, having to be a real detective was going to need some attention. Luc's palms started sweating again. He thrust his napkin into his lap and busied himself smoothing it out. After a few long moments, the busboy managed, "Uh, let me think."

"I can introduce you to some people around here who might remember Dorian Thibault, Armande Marwane, and Tag le Tier."

"Do you think they'd be able to help?" Luc asked.

"Who knows? But, they might be able to help you understand who those men were as people—their personalities."

That's a great idea, Luc thought.

The other table erupted in drunk laughter. Alaina noticed Luc glance in their direction.

"I've never spent a lot of time talking to Madame Merriweather, but the one or two times I have, she was alright."

"What do you mean?" Luc asked. He was relieved that Alaina seemed to have suggestions on the case, as well as her apparent ability to notice his nerves and change the subject. It helped calm him down.

A waiter appeared with a large silver carafe. The man flourished and made a grand show of pouring a small amount of liquid on a saucer in front of Luc.

"What's that?" Luc asked.

"It's hornet honey, sir. Pairs wonderfully with the bread."

"Hornet honey? I don't think I've heard of that

before," Luc said.

"Ours is particularly sweet, sir. We add hornet milk," the waiter replied.

"Hornet milk?"

"Yes, hornet milk," Alaina confirmed.

"I don't understand. What is that?" Luc asked.

"Well, just like most mammals, hornets nurse their young. We extract the milk, and use it for flavor," the man answered, looking at Alaina in shock that their guest didn't know what hornet milk was.

"I don't think hornets are mammals," Luc said.

"Common misconception," the waiter answered.

"And I don't think they make honey, either."

"Oh, they do. We have a hornet farm onsite," the waiter replied.

"I'll show you later if you want," Alaina added.

"I'm not sure I need to go near a hornet's nest," Luc answered.

"It's a hornet *farm*, sir. You should try the hornet meat sushi," the waiter suggested.

"Hornet meat?"

"It's a delicacy. For the elite."

Luc looked at Alaina. She just smirked.

"We harvest it right onsite," the waiter continued. "We don't let a single part of the hornet go to waste."

"How many parts can a hornet have?" Luc asked.

"Just try the hornet honey," Alaina said.

Luc dipped his bread in the honey and hornet milk. It tasted like honey with butter and hot pepper in it. Luc's face twisted.

The waiter seemed satisfied with himself and disappeared.

"Anyway, about Marianne Merriweather," Alaina continued. "I was 15 or so. I wanted to know how to play plouquette, but my parents said I would probably not be good enough."

"That's not very encouraging of them," Luc noted.

"No, but that's always what it's been like around here. When I was a kid, I loved club life. My parents' friends were nice to me, and I wanted to grow up here, be good at plouquette, and be someone around here that was respected. Maybe even club leadership."

"But not anymore?"

"Well, as I got older, I started hearing a lot more about things I couldn't do—either because I was a girl, or because no one thought I'd be good at something."

"That's awful," Luc thought aloud.

"Well, it turned me against this place. But Marianne Merriweather remained someone to look up to. Once, my dad was trying to show me the basics of the sport. It took some coaxing, but he started giving me lessons."

"But you still don't know anything about it now?" Luc clarified.

"Right. He was a horrible teacher," Alaina said.

"Sorry about that."

"Whatever. Anyway, I must have been bad at it because my dad was getting furious with me, but I didn't understand what I was supposed to do to get it right. Then,

Marianne appears out of nowhere and says, 'Mitch, go easy on her. It's just a silly game. Then my dad says 'How dare you?!' in this big, insulted voice, and Marianne grabs his cocktail out of his hand, downs it in one shot, hands the empty glass back to him, winks at me, and says 'C'mon, let's go shopping.'"

Luc raised his eyebrows.

"I didn't get to go, though," Alaina continued. "My parents just walked me away, and I had to go back to my lesson."

"What a shame."

"But, that's always stuck with me," Alaina replied.

Six or seven waiters swirled around them again. They delivered crackers. And then they were gone.

"Like I said, I can introduce you to some people around here who might remember Dorian Thibault."

"Well I was thinking," Luc said as he noticed his palms were sweating a little less than before. He must have been gaining confidence in his new role as a detective. "I think the obvious first step might be to go to the jail, and see if they'll let us talk to Tag le Tier."

Chapter IV.

A fluorescent light buzzed above Luc and Alaina. The two waited, staring at an empty chair on the other side of the thick glass in the police station visitor's room. The chair itself looked like it was built for a 10-year-old. Pea green walls almost looked like the sides of a dirty aquarium. Luc and Alaina waited alone for Tag le Tier.

"Do you think the others are still alive?" Alaina asked Luc as they waited.

"I'm not sure yet," Luc answered as he shrugged. "I think it would be very hard to sustain a lie like that for so long."

"Faking a death, you mean?"

"Yes, exactly."

The two sat in awkward silence. Luc couldn't keep his leg from jittering. The busboy knew he was about to be face to face with one of the perpetrators of the crime, but he was distracted. His thoughts kept drifting back to the idea that Alaina had a boyfriend.

"So…" Luc began. "How long have you been seeing Dolt?"

"It's been a few months. I started dating him because my parents hate him."

"Why do they hate him?"

"They think he's an idiot."

"But he's not?" Luc asked.

"Get your head in the game, Detective," Alaina said,

changing the subject. "What's your plan for le Tier?"

Luc felt his face become numb. He had no plan. The busboy couldn't find a single reason to believe that Tag le Tier would reveal anything to them. *Just sound professional, just sound professional, just be cool,* Luc thought to himself over and over again as his glasses began to fog from the heat and sweat of his brow.

On the other side of the glass, a large steel door opened, and two officers escorted a small, round-faced man to his spot across from Luc and Alaina. His chair shrieked as he pulled it back and sat down. His eyes were so round that it looked like it took extra energy just to blink.

"Fifteen minutes," the guard warned, leaving Tag with Luc and Alaina.

"Certainly, sir, certainly," Tag stated as he fidgeted in his handcuffs.

"Uh... hi," Luc started. "I'm Luc Martin, and this is Alaina Amandine."

Alaina shot him a look. Luc realized that he hadn't told her his last name yet.

"But," he exclaimed, "you can call me, 'Detective.'"

"Detective?" Tag le Tier asked. "I was sure they were through interrogating me."

Luc looked at Alaina, at a loss for words.

"The police might be," Alaina said, "but we are here on behalf of the Paris Publique Plouquette Pitch, Grounds, Gardens, Grass Court, and Lawn Club."

Tag smiled. "Certainly, certainly. The PPPPGGGCLC. I see now. Love that place."

The man never sat still. The small wooden chair creaked beneath him with every move.

"I work there, and we have hired this man," Alaina said nodding at Luc, "to investigate you—independently of the police."

"A private detective then?" Le Tier asked.

"Yes. I'm a detective. Private detective. I am the greatest detective of all time." Luc winced, not believing himself.

"Certainly, certainly. Congratulations on that," Tag chirped. "They sure had a lot of detectives chasing us back in the day."

"I'm sure," Luc answered, not able to sit still himself. "But that didn't last long, did it? I mean, they all thought you died."

"Yep," Tag answered. He stuck his chin in the air and smiled.

"So…" Luc mustered his courage. "Are Dorian Thibault and Armande Marwane still alive too?"

Tag squirmed. "Oh no. Unfortunately, they died in the fire."

"I'm sorry to hear that," Luc answered.

"Yes, I miss them so much. They were my best friends."

"They were?" Luc asked. "Where did you meet them?"

"At the PPPPGGGCLC, of course. I was a busboy."

Luc could picture him wearing the apron. He wondered if he was just as awkward in his parents' café.

"Were Dorian Thibault and Armande Marwane members when you started?" Alaina asked.

"Yep, they were."

She looked skeptical. "I'm a current member, and the busboys aren't my best friends."

Luc decided not to remind her that she was dating the bartender.

"Must have been different back then," Tag answered. "These guys were the best. They talked to me every day."

"President Cravenmoore," Luc added, "seems to think they were not the best. He made it sound like they were cheaters and crooks."

"Never. They were so great. In fact, President Cravenmoore is the crook."

"Is that so?" Luc asked. "Why would you say that?"

"He hired you, didn't he?" Alaina added.

"Certainly, certainly. But not really. I was hired by the supervisor who handled all the busboys. I never met President Cravenmoore. But he hated my friends, that's for sure."

"Why did he hate your friends?"

"Because Dorian Thibault was the best at plouquette. Ever. His game was the best. Best player ever. Greatest of all time."

"You know," Luc said as he leaned in, "I still am not quite sure how to play."

Tag laughed. "Don't worry about that."

Luc looked to Alaina, who frowned at Tag.

"President Cravenmoore stole my friend's trophy,

though," Tag added. "Just because he was jealous."

"I thought it was because he was a cheater," Alaina said.

"Dorian Thibault doesn't grease his balls. Certainly not. Certainly not."

"Okay," Luc continued as he felt himself becoming more comfortable with his role as a fake detective. "So, where have you been for the last two decades?"

"Everyone has been asking me that," Tag said as he fidgeted. "I was hiding. Hiding from everyone."

"Where were you?" Alaina asked.

"I was around."

"Around where?"

"I don't know. I've been right here in Paris most of the time."

"What about Dorian Thibault and Armande Marwane? Were you with them?" Alaina pushed.

"I told you. They're gone."

Alaina made a face, and Luc could tell she was frustrated by the man.

"Tag," Luc said, "tell me about plouquette life back when you were a club member."

Tag straightened up. "Thank you for asking me about that. Everyone here has not been nice. All they want to know about is the fire. It's as if they don't care about me, as a person."

"I'm not surprised. You're in jail," Alaina answered.

"Not for long. I'm going to break out of here pretty soon probably," Tag said.

"Is that so?" Alaina asked.

"Yes. I'm a martial arts expert." Tag said with pride as he hacked at the air.

"Incredible," she said without enthusiasm.

"Yep. I can break boards. Probably cinder blocks. So, these walls aren't going to be too tough."

"You plan on kicking through a wall to get out of here?" Alaina asked.

"You never know," Tag le Tier answered.

"Here's a question," Luc interrupted. "Why were you trying to steal a raccoon?"

"Well." Tag straightened in his chair again. "First, it wasn't just a raccoon. It was a very special raccoon. It was a re-venomized raccoon."

"Yeah, I'm still struggling to understand what that is," Luc answered.

"It's a raccoon that's been given his venom back. I would assume that you'd know about them."

"We don't," Alaina said.

"Well, I've heard they make great pets. I've always wanted one, and they are very affectionate and loyal."

Luc was puzzled at the thought. He looked at Alaina, who seemed disgusted.

"So," Luc said, changing the subject. "How did you survive the fire?"

"Oh, I was lucky. Not many people get out of fires. I had been knocked unconscious when I fell trying to escape the burning house. I couldn't have been out long, but I woke up surrounded by flames. I just ran out as fast as I could."

"What about the police waiting outside?" Alaina asked.

"I got by them."

"How?"

"I don't know. They must have been distracted by the blaze," Tag answered. He seemed satisfied, as if that answer should be the end of it.

"Who was inside the house with you?" Alaina asked. Luc liked how she already knew the answer to almost every question she asked.

"Dorian Thibault and Armande Marwane, of course."

"There wasn't anyone else?" Alaina asked.

"No."

"I suppose that makes sense," Luc added. "The fire was so bad that they didn't find many human remains."

"Right," Tag agreed. "Hey, tell me something. Is the club still the same?"

"I don't know. Alaina?" Luc asked for help.

"Probably, I don't know," she answered.

"Are you new?" Tag asked.

"No, I've been there all my life. I'm a lawn girl, but it's just a temporary job."

"Do you know Hugo Trickets?" Tag asked. "He was also very nice back then."

"Hugo?" Alaina asked. "The guy who runs the plouquette pro shop at the club?"

"Yes, that's him!"

"He's still there," Alaina confirmed. "And Yelly Reardon, you probably remember him."

"Poor Yelly," Tag said.

"Yes. Poor Yelly," Alaina answered.

"He always wanted to win so badly," Tag lamented, shaking his head. "I hated to steal the trophy away from him. I always liked him. He was very nice too. But, he didn't win it. Dorian did."

"Well, Dorian Thibault cheated," Luc reminded the would-be re-venomized raccoon thief.

"Dorian Thibault was the best," Tag said. "Truly. Yelly couldn't have ever beaten him. Period."

An officer entered and approached Tag.

"Time's up, le Tier."

Tag looked at Luc and Alaina. "Well, thank you for coming to see me. It was certainly, certainly a pleasure. Say hi to everyone at the club for me!"

"Let's go," the officer grunted.

"Bye," Luc said as Alaina only watched the man get taken away.

"Well, what do you think?" she asked Luc once they were alone again.

"I'm not sure. But don't you think we should talk to someone like Hugo Trickets? Someone who's been around that long might have some insight into these guys."

Chapter V.

"I don't believe it," Charlie mumbled at the kitchen table the next morning. He tore a piece of baguette, exploding bread dust into the air.

"I know, it's crazy," Luc answered, standing, pouring coffee. "And I'm going to meet this Hugo guy after my shift today."

"Back up. I mean, what made you do it? What made you tell them that you were the greatest detective of all time?"

"Uh, the money?" Luc answered as he placed the coffee pot back on the maker.

"Yeah right," Charlie laughed as he chewed bread. "I bet it's this girl."

"No, that's not it," Luc insisted as he sat at the small kitchen table across from Charlie.

"Please. Of course, it is."

"It is not." Luc tried not to smile.

"You are acting like a kid. You. Luc Martin. The guy who's been acting like an elderly man his entire life."

"I am not."

"What is Janet going to say?" Charlie asked.

"Nothing. I broke up with her."

"She called twice yesterday."

"No, she didn't," Luc said in disbelief as he looked up from his coffee.

"She sure did, my friend."

Luc's forehead moved as he tried to process the

information. "Why?"

"Allow me to restate my concern," Charlie continued. "Are you sure you broke up with her?"

"I did. Definitely. Yes." Luc took an unconvincing sip.

"Whatever you say. I'm just sitting here thinking, you don't grow up as the only girl with 17 younger brothers and not feel like you should be the center of attention from guys."

Coffee burned Luc's tongue.

"What are you going to do about work?" Charlie continued.

"I don't know. I have the short lunch shift today, but that's okay because Alaina isn't expecting me until the afternoon. What do you mean 'do' about work?"

"Are you going to be able to hide this from your folks?" Charlie asked as he thrust a dull knife into a small jar of jam. The utensil made a clinking sound as Charlie swirled it in the glass container. The noise annoyed Luc.

"As long as you don't tell them that I'm working a side job, they won't find out," Luc said.

"Why would I tell them?"

"Because it seems like you and my mom are somehow best friends. You told her about Janet."

"Well, I went down there for a few beers. I had to talk about what was on my mind. You know how I get."

"Just don't say anything, okay?" Luc asked.

"Sure. But what if they find out another way?" Charlie asked as he spread jam on his bread. He was making a mess on the table.

"Don't you want to use a plate for that?" Luc asked.

"No thanks, it's okay. Don't want to have to do the dish later."

Have you ever done a dish? Luc thought. "How else would my parents find out?" Luc asked.

"I don't know. They might just figure it out. It's like you're taking a second job."

"I doubt they'd just 'figure it out.'"

"It's going to be a lot of work, man," Charlie warned as he stuffed bread into his mouth.

"I know."

"Seriously. Professional detectives have tried to solve this case."

"I know," Luc repeated.

"So, you're going to be a busboy who solves crimes now?"

"I don't know. Let me drink my coffee in peace."

"Okay, fine," Charlie said. "Do you really think these guys are still alive?"

"Yes. I think they are."

"So where have they been?"

"Who knows? That's what I'm going to try to solve."

"Obviously. Right. Good luck with that. Here's another question for you," Charlie continued. "Up until now, what's the riskiest thing you've ever done?"

Luc paused as he thought. "I talked to Janet at the market. Remember that? You said you thought she was cute, so I asked her out."

Charlie laughed and brushed crumbs off his hands. "*You* said you thought she was cute, and I just agreed. By the way, I don't think that anymore. Plus, back then, you weren't the one who approached her. I was. And I introduced you two, and she said 'Hi, I'm Janet,' and you said, 'Fine, and you?'"

"Maybe that was a bad example."

The pigeon flew in from the living room and landed on the kitchen table.

"Dammit," Luc said. He cowered and covered the top of his mug as if the bird wanted coffee. "What the hell is that bird still doing here?"

"He came in yesterday. Through the window. You know this. We had a whole discussion about it."

"He's been in the apartment since yesterday?"

"He spent the night."

"What?!"

"We're friends. And it was raining," Charlie answered. Luc's roommate stroked the top of the pigeon's head with his index finger. The pigeon closed its eyes and leaned into it.

"Get him out of here! He's a bird. They carry disease."

"Calm down, my friend. Richard is great."

"No, Richard is dirty," Luc protested.

"I appreciate you calling him by his name. Finally."

Luc rolled his eyes so hard it gave him a headache. Or it was just the fact the bird was there. Either way, he had a headache.

The bird tilted his head as he blinked at Luc.

"The pigeon head tilt," Charlie muttered. "Classic Richard. You know what the best part is?"

"No, what?" Luc asked, scooting his chair further from the table. He only made it an inch or two before he hit the wall of the tiny kitchen.

"We don't know if it's a boy or a girl pigeon. But I've named it Richard."

"So?"

"What if it's a girl?! That's hilarious!"

"Okay, I've got to head down to the restaurant," Luc stated, setting his mug down.

"But your shift doesn't start for another two hours."

Luc stood and marched towards the door.

"Before you go, one more thing," Charlie mentioned.

"What?"

"You know, for a guy who has pretty much never told a lie in his entire life, you are lying a lot in the past 24 hours."

"What?!" Luc spun to face Charlie, who now stood in the doorway of the kitchen. The pigeon rested on his shoulder.

"When have I lied to you?!" Luc asked.

"Just now when you said it wasn't about the girl. But more amazingly, when you told some really rich and powerful people that you were the world's greatest detective, and then agreed to take 2 million euros from them."

Luc blinked. "Oh."

"I mean, you know you aren't going to solve this case, right?" Charlie asked.

"I don't know." Luc grabbed his apron from the hook by the door.

"Oh no," Charlie sighed. "You actually think you can solve this case."

"I don't know. Leave me alone, man."

"I mean, the police have had thirty years to solve it, right?"

"That's not necessarily true." Luc was still hovering by the front door. "They tried to solve it for a few days, and then stopped working on it because they thought the suspects were all dead."

"But still. Do you have any idea how hard it is to figure out something that happened 30 years ago? Do you even know where you were 6 weeks ago?"

"Probably."

"Okay, bad example," Charlie said. "You do the same thing every day. Look, all I'm saying is that 30 years is a long time."

"It was 22 years."

"Whatever. I'm saying a lot has changed since then. How will anyone remember anything they didn't back then?"

"I don't know. But I'm counting on it. That or maybe the idea that people have changed enough to want to get this thing resolved."

"What makes you think the suspects want anything resolved? If the others are still out there, why would they want to be found?" Charlie asked.

"I don't know." Luc resigned.

"Here you go, Richard," Charlie said as he gave Richard a pinch of bread.

"When is the bird leaving?" Luc asked.

"I don't know. Why?"

"Well, this is my apartment, and I don't want a pet

pigeon."

"No, it's *our* apartment, and Richard is not a pet. He's a friend. Or maybe more like a roommate."

"But I don't want a roommate. Especially one who doesn't pay us any rent."

"He's free to go at any time."

"But you're feeding him right now!"

"So?"

"So, he's not going to want to go anywhere if you feed him all the time."

"I never feed you and you still live here," Charlie answered.

"But this is *my* apartment."

"*Our* apartment. And if it makes you feel any better, I can ask him not to go in your room."

"*Ask* him?!" Luc exclaimed. "What good will that do? Does he understand or obey you?"

"Take it easy. I'm giving you a hard time," Charlie said, while giving Richard another few crumbs of bread.

* * *

"I'll have another glass of wine," some lady told Luc without making eye contact.

"I'll tell your waiter," Luc said as he removed an empty plate from her companion's spot. His mind was on his meeting later with Hugo Trickets, and he could barely hear the woman's voice above the din of the crowded café.

"No, I'm telling *you*," she answered.

"Oh, okay." Luc started for the kitchen.

"Don't you need to know what I'm drinking?"

"Yes," Luc answered. He turned to fully face the woman again. "Sorry. What are you drinking?"

The woman exhaled. "It was a sauvignon."

"Okay. Was it a white?"

"Obviously." She waved her glass in the air, displaying the last drops of the wine. Her companion snickered.

"Do you know which one?" Luc asked.

"You're the one who works here. Aren't you a wine expert or something?"

"I'm a busboy."

"Then bus me up another glass of wine."

"I'll let my mother—I mean your waitress—know."

"Of course." The woman said as a loud aside to her companion. "He got the job because his mom works here."

"Everything okay here?" Luc's mother asked as she approached the table.

"Well, I'd like another glass of wine," the woman repeated. "But your son is more interested in talking about it than running to go get it."

"We'll have it right out," Luc's mother answered as she escorted Luc away. "What's the matter with you?" She whispered.

"What do you mean?"

"That wonderful, beautiful, paying-customer-of-a-woman wants another glass of wine."

"I didn't know what to get."

"When that happens, come find me. I'll get it for her."

"I know. I tried. But she wouldn't let me leave."

"Let you leave? You're not eight anymore." Luc's mother sighed. "There's syrup on your cheek." She dabbed a corner of Luc's dry apron on his cheek. "Listen. In the future, just answer with 'yes, of course.' Then walk away."

"But, I thought you said I should be seen and not heard around here."

"Very true, but you still have to make our customers happy."

"Can I ask you a question?" Luc asked as they entered the kitchen.

"We need another glass of the sauvignon to table seven," Luc's mother announced to her husband as he walked by.

"Could I have a little time off?" Luc ventured.

"What?"

"Could I get a little time off? I've never been on vacation, and it might be nice to get a little breathing room."

"Is this what Charlie was talking about? Your weekend train trip or something? Because that sounds dangerous. I don't like it."

"No, definitely not. I just could use a little break."

"Are you sure you need it right now? I mean, we're in the middle of the busiest season."

"No, we're not."

"Well, sure. Maybe the holidays get a little hectic also. But listen. You know I love you, but you made a commitment to us, and we're depending on you."

"But you said if I let you know ahead of time, we could work it out," Luc said.

"We need some help here," his mother pleaded. "And you're great at it. We just count on you, that's all."

"I know, but some time away would still be great," Luc persisted.

"We'll discuss it later," the woman said as she walked away. "Please, we need to get table four reset."

"Excuse me, sir?" The belligerent customer's voice echoed behind Luc.

"Yes?" He answered.

"Wine?"

* * *

Coat-check Carl eyed Luc's non-white corduroys as the busboy entered the club. The old man said nothing, but Luc knew he might not be allowed to pass again if he didn't find some white pants before his next visit.

Luc met Alaina at the club standing in the bright hallway off the club's glum entryway, just inside two ornate glass doors that led to the plouquette lawn. The view of the courtyard yielded Dolt in the background, picking up plouquette mallets and balls. The horse stood grazing nearby.

"I didn't realize that he also worked as a lawn boy," Luc commented, nodding at Alaina's boyfriend. "I thought he was a bartender."

Alaina turned to look outside. "He usually doesn't do

that, but everyone does pretty much everything around here at some point."

"Have you ever bartended?"

"Not me, no," Alaina answered. "And luckily, I've never had massage cleanup duty. C'mon. Let's go say hi to Dolt."

"Great," Luc whispered to himself.

The grass of the plouquette grounds was thick and short. Luc wasn't even sure if it was real. It could have been carpet. Several couples stood around chatting. Luc still never felt like he saw them play.

"Hey babe," Dolt said as they approached. "Hey Pigeon."

"Hey," Luc mustered.

"What are you two up two?" Dolt asked.

"Nothing," Alaina answered. "We're about to go talk to Monsieur Trickets."

"For what?" Dolt responded.

"To talk about the case."

"Of course," Dolt said, nodding. "The case. You guys are so cool."

"I have a question," Luc asked.

"Shoot, Monsieur Pigeon."

"Stop calling him that," Alaina said.

"Why? That's his name, right?" Dolt said.

"*Code* name," Alaina corrected.

"What's the difference?"

"A code name is given by someone. A regular name is something you're born with," Alaina explained.

"I say," Dolt responded, "be happy with your name. No code needed."

"I'm good," Luc added.

"What's your question, Pigeon?" Dolt asked.

"Well, I've noticed the horse in here."

"A horse?" Dolt asked.

"Yes. That white horse over there, grazing in the corner."

"Oh, Phyllis. Yes. Her," Dolt confirmed.

"Okay. Phyllis. What's the deal with her?"

"What do you mean?" Dolt asked as the wooden mallets in his arms knocked together.

"I mean, no one ever seems to acknowledge her. Isn't it strange to have a horse on a lawn for playing a game?"

"What makes you think she's not part of the sport?" Dolt asked.

"I don't know. Is she?" Luc asked.

"I don't know. I'm not sure how to play," Dolt answered.

"Of course."

"I know she's for riding, though" Dolt went on.

"She *is not*," Alaina said.

"Who feeds her? Where does she sleep?" Luc asked.

"Oh. Good questions. I'm not too sure about either of those as well," Dolt answered.

"Me neither," Alaina added.

"Huh," Luc muttered as he thought.

"I'm telling you two. She's for riding," Dolt insisted.

"No, she's not," Alaina answered.

"She is too," Dolt complained. "She's pretty much the best ever."

"I agree that she's the best ever, but she's not for riding."

"Why not?" The bartender asked.

"Have you ever tried to ride her?"

"No," Dolt answered, picking up another mallet. He shifted his bear hug on the items to accommodate the addition.

"Well, see what happens," Alaina urged.

"Maybe I will," Dolt said.

"Go ahead," she urged again.

Dolt looked at the horse and dropped his armload. The bartender walked over to the horse, who didn't flinch as he approached. Dolt touched her mane. Phyllis still ignored him. Luc liked how he could see every muscle underneath Phyllis' pristine white horsehair. Dolt lifted himself up to her and swung one leg over her bare back.

"See? Couldn't be easier," he noted one half-second before Phyllis thrust her legs in the air, bucking Dolt to the ground with one single violent motion.

"What an idiot," Alaina whispered as half of the players turned their heads in time to see Dolt hit the grass. A cracking sound made Luc believe that Dolt snapped his coccyx. The bartender let out a short, throat-tearing scream.

"Anyone who has ever ridden Phyllis has been bucked," Alaina whispered to Luc as Dolt writhed on the ground. "She isn't tame."

"So why does the club have her?" Luc asked.

"Who knows?"

Dolt squirmed on the ground. Luc took a secret pleasure in seeing him get bucked.

"Should we do something to help him?" Luc asked, but Alaina was already walking to her boyfriend's side.

"I'm fine. I'm fine," Dolt insisted as he gingerly rose. Alaina reached him as he got to his feet.

"Are you sure? That looked pretty bad. I didn't think you'd actually try to ride her," Alaina said.

"I didn't think she'd buck me," Dolt countered.

"She bucks everyone, and you know it."

"I thought we had something special," Dolt said.

"Why would you think that?" Alaina asked as she watched her boyfriend rub his tail bone.

"Mostly, it's the way we look at each other," Dolt said.

Alaina rolled her eyes. "Well, if you're sure you're okay, Luc and I need to go meet Monsieur Trickets."

"Okay, I'll catch you two later," Dolt said as he turned.

"You should take it easy," Alaina said to him.

"I will. But first, I'm going to try to ride Phyllis again."

"What?! Why?!" Alaina exclaimed as her boyfriend walked back towards the horse.

"Horse isn't going to ride herself," Dolt answered.

"That makes no sense," Alaina said.

How could a horse ride itself? Luc wondered.

"Look," Alaina said to Dolt. "Just go back into the bar

and have someone else clean up these mallets and balls. Just take it easy."

"Maybe I will," Dolt answered, limping away.

"Luc and I have to go."

As Luc and Alaina turned, Luc was positive Dolt was going to wait until they were out of sight before immediately trying to ride Phyllis again.

*   *   *

Luc and Alaina stood at the doorway of the pro shop at the Paris Publique Plouquette Pitch, Grounds, Gardens, Grass Court, and Lawn Club. It was located on the second floor, and more closely resembled a high-end jewelry store. Most of the mallets, balls, apparel, and other merchandise were behind glass cases, on display and dramatically lit as if they were items in a museum.

"I don't come in here very often," Alaina said.

"Why's that?" Luc asked.

"My father is very strict with his club account and won't let my mom and me buy anything without his permission. Besides, I don't need any plouquette equipment. He's bought it all for us."

"Even the clothes?"

"Please. I don't buy my clothes at the pro shop at the club."

"Why not?" an old-sounding voice asked. Luc and Alaina looked up to see a little bald man in a tuxedo seated on a high stool behind the counter. They hadn't realized he could hear them as they wandered into the store.

"Um, I don't know," Alaina answered.

"Relax," the old man said, hopping off his perch. He waddled out from behind a glass case full of plouquette shoes to greet them. "I'm kidding. You're young and pretty. Why would you shop somewhere that Yelly gets all his clothes from?"

"Poor Yelly," Alaina sighed.

"And you must be the detective," the old man said, extending his hand.

"I am," Luc answered. He hoped the pro shop manager wouldn't notice the amount of sweat on his palms.

"I've heard about you. I'm Hugo Trickets," the man said as they shook hands. "Heard you got to talk to Tag le Tier."

"Nice to meet you. And yes, I did."

"How is he? Is he okay?"

Luc shrugged and looked at Alaina. "He seems okay—for being in jail."

"Never was the brightest guy on earth," Hugo said.

"That's what I hear," Luc confirmed.

"Anyway, let's cut the small talk. I know why you're here. The white pants are right over here."

"Oh, it's okay," Luc started. "That's not why—"

"Just follow him," Alaina sang.

"Please allow me to don a new pair of pants-handling gloves, detective," the pro shop operator said as he pulled a small plastic package out of his tuxedo jacket pocket. Hugo tore the seal and removed a new pair of pristine white gloves.

"No one will take you seriously around here without white pants. Plus, after a day or two, that little gnome of a man at the front door will stop letting you in."

"Who?" Luc asked.

"Coat-check Carl," both Hugo and Alaina answered in unison.

"Oh. Okay."

He floated with ceremony to a glass case holding a folded pair of white pants and pressed his thumb to a small pad. Luc watched the glass lower as Hugo donned each glove with care. Then, with a flourish, the pro shop operator ceremoniously lifted a pair of pants from the display. He presented them to Luc.

"I think you'll like these. Center seam. Triple pleat, double fly. No pockets."

"No pockets? Why?" Luc asked.

"Most people around here are so rich," Alaina said, "that they don't need pockets."

Luc didn't understand that. "It's so bright. Do you have something with a little less glow?" Luc asked.

Hugo stood stone faced.

"Ew," Alaina offered, disgusted. "Less glow? Are you serious?"

"Sir, we offer only the club color: crisp snowdrift," Hugo said. "My apologies if you can't handle its glow."

"Never mind." Luc glanced at the price tag on the pants in Hugo's gloved hands. "How much are they?"

"7,000 euros."

"7,000 euros?!" Luc jumped. "I'm can't... I mean, I'm

not paying that."

"Sir, this is one of our most modestly priced pairs," Hugo pitched. "But the fabric is very fine. It's a cobweb and spilk blend."

"A what?"

"A cobweb and spilk blend."

"What's spilk?"

"Fake silk."

"I've never heard of it," Luc said.

"It's what we, in the industry, call a silk-alike," Hugo said with a smile. "We do offer cobweb and real silk blends, but those are much pricier.

Alaina nodded.

"But rest assured," Hugo added. "The spilk feels real and can sustain a little more of the wear-and-tear caused by plouquette—especially in the knees, where the sport is hardest on a pair of pants."

"I swear, I do not understand this sport. Why the knees?"

"Don't worry about the details of plouquette," Hugo urged. "For a cobweb and spilk blend, these pants are top quality. Can't get any whiter. The spider farm that produced this fabric has a large population of albino spiders, fed only milk from albino cows, so you know the cobweb is really, really white."

"Okay," Luc answered. "I don't doubt the whiteness of these pants. But I'm still not paying all that money for them."

"Very well. Although I like the look of white pants

with the black in your glasses frame," Hugo said, placing the merchandise back in the case. "You may borrow a loaner pair. I keep some behind the counter in case of emergency. They fabric isn't as fine, and they've never been dry cleaned, but I do spray them with disinfectant after each use by one of our guests."

"Uh... okay," Luc stammered. Alaina looked disgusted.

"Just don't get any blood on them in a plouquette game until then or anything, okay?" Hugo said as he led the two back to the manager's stool.

"Blood? How do you bleed in plouquette?"

"You are so naïve," Hugo said as he reached below the counter and produced a foggy-white pair of pants. "Here."

Luc accepted the garment with the tips of his fingers. The pants were unusually stiff and a little sticky, like a piece of felt that had been dipped in milk and hung out to dry in the sun.

"You may change in the back before you go."

"Well," said Luc. He swallowed hard at the idea of putting the pants on, but decided to get to the heart of his visit with the club pro shop manager. "I came to ask you about Dorian Thibault and Armande Marwane."

"Is that so? What do you want to know about them?" Hugo asked as he scooted his way back on to his stool.

"We don't know much about either one at all. Only their names. What were they like?"

"Well, I'm not sure that I could tell you much."

"Tag said you knew them all," Luc added.

"I guess I knew them as well as anyone. I thought they were great guys. Tag just followed them around. I knew Armande ever since he was a little boy. Typical 'grew up in the club' kind of person. Not unlike you, young lady." Hugo pointed at Alaina.

Alaina raised her eyebrows and frowned.

"He was always very nice. A little quiet, but when Dorian showed up, they were fast friends. Dorian brought out a different side of Armande. A brighter, more charismatic side."

"When did Dorian first join?" Alaina asked.

"I'm not sure. Couldn't have been more than a year or so before he was kicked out."

"Why would you guess that?" Luc asked.

"That tournament that he won—I mean, Yelly won—was the first one Dorian had played in."

"He technically won the first tournament he'd ever played in?" Luc asked. "Does that happen often?"

"Never. He was a special player. But you've already heard that, I'm guessing."

"I have," Luc answered. "How did Dorian Thibault learn to play plouquette?"

"I never knew. Never asked him."

"How did he even get in the front door of the club? Was he brought in by another member? Armande maybe?"

"No, Dorian and Armande met here," Hugo answered. "I know that much. Not sure where Dorian came from. It's been kind of an interesting mystery around here. Other people have wondered that."

"So, no one knows where Dorian Thibault came from?" Luc asked.

"No one I know, at least."

"And, does anyone know how he got so good at plouquette?" Alaina asked.

"No. I'm sure he told Armande, and probably Tag. But I've never heard that they told anyone, so who knows?"

"You said they were great guys. What made them so great?" Alaina asked.

"I don't know," the club shop operator said as he ran his finger along the top of the glass case in front of him. He inspected it closely as he spoke. "They were very nice. Dorian was a charmer. All the women loved him. He was very friendly with all the guys. He was always the center of attention either out on the lawn, in the bar, the cigar room, anywhere really. People were just drawn to him. He treated everyone well—and they loved him."

"Even President Cravenmoore?" Luc asked.

"At first, definitely. The President was so excited to have the best plouquette player in the world here."

"How did you know he was the best in the world?"

"I guess we don't. But we'd never seen anyone play like him. He was incredible."

"When did Cravenmoore change his mind about him? Was it after he was caught cheating?" Luc asked.

"I'm not sure. You know, I've always wondered about that cheating thing. It seemed so unlike Dorian. He was an amazing player who didn't need to cheat. And greasing your balls? That's the least original way to cheat at plouquette. You can't do it at all without being caught these days. Same back then."

"So, do you think he maybe didn't cheat?" Luc asked.

"Well, the evidence is stacked against him. Maybe he wasn't as good as we thought and he cheated the whole time. But that seems unlikely. I thought he was an incredible talent." Hugo sighed, before raising his eyebrows with a new idea. "You know what might be helpful?"

"What?"

"The chief of police who worked the case is retired now, but he's still a member here. I'm sure he could give you so many more details than I could."

"Of course," Alaina said. "I should have thought of him. Monsieur Pompousselpeck, no?"

"That's right. Flive Pompousselpeck," Hugo confirmed. "I'm not sure how much help he'll be, but it's worth a shot. He managed the whole investigation for the police. But he's been retired a while. I saw him here this morning. He's probably out on the lawn still."

"That's great. Thank you. Let's go talk to him," Luc said to Alaina.

"One last thing," Hugo added as Luc and Alaina were turning to leave. "Ask him about the remains of the Waterford Cup that they found after the fire."

"Okay. Why's that?" Luc asked.

"I've always wondered about that, too," Hugo said. "If you believe everything you hear, the rumor was that they only found a little part of the cup."

"Is that right?" Luc asked.

"The cup itself was never recovered, according to the gossip. I heard the only thing they got out of the fire was the winner's nameplate, melted off the face of the trophy, lying among ashes. Just a mangled little piece of metal that said 'Yelly Reardon.'"

Chapter VI.

Luc and Alaina stood on the grass in the courtyard at the Paris Publique Plouquette Pitch, Grounds, Gardens, Grass Court, and Lawn Club. Several groups of people milled about, chatting amidst their mallets and balls. The busboy didn't think anyone seemed invested in the actual game. A quartet of short musicians on stilts played on the veranda at one end of the courtyard. Luc grimaced.

"What's the matter?" Alaina asked.

"Nothing. It's just that I've never seen any of those instruments before."

"Really? That is the most premier super-soprano clarinet quartet in Paris," she answered.

"A super-soprano clarinet? I don't think I've ever heard of that. What is it?"

"It's exactly what it sounds like it is."

"Why are they on stilts?"

"Who knows? Nice pants by the way," Alaina said.

"Thanks," Luc managed as he squirmed. He'd changed into the loaner pair of pants from Hugo. They fit a little tight, and rubbed his legs the way a piece of felt covered in sand might.

"Do they breathe well?"

"No, I'm sweating a little because of it," he said. His glasses slid down his nose. Used his middle finger to correct their position.

"Imagine trying to play plouquette in those," Alaina

said.

"I can't imagine playing in anything. I don't know the sport and no one seems interested in telling me about it." Luc dipped at the knees to try and loosen the pants' grip on his legs.

"My skirt is made out of the same stuff."

"Really? I thought you'd be in a real cobweb and silk fabric, like Hugo mentioned."

"Please. I only wear this because I have to."

Luc loved her defiance. He wished he could rebel at the café the same way she did at the club. But he reminded himself to focus. He was still there to pass himself off as the greatest detective of all time, and he was about to talk to a law enforcement professional. The busboy rubbed the sweat from his palms on to the sides of his white pants.

"Hey, so are you thinking what I'm thinking about the fire?" Alaina asked.

"What are you thinking?"

"Well, if they only found the name plate in the ashes—"

"Then maybe Yelly's name plate was the only thing in the fire, and the trophy is still out there?" Luc guessed. "It crossed my mind, too."

"I'm wondering what the former chief of police will say about that," Alaina said.

Luc surveyed the lawn. He noticed the woman from the restaurant, Marianne Merriweather, laughing with a group of people at the far end of the courtyard. Otherwise, there wasn't anyone else he seemed to recognize out there, except for Yelly.

"Do you know who we're looking for?" Luc asked.

"Yes, Monsieur Pompousselpeck has been around here forever. Then again, most of these people have."

Luc noticed the gentle breeze moving the delicate ends of her straight red hair. For a moment, he was lost watching them.

"There he is," she said, pointing.

Luc snapped out of it. Alaina led him to a plump, older man, speaking with a small group of people. They all rested their hands on the tops of their overturned mallets.

"Excuse me, Monsieur Pompousselpeck?" Alaina asked.

The man turned. Red flesh on his face consumed his jaw, erasing any distinction between head and neck. His face was topped with a shock of reddish and white hair, the only hair he hadn't lost yet.

"Yes?" The man asked.

Alaina nudged Luc.

"I'm uh... a detective..."

"Monsieur Pompousselpeck," Alaina interrupted as she rolled her eyes. "This is the detective hired by President Cravenmoore to investigate Tag le Tier's reappearance."

"Ah, I see. Excuse me a moment, my friends," Monsieur Pompousselpeck said to his group. "This is a matter for law enforcement professionals. I must excuse myself from our game. Per section D of rule 91 in 'The Plouquette Code: A Rulebook and Style Guide,' I inform you that I will now remove my balls."

"There's a rulebook?" Luc whispered to Alaina.

"I've never seen one," she replied.

The former chief of police lifted his balls from the field of play and presented them for the group. They nodded their approval.

"Please," he whispered to Luc and Alaina. "Let's talk over here." He motioned to a less crowded area of the courtyard, not far from Phyllis, the horse. "Plus, I would like to keep playing plouquette while we chat."

"Thank you," Luc began. His voice shook with nerves. "I hate to take you away from your friends. I really appreciate you talking to us."

"Have you been introduced to many people here at the club?" Monsieur Pompousselpeck asked as they walked.

"A few," Luc answered. "There's President Cravenmoore, and Maurice de Mouton. Hugo Trickets in the shop. And Alaina here, obviously."

"And he's met Coat-check Carl," Alaina added.

"Of course, he has," the former chief of police said. "Marianne Merriweather?"

"I've seen her around, but we haven't been introduced," Luc answered.

"You will discover, young man, that the elite of Parisian society are all here."

"Yes, I've heard."

"The group I was just with is extremely impressive," Pompousselpeck commented, dropping his balls to the ground as he turned to point out the individuals he was just with. "The man in the green sweater is the head of medical practices and coach of the handball team at St. Helmut Disciplinary Academy for First-Time Juvenile Offenders. He is a triple PhD on the human thumb. Incredible stuff. The man next to him is Pierre Pantsuit."

"Pierre Pantsuit?" Luc asked.

"Have you not heard of him? He is a premier one-ball juggler."

"Okay."

"Anyway, the man next to him with the tie tucked into his sweater is the owner of 'Recycloscopes.' Ever heard of it?"

"I don't think so," Luc stammered.

"It's the shop on the left bank that sells high-end telescopes made from recycled telescope parts. It has an elite clientele. Did 4.5 million in profit—*after lawsuits*—just last year alone."

"Wow."

"You got that right. Also, the man to his left is the founder and President of the non-profit group that promotes Pterodactyl remembrance."

"Pterodactyl remembrance?"

"Yes. I'm a board member myself. Never forget the mighty pterodactyl. Gone too soon."

"Okay," Luc said, stealing a look at Alaina.

"And the other gentleman is our resident actor. He stars in many of our zarzuelas."

"I just learned what a zarzuela is."

"You didn't know? Don't you own a word-of-the-day calendar?"

"He doesn't," Alaina chimed in.

"Well, as you know, we have a theatre space on the second floor here dedicated just to zarzuelas. We put millions into it. It's beautiful. Our productions are 80% funny, and 20% meaningful. Just the right mix for operettas, in my opinion. Plus, the word alone is great. Just say it: 'Zarzuela.'"

"Zarzuela."

"See? Doesn't get any better than that." Pompousselpeck continued. "But, that isn't what you came to talk to me for. What may I do for you, young man?"

"Well," Luc shifted. *Here we go,* he thought. "I'd like to ask you about Dorian Thibault, Armande Marwane, and Tag le Tier."

"What's there to ask?" Pompousselpeck replied, readying his mallet as he stared at his balls. "Those guys were losers. Hardened criminals. Liars. Cheaters. They're gone, and thankfully, no longer an issue." The former chief of police grunted as he adjusted the grip on his mallet.

"But Tag—"

"Yes, yes, I heard. Tag le Tier has turned up," the man said.

"Do you think the others are still out there then? Dorian Thibault and Armande Marwane?" Alaina asked.

"They are definitely not."

"Why not?" she asked.

"Dorian and Armande were the real targets. Tag was such a cretin. Honestly, he wasn't the one we cared about at all. That Dorian Thibault was the troublemaker of the bunch."

"Did you know him personally?" Luc asked. "Before

he won the tournament?"

"He didn't win," Pompousselpeck said, jabbing a look at Luc. "But, I did know him personally. We were both members back then."

"What was he like?" Luc asked.

"Listen boy," the former chief said. "I get it. You have a job to do. And I've heard you're good. But you must have also heard that I *was* the law in Paris for decades before you came along."

"Of course, sir," Luc answered. He spine tingled as his nervous system went haywire. Instant palm sweats.

"Let's at least play a little plouquette though while we talk," the man added. "As you know, I'm retired. I didn't retire to talk cases. I retired to play plouquette."

"Sure," Luc answered as he exhaled. "I don't get this game anyway. It might help to get a little instruction."

"Great. Take this mallet," Pompousselpeck instructed.

"We also need to ask you about the part of the cup you found in the wreckage of the fire," Alaina pressed. Luc wished he had her courage.

"Ah yes. The cup. Such a shame," Pompousselpeck said as he helped Luc situate his hands on the mallet.

"We heard that the only part of the cup that was recovered was Yelly's nameplate," Alaina said.

"Correct, young lady," Pompousselpeck answered. "Now detective, right hand over left, and take a short, quick swing at the ground."

Luc tried.

"That was awful," the man chuckled. "Don't worry. You'll get it. And yes. We found Yelly's nameplate. In fact, after it was cleared from evidence, we gave it to Yelly himself."

With this, Yelly, who was practicing nearby looked up at the small group.

"Are your ears burning, Yelly?" the former chief of police shouted over to him.

Yelly waved.

"Poor Yelly," the chief whispered as he smiled and waved back. He raised his voice again. "No doubt trying to perfect your impossibly-majestic-high-arc-rainbow-hammer-mallet throw, Yelly old boy?!"

"Yep!" Yelly shouted back.

"How's it coming, my good man?"

"I think I'm about to get it!" Yelly answered.

The former chief of police turned back to Luc and Alaina. "He's definitely not about to get it. Yelly's good, but he's not *that* good. 'Hope' is his greatest downfall."

"But he's come in second every year. So Yelly must be good?" Luc asked.

"He even won once," the former chief corrected him.

"Well sure, but that was a technicality, right?" Alaina asked.

The chief scowled. "Listen you two. Any man who greases his balls to get ahead in this world is not a man I'd ever shake hands with. And that's Dorian Thibault. He's a scoundrel. He deserved to lose that."

Luc let the subject drop for now. "I've been wondering, Monsieur Pompousselpeck. What's with the horse?"

"Who, Phyllis? She's the club horse."

"Is she part of the game of plouquette?"

"Well, she's not for riding, if that's what you're asking."

"No, I know that," Luc answered, looking over at Alaina.

"She's unrideable. No one has ever succeeded. In fact, watch this. LAWN BOY!" The chief called to no one specific.

Luc turned to see a lawn boy come jogging over to the group.

"Yes, Monsieur Pompousselpeck? What may I do for you?"

"Good afternoon, young man. Go give Phyllis a good ride, will you?"

The lawn boy showed no sign of disappointment. "I'll try, sir!"

The boy jogged over to Phyllis, mounted her with enthusiasm, and looked back with a smile and a wave one second before he was bucked high in the air. He landed face-first on the ground and remained motionless.

"See!" Monsieur Pompousselpeck turned back to Luc. "Unrideable!"

"Ah! Flive!" A voice called from behind Luc. "I see you're demonstrating the insolence of our lawn boys for our guests."

Luc turned to see President Cravenmoore approaching with Maurice de Mouton in tow.

"Ah yes, Keveen. Exactly." The former chief of police

squared off his stance, puffed his chest and saluted the President. "Skeeeerawwwww!" He shouted.

"Skeeeerawwwww!" The President shrieked as he mirrored Pompousselpeck's actions.

"What was that?" Luc asked the men.

"That, my boy," Pompousselpeck answered, "is how one member of the Pterodactyl Remembrance Society greets another."

"Oh, I didn't realize that's what a pterodactyl may have sounded like," Luc said.

The men looked at one another and burst out laughing.

"What makes you think," Pompousselpeck managed as he coughed on his own chuckles, "that's what the pterodactyl sounded like?!" Both men doubled over.

"Yeah, crack a history book every now and then, boy," Cravenmoore added with tears in his eyes.

The laughter began to die down as Luc looked at Alaina. She stood, unimpressed.

President Cravenmoore laid a hand on his belly to control his chortles, and eyed the lawn boy, still motionless on the grass. "How foolish for the youth to believe Phyllis could be ridden," the President said.

"My thoughts exactly," the former chief of police added, also recovering from the fit of laughter.

"Anyway, Monsieur Pigeon. I like your white pants. How is the case coming?" Cravenmoore asked.

"Thank you, and it's coming along," Luc answered.

"I was just lending some insight for the boy,"

Pompousselpeck added. "After all, I am a valuable resource for this young man."

"Careful Flive," the President warned. "You're talking about the greatest detective of our—or any—generation there. He's not just a boy."

The former chief of police scoffed at the thought. "I've been showing him the finer points of plouquette along the way as well."

"Very good. I'm sure with a little bit of work, he could be just as good as my terrible ex-wife!" The President erupted in hysterical laughter again.

"Good one, Keveen," the former chief answered with an eye roll.

"Monsieur Pompousselpeck has been helpful," Luc assured the President. "Alaina and I have spoken with Tag le Tier already as well."

"Very good. I trust that little bastard is finding his cell quite accommodating after so many years on the lam?" the President asked.

"He wasn't much help," Alaina added.

"You know who's *really* behind all this, don't you?" the former chief of police asked Luc with a serious look in his eye.

"What do you mean?" Luc asked.

"I mean that Dorian Thibault, Armande Marwane, and Tag le Tier were all just pawns. They're losers. They could never have pulled this off."

"No, they're not the masterminds. They're too dumb," the President added.

"Who should I be looking at, then?" Luc asked.

"It's those scoundrels at the Private."

"What's that?"

"The Paris Private Plouquette Conglomerate. It's our rival club," Cravenmoore said without separating his teeth.

"Wait. There's a rival plouquette club?" Luc asked.

"Of course," the former chief answered.

"I didn't realize there were multiple clubs. How have I not heard of this sport before?" Luc asked.

"It's for the elite," Pompousselpeck answered.

"You see," the President explained, "when plouquette was invented in 1644 by Paul Plouquette Sr., there were clubs all over the city. Originally, they were all private."

"But your name suggests that you are public," Luc noticed. "The Paris *Publique* Plouquette Pitch, Grounds…um…"

"Right, the Paris Publique Plouquette Pitch, Grounds, Gardens, Grass Court, and Lawn Club," the President continued. "We went public for a brief period in the wild 1650s."

"Those were crazy times," the former chief said. "Famous for rampant drug use and greasing of many balls."

"But the 'Publique' name stuck," the President said. "And even today, the 'Publique' and the 'Private' have remained heated rivals."

"Nothing but a bunch of losers and cheaters over there," the former chief of police added.

"So that's who you think started this whole thing?" Luc asked.

"Undoubtedly," Pompousselpeck answered. "I suspected them 20 years ago, and I've known in my heart that it's been them ever since. I'm sure they put Dorian Thibault, Armande Marwane, and Tag le Tier up to it. I just can't prove it."

"Interesting," Luc answered. "Maybe that should be my next stop."

"They are as exclusive as we are," Alaina added. "How can we get in over there?"

"My wife is a member," Pompousselpeck grunted.

"Your wife?" Luc asked.

"That's right," the former chief of police confirmed. "She's been a member there for years."

"Why isn't your wife a member here?" Alaina asked.

Both Flive Pompousselpeck and President Cravenmoore exploded in red-faced laughter again. A solid minute passed before either man could find the breath to speak.

"Who would ever want," the former police chief managed between breathy giggles, "to attend the same club as their wife?!"

Chapter VII.

The next day, Luc and Alaina walked through Paris on a fair-aired afternoon. The presumed greatest-detective-on-earth tried not to think about work in his parents' café—or the fact that a pigeon might be defecating on his pillow at that very moment.

Luc just wanted to take in an afternoon with the girl as they walked by tiny Parisian shops and sidewalk cafés. The autumn breeze carried the occasional orange or brown leaves away from small parks in the city, as the couple lumbered over uneven cobblestone side streets. They talked about Cravenmoore and Pompousselpeck. Luc couldn't muster the courage to ask about Alaina's love life again.

Before long, they found themselves at the unmarked door to the Paris Private Plouquette Conglomerate. The building looked like a small cathedral compared to the Publique. Its ancient carvings looked lost in time, dirtied by years of car exhaust and cigarette smoke from the sidewalk.

"This is it," Alaina confirmed.

The walk had been too short for Luc. He could have strolled with her until dark.

"Have you ever been here before?" Luc asked.

"No. Why would I ever have?" She answered.

"I don't know."

"My dad was never keen on letting us fraternize with other clubs. The social circles just don't mix."

"Seems as though the President and former chief of

police don't think too much of these guys either," Luc added.

"Yes. Both clubs hate each other, I'm told."

"Will they even let us in? Don't they know we're from the other club?" Luc asked.

"Pompousselpeck told me that he'd phone ahead for you, and his wife would let you in," Alaina answered. "You were too busy trying to hold the plouquette mallet correctly to be paying any attention."

Luc huffed.

"Besides. If these guys didn't do it," Alaina added, "I'm sure that they'll be eager to clear their name."

"Or, they'll love watching us fail to help their rival," Luc offered.

"True," Alaina answered. "I guess we'll just have to see."

"Guess so," Luc conceded as he watched Alaina ring the bell.

"Yes?" A voice came over the intercom.

"Hi, my name is Alaina Amandine, and my guest and I are here to see..." Alaina checked a handwritten note from the former chief of police, "...Flova Pompousselpeck."

"Of course, Madame. She's expecting you."

Just as the intercom sparked to a stop, the door opened.

The foyer of the rival club was bright white—a stark contrast to the entrance that Luc and Alaina were used to at the PPPPGGGCLC. An enormous black man was waiting for them.

"Please, come in," he said. "Do you have a coat to

check?"

"We don't," Alaina answered.

"Excellent," the man replied. "Madame Pompousselpeck will be right down. In the meantime, I'd like to introduce myself. I'm Chad Claude, and I'd love your vote in the upcoming parliamentary elections.

Luc and Alaina looked at one another.

"The education of our youth is very important to me," the man continued. "It's second only to an issue that gravely concerns me: the unfair jurisdictional boundaries of my—and my fellow party members'—parliamentary districts, which are drawn up based on population, which makes it harder for us to win. That is unfair and must be changed. That, and the education of our youth."

"That's enough, Coat-check Chad," a woman's voice said from behind the towering man.

He stepped aside to reveal a short, round woman in her mid-sixties. Her bright white hair was pulled back, and her natural beauty was evident.

"Spare them the lecture. I'm sure they're sympathetic to your struggle," she added.

Coat-check Chad smiled at the two visitors. "Thank you for listening. Look for me on the ballot, and remember—together, I can achieve," he said as he closed the door behind Alaina and Luc.

"Thanks," Alaina answered. "Flova Pompousselpeck?"

"You must be Alaina Amandine," the woman answered. "Nice to meet you. Follow me."

Madame Pompousselpeck led the two beyond the foyer, into a grand hall. Unlike the PPPPGGGCLC, the actual plouquette-playing surface was nowhere to be seen. Large chandeliers hung high above pristine carvings and a glimmering marble floor.

"I must apologize for Coat-check Chad," the woman began. Her voice echoed in the large space. "He's aggressively seeking another term."

"He's really a member of parliament?" Luc asked.

"He is," she confirmed. "I'm not sure how familiar you are with this network of clubs, but most of the doormen are members of parliament. They want to get close to people with money, but they only ever score a doorman job. Now, you'll have to forgive me for not giving you the grand tour. The club execs don't know who you are, and I'd like to keep it that way. Young man, your white pants would give you away in a moment, and the brass around here would not be impressed that I invited members of the rival club. They might believe you're spies."

"I'm not a member of the other club," Luc mentioned.

"Yes, that's true," Alaina added. "He's the detective that they've hired to solve an old mystery."

"Yes, I've heard. Monsieur Pigeon here is said to be the greatest detective of all time," Madame Pompousselpeck confirmed as she led the two up a steep and narrow spiral staircase off the grand foyer.

"It sounds like your husband filled you in," Luc answered. The stairwell was dimly lit and he began to feel dizzy as they climbed.

"I'm familiar with the case. I remember when it happened," she said. "There are few in these circles who don't. Everyone here was talking about the disappearance of the Waterford Cup for years after it happened."

When they reached the top of the staircase, Luc and Alaina found themselves in another well-lit hallway. This one was lined with classical-looking busts and other statues.

"Here," Madame Pompousselpeck continued. "We can chat on this bench. This is one of my favorite spots. I feel as though I can be candid here."

"Okay," Luc answered as he continued to take in the ornate hallway. "Who are all these statues?"

"The busts?" Madame Pompousselpeck responded as she eased onto the bench with a grunt. "They're various luminaries. Visionaries from another time. All members or deceased members of this club. Sort of our hall of fame."

"Oh, cool," Luc answered.

"I won't bore you, but we have a few interesting ones. The one third down on your left is the famous camel trainer and shaver Bobby Warlust. Then of course, you'll notice the famous oboe artist Wazoo Nichols."

"An oboist? Interesting," Luc said.

"No. An oboe artist. That's someone who makes art out of oboes. Statues and things. But enough of that. Please," she said. "Take a seat. What may I help you with?"

Luc and Alaina sat down.

"Well," Luc began, "Your husband seemed to think that..." he looked around to double-check that they were alone, "...that people from this club might be in on the Waterford Cup heist."

"Oh, I don't know about that," Madame Pompousselpeck answered. "That would surprise me. I'm sure I would have heard about it by now."

"Did you know Dorian Thibault, Armande Marwane, and Tag le Tier?" Alaina asked.

"I didn't know them personally," she said. "Our two clubs don't mingle socially. But, the guys were famous among the elite. Even before the heist. Dorian Thibault and Armande Marwane were extremely popular people. I heard a lot about them from my husband, but their popularity even made them well known here. To a degree, at least."

"Have you heard that Tag le Tier has been found alive?" Alaina asked.

"I did. The story was of obvious interest to my husband."

"So," Luc asked. "Do you think Dorian Thibault and Armande Marwane are still out there?"

"I think that would surprise me," the woman said.

"Why?" Luc asked. "If le Tier has been hiding out, why couldn't the other guys be out there? And what about the cup for that matter?"

"I suppose you're right," Madame Pompousselpeck answered. "But keeping a secret for that long is very difficult. Especially around here. If someone at this club were also behind it, I think I'd know about it."

"Why's that?" Luc asked.

"Because no one around here can keep any kind of

secret. For instance, when Coat-check Chad had an affair with our club pro's wife, they swore to each other that they'd never tell another soul."

"But he did?" Alaina asked.

"Obviously. He ran right to the center of the plouquette grounds here and announced the liaison."

"Why?" Luc asked.

"I don't think he sees too much action," Flova Pompousselpeck replied. "He was proud. The woman was beautiful, and as a member of parliament, he was waiting for a sex scandal to really get his name out there. Regardless, I have no reason to believe anyone here was involved in the heist of the Waterford Cup.

"Do you ever go over to the Publique with your husband?" Luc asked.

"I don't. My husband doesn't invite me, and I don't invite him here. But, I *am* curious to see what it's like. I convinced him to take me to this year's Waterford Cup."

"That's coming up," Alaina mentioned.

"Very true. End of next week, and I'm looking forward to finally seeing the club," she said before pausing. "You know, there's someone I'd like you to meet. It didn't occur to me until now, but perhaps he can be of help."

"Okay, great," Luc said.

"Follow me," Madame Pompousselpeck suggested as she stood. Her knees creaked. Luc and Alaina joined her as they started walking down the hall of busts.

"Our barber here has been a member at both clubs. I think he knew Dorian Thibault, Armande Marwane, and Tag le Tier all at least a little bit. He cuts everyone's hair at some point."

"Sounds good," Luc said.

"His shop is on this floor, through the door at the end. It's nice and quiet up here. I don't think he gets too much traffic."

"Let me ask you a question before we talk to him," Luc said. Flova Pompousselpeck had a motherly look—while being a little more kind than his own. She made him comfortable.

"Go ahead."

"Do you think Dorian Thibault greased his balls in the championship game?"

"Well, that's the rumor. But, I didn't know the situation well enough. My husband thinks he did."

"Okay," Luc said.

"But you don't think he did?" Madame Pompousselpeck asked, sensing some doubt in Luc.

"I didn't say that," he answered, looking at Alaina. "It's just that, we've heard some conflicting reports about Dorian Thibault, Armande Marwane, and Tag le Tier. Dorian and Armande especially."

"What kind of conflicting reports?" Madame Pompousselpeck asked.

"Well," Luc thought aloud, "it's just that some people we talk to say they were crooks. And then there are others that say they were great guys."

"I see," Madame Pompousselpeck answered as they stopped in front of the barbershop.

"It seems like senior club leadership has a different opinion than many other people," Luc added. He wondered if speaking behind Cravenmoore's back was wise, but he somehow trusted Madame Pompousselpeck.

"Interesting," the woman answered. "You know, you should keep something in mind. The kinds of people that you're dealing with—they're people who will do anything to protect their legacy."

"Okay," Luc answered.

"I hate to tell you this, but my husband is one of those people. You may have already guessed, but he assumes that their original result on this case was absolutely correct, and he may be blind to any evidence to the contrary."

"We get that," Alaina said.

"Just know, if you need anything along the way in your case, don't hesitate to ask me for help. I can't imagine what it might be, but my door is always open to you—even if it's something that you'd like to maybe keep a secret. Happy to help. Anyway, here we are. The barbershop," Madame Pompousselpeck said.

She opened the door. The room had four ornate barber chairs set up across from a wall-length mirror. Marble floors and gold cosmetic utensils accented the classic barbershop feel.

A man jumped to meet them. He was dressed in a smock as if he were the one receiving a cut. His mustache quivered with excitement at the sight of them.

"Flova!" He exclaimed as he jumped. "How great to see you!"

"Snippy. What's with the smock? Giving yourself a trim?"

"It gets a little slow up here. Thought I'd try out a new shearing technique."

"Well, you don't have to leap up just for me."

"Why not?" He answered. "Seeing you is a real treat. And you've brought some friends along!"

"I have," Madame Pompousselpeck said with a nod. "Snippy le Coif, this is Alaina Amandine and Monsieur Pigeon. They are my guests."

"Pigeon? Given name?" Snippy replied, looking at Luc.

"We could ask you the same," Alaina answered.

"Touché, young lady. I did have it legally changed back in '11." Snippy answered.

"What was your name before it was Snippy?" Alaina asked.

"Dave."

"Cool," she deadpanned.

"Anyway, my friends, it is my absolute pleasure to host you in my barbershop today. Monsieur Pigeon, I believe we'll start with you."

Snippy motioned to the empty barber chair.

"Oh, no thank you," Luc said. "I didn't come here for a haircut."

"My dear boy, please have a seat. I insist."

"No, no thank you," Luc said again.

"Absolutely not, young man," Snippy interrupted. "I said, have a seat. You'll never get ahead in plouquette with arms like that."

"Arms like that?" Luc asked.

"All that arm hair," the barber replied. "Seriously, you'll never be able to play like a pro with all that."

"I don't see what arm hair has to do with the game of plouquette," Luc replied.

Snippy looked at Madame Pompousselpeck. The pair giggled.

"Don't get distracted by the details, my boy. Just let Snippy get you taken care of. Let's go," he urged. "Take a seat."

Luc sat down, and Snippy fitted a smock across the fake detective's body, leaving the arms exposed. Oddly, the smock had a hood, and Snippy made a small show of covering Luc's head.

"I've never been to a barber before who covers your head," Luc observed.

"It's a practice of the elite," Snippy said.

"Snippy, while you're doing that," Madame Pompousselpeck said, "I brought them to you for a specific reason. These two are interested in knowing about the heist of the Waterford Cup."

"Ah yes," Snippy replied, rummaging through his supplies. "That's been a popular topic lately."

"Oh yeah?" Alaina asked.

"Well, with Tag le Tier turning up and all."

"So, you've heard," Luc said.

"I told you," Madame Pompousselpeck mentioned. "It's a hot topic."

"Did you know him?" Alaina asked Snippy.

"Sure, I knew Tag. I was a member at the Publique when I was younger. We'd met. I knew all three men."

"Snippy here has been a member of both clubs off and on for years," Flova Pompousselpeck added.

"Oh yeah?" Luc answered. "I didn't realize that someone could be a member of both clubs."

"I should clarify," Snippy said. "I've never been a member of both clubs—*at the same time.*"

"Ah, I see," Luc answered.

Snippy began to lather shaving cream onto one of Luc's arms. By almost any account, it was way more than one might need to shave arm hair.

"I started as a member at the Publique from sixty-seven to seventy-one. Then, I came here to the Private from seventy-one until seventy-six. Then it was the Publique again from seventy-six to eighty-five, and then the Private again from eighty-five until ninety-five. In ninety-six, I was back at the Publique, but in ninety-seven I came here, and I've been here ever since.

"Why all the back and forth?" Alaina asked.

"I don't know. I love the Publique for the Zarzuela Theater and the upstairs gallery of post-impressionist all-blood paintings. But I like this place for the meat-only breakfasts, organic shoe store, and ping pong tables in the shower rooms," Snippy replied after a moment of thought.

"I could handle an organic shoe store," Alaina commented.

"Hold still, son," Snippy said as he took a razor to

Luc's arm.

Luc squirmed. Alaina smirked at his insecurity.

"Maybe you know my parents?" Alaina asked. "The Amandines?"

"Name rings a bell," the barber said without looking up. "But I haven't been over there in years. I knew President Cravenmoore, though."

"And probably Madame Pompousselpeck's husband? The former chief of police?" Alaina asked.

Snippy glanced at Madame Pompousselpeck, who smiled back. "Yes, I know him. Forgive me, Flova, for telling our guests that I have no love for your husband."

"That's okay," she answered. "Your disdain for him is well known. Thank you for not hating me just because you hate him."

"You're welcome," Snippy answered.

"Why do you hate him?" Luc asked. His rigid body almost lay straight in the chair.

"Just could never beat him at plouquette. He was always so in-my-face about it too. Not sportsmanlike. Then, to be so confident in his ability as the chief of police. Always bragging. He and I just didn't click most of the time."

Luc knew what the barber meant, but he didn't want to agree with him in front of Madame Pompousselpeck.

"So, I'm hoping you can tell us something about Dorian Thibault and Armande Marwane." Sweat from Luc's brow made his glasses creep down his nose.

"Sure. What do you want to know?"

"Well," Luc continued, "we've heard conflicting

opinions of these guys. I'm just trying to get a feel for who they were—and I'm trying to figure out if they're still out there." He paused to wince under the razor. "So, it would be great to know maybe where they are from, where they hung out, that kind of thing? Are you finished yet?"

"Not quite," the barber said as he worked. "But let's see here. Armande had been a member of the club almost his entire life. At least as long as I could remember. He's from right here in Paris, but I can't think of any place I knew he hung out other than the club itself. That's about right for the elite society. They'd never be found in just a normal café."

"I see," Luc answered.

"And Dorian Thibault," the barber said, "well, he was the great mystery."

"That's what I've heard," Luc said.

"Thing about him is that none of us knew where he came from at all. So, I couldn't tell you where he would have run to hide out or anything—if that's what you're asking."

"I see," Luc answered.

"I'm going to take care of your other arm. You are going to be in top shape," Snippy continued. He moved to Luc's other side.

"We were just telling Madame Pompousselpeck," Alaina chimed in, "that we've heard from some people that Dorian Thibault and Armande Marwane were the greatest guys ever. Others have said they were crooks and cheaters."

"Why not both?" Snippy answered.

Luc thought for a moment.

"I'm not saying that I think they were crooks and

cheaters," Snippy went on. "In fact, just the opposite. I'm one of the ones who think they were great guys. I'm just saying, being a great guy and being a cheater and a crook are not mutually exclusive."

"Sounds pretty cut and dry to me. I don't think crooks are good guys," Luc ventured.

"Well, think about it though," Snippy continued as he worked. "What's a great guy? Someone who treats people well? Thinks of others? Inspires others?"

"And someone who doesn't steal," Luc replied. His voice shook with nervous energy as Snippy went to work on his other arm. Luc shortened his breath with anxiety.

"Well wait. Let's say the man steals. Ask yourself: 'what was his motivation?' Was he stealing to hurt someone? Or was he stealing to help someone else? Was he righting a wrong? Was it a victimless crime? It's all about perspective. And don't make a judgment without all the information."

"That's good advice," Luc managed.

"Cravenmoore should follow it," Alaina interjected.

"You're not wrong," Snippy answered.

"So, you're saying that they could be great guys and still grease their balls?" Alaina asked as Luc lay frozen.

"Oh, definitely not. I firmly believe Dorian and Armande didn't grease their balls. All I'm saying is you can be a great guy and still lie to someone," Snippy answered.

"You don't think they cheated?" Luc asked.

"I know they didn't."

"How do you know?"

"I played plouquette with them many times. There

wasn't even a whiff of cheating. Ever."

"Maybe they only did it on the morning of the tournament?" Luc guessed.

"Look," Snippy paused the shaving. "Dorian Thibault was so good at this game. Every shot was perfect. Plus, he played with a lot of swagger. He condemned people who greased their balls. When others would do it against him, he'd still win. He was proud to not have the need to cheat."

"I see," Luc answered.

"In fact," Snippy continued, gesturing too close to Luc's face with the razor, "When he felt threatened by an opponent, he just buckled down even harder to beat him."

"I see," Luc repeated. The busboy gulped as he watched the foamy blade pass in front of his nose several times.

"If anything," Snippy went on, "those guys were pranksters. They loved a good laugh. Always had a little joke ready. They never would have greased balls. That's too serious. In the context of the tournament, Dorian was all business."

"Could you not wave the razor around like that?" Luc asked.

"Oops. Sorry. I've nicked too many people in my day. You'd think I'd have learned by now!" Snippy exclaimed with a chuckle.

Luc didn't find it funny.

"Anyway, the day of the tournament," Alaina interrupted, "Dorian's toughest competition would have been Yelly Reardon, right?"

Snippy scoffed. "Yeah right. Yelly couldn't touch Dorian. Dorian knew it. Yelly knew it. Everyone knew it. The final score wasn't even close. Greased balls couldn't have saved Yelly."

"I don't get it," Luc offered. "President Cravenmoore said they caught Dorian with greased balls."

"No. They framed Dorian Thibault," Snippy answered as he went back to shaving Luc's arm.

"Why would they do that?" Alaina asked.

"Yeah, it doesn't make sense," Luc continued. "If the best plouquette player of all time is a member of your club, isn't that a good thing?"

"You haven't heard yet," Snippy said.

"Heard what?" Luc asked.

"Cravenmoore never wanted it to get out. Thought it would sully the prestige of the club."

"What would?" Luc asked again.

"Dorian Thibault was an imposter. He was penniless."

Chapter VIII.

Luc thought for a moment. "Penniless? What do you mean?"

"What do you think I mean?" Snippy answered, running the razor down Luc's arm. "I mean he wasn't rich. He was posing as a rich person at the club. He wasn't elite at all. He had nothing."

"He had nothing? Like *nothing* nothing?" Alaina asked.

"I mean I'm sure he had a little something," Snippy answered. "But he wasn't even middle class. He was broke. Paycheck to paycheck."

"And they framed him?" Luc asked as he pieced the story together.

"Remember," Snippy continued. "It's called a plouquette club, but it's for wealthy people first, and the sport comes second."

"How'd he even get in in the first place?" Luc asked.

"Like I said," Snippy answered. "Dorian Thibault was the great mystery."

"And how'd he get so good at plouquette?"

"Well, that's all part of it. Who knows?" Snippy replied.

Luc sat up as Snippy wiped the excess shaving cream from his forearm. "So, let me get this straight. One day Dorian Thibault, who has no money, somehow sneaks in and gets accepted in one of Paris' most elite clubs. Plus, he shows up being better at a sport that usually people only learn how to play at the actual club. He becomes friends with Armande Marwane, who's already on the inside, they befriend a busboy, Tag le Tier, and somehow the bond is so strong between the three that they wind up dying together in a fire to protect a treasure they stole from the club?"

"That's it," Alaina nodded. "Supposedly."

"I think I have one more thing that could help you," Snippy continued.

"What's that?" Luc asked.

"An address. It's for one of our club members here at the Private. But, he was also a member of the Publique at the time of the tournament. We don't see him a lot around here anymore, but if he still lives there, he could be of help to you."

* * *

Luc and Alaina walked down Rue des Riches after leaving the Paris Private Plouquette Conglomerate. Orange and brown leaves dotted the dirty sidewalk, sometimes mingling with the legs of postcard carousels. The bright afternoon sun had turned soft, adding visual warmth to the sky and coolness to the autumn air.

"It's getting a little late," Luc said, checking his watch. The reluctant busboy was dreading his breakfast shift at the café. "Should we visit this guy tomorrow afternoon maybe?"

"Really? Just when this is starting to get interesting, you want to stop now?" Alaina pulled a cigarette from her small purse.

"No, it's just that I don't want to knock on someone's door if they're getting ready for dinner or anything."

"Let's not worry about it. Don't you want to break this thing wide open?" Alaina reached for her lighter. Luc watched her lips seal on the end of the cigarette. She inhaled as the flame cast a soft orange glow on her face.

"I guess I do… want to break this thing wide open," Luc answered, distracted.

"Tell you what, if it goes nowhere tonight, I'll buy you a drink somewhere. But this address is just a few blocks away. Aren't you curious to hear what this guy has to say?"

"Definitely." Luc almost hoped the encounter would fail after hearing Alaina's offer. He tried to play it cool. "I guess we can keep going."

As they strolled the Paris streets, the busboy wanted a little time off from the café now more than ever. His shifts in the last few days felt longer than normal.

Luc was looking forward to filling Charlie on his day. And while thinking of Charlie, Luc also wondered if there was still a pigeon in his apartment. Was it sleeping in his bed now? And what about Janet? Had she kept calling? He hadn't given her a second thought until now. When Luc was around Alaina, he forgot everything about Janet. Luc hoped she wasn't harassing Charlie.

"Here we are," Alaina said as she stopped in front of an impressive townhouse.

"Wow. Some place," Luc muttered.

"The guy's name is Roman Lubin," Alaina said,

checking the address Snippy le Coif had given them. "After you, detective."

Luc ascended to the door and rang the bell. After a moment or two of waiting, a good-looking black man in his fifties answered. The busboy thought the man was dressed as if he was in an ad for an expensive watch. Classical music played in the background.

"Yes?" the man asked.

"Good evening," Luc answered. "We got this name and address from Snippy le Coif at the Paris Private Plouquette Conglomerate."

"Oh yeah? What may I do for you?"

"Are you Roman Lubin?" Luc asked.

"Yes, that's me."

"I am a detective, and I'm investigating the reappearance of Tag le Tier…"

The man's face became serious. "Tag le Tier?"

"That's right. I'm just hoping to ask some questions about Dorian Thibau—"

"You know," the man interrupted. "Actually, this is not a great time. It would be helpful if we rescheduled."

"Oh, I'm sorry," Luc answered. "When would be a time—"

"Thank you. I'm sorry," the man interrupted again. He shut the door.

"Okay?" Alaina muttered.

"Huh," Luc thought aloud, still facing the closed door.

"Well, that was interesting. Not too talkative."

"Not at all," Luc said as he turned around.

"That seems like a dead end."

"I guess. He did say we could reschedule."

"Are you kidding?" Alaina asked. "He just shut the door in our face. Who are you going to call to reschedule?"

"Snippy got us the appointment," Luc guessed.

"Snippy's not his secretary."

"Good point."

"So. Ready for that drink, detective?"

* * *

Luc sat across from Alaina at the last spot in a row of empty tables at a sidewalk café. The warm evening was pleasant. Plenty of passersby moved near the couple, and the occasional dog stopped to scavenge under the café tables until its owner pulled it away. A deep navy-blue sky domed Paris. No stars.

"So," Alaina began. "How often do you have a 'nobody' like me tag along on your cases?"

Luc shifted in his chair. He was even more uncomfortable than the pants were already making him. The corners of his glasses near his nose started to fog up again as he got nervous.

"Uh, not often," he said.

"Well, I'm honored. The greatest detective of all time. That's something."

"I guess."

"So, tell me about the most gruesome case you've

ever seen. You've probably been to plenty of murder scenes."

"You know," Luc said as he shifted again in his chair, "I think we better stick to talking about this case."

"Okay, sorry," she said as she sipped from her drink.

A moment of silence passed, and Luc regretted lying to her. He'd never had a female friend with her type of self-confidence. The busboy liked that.

"Here's my question," Alaina said. "Don't they do a background check of any kind when you join the club?"

"I don't know. You're the one who is a member there."

"Yeah, but I was born in. How did Dorian Thibault get by them if he had no money? Coat-check Carl usually won't even let you in the door if you're not wearing some ten-thousand-euro suit."

"Maybe Dorian knew someone on the inside already? I mean, I wasn't wearing a suit like that and Coat-check Carl invited me in."

"That's true, but so far, we haven't heard anything concrete that says Dorian Thibault was anyone's guest," Alaina said. "What if 'Dorian Thibault' isn't his real name?"

"Interesting," Luc answered. "He seems to have come out of nowhere, I guess. Plus, no one knows anything about him outside club life." The busboy couldn't stop looking at her lips. It was either that or her eyes. The black eyeliner seemed to make her blue eyes even lighter to him.

"Okay," she answered. "And if I were to infiltrate a swanky club, I would try and lie about who I really was too."

"Yes, good point," Luc answered, squirming.

"You know," Alaina continued, "why don't you join the club?"

"What?" Luc choked on his drink a little.

"Just seems like you'd be a top catch. I have nothing to do with membership, but I don't get it. You're rich. You're at the top of your field. You're young. It all makes sense."

Luc felt invisible weight, and he sighed into his drink. She was more than a beautiful girl to him. He was attracted to everything about her that he wasn't: a risk taker, fearless. He liked it that she brought these things out of him. And here she was, suggesting he should join the club. Did it mean she liked him? Did she want to spend more time with him? She *did* ask him to join her for a drink. *This was her idea*, Luc reminded himself.

"Just a suggestion," she offered as she took another sip.

"Alaina. I have something to tell you."

"Okay?"

Luc had Charlie's voice in his head again. Yes, he had a lie to perpetuate, but he couldn't bear to do it any longer with the girl he couldn't stop thinking about. Besides, what was riskier than going all-in on a girl? Luc convinced himself Charlie would be proud.

"I don't know what I'm doing," Luc said.

"What do you mean?"

"It's just that—"

"Are we not giving you everything you need? I'm pretty sure I could ask President Cravenmoore for almost anything and he'd give it to you."

"No, it's not that. It's just that... I'm *not* the greatest detective of all time."

Alaina leaned back in her chair. "Come on, man."

Luc watched her. He wanted to tell her how beautiful he thought she was, but for some reason he couldn't make his mouth say it.

"You're not going to make me give you some kind of pep talk, are you?" Alaina whined.

"What?"

"I know what you're doing. A lot of guys do this. They downplay their egos just to get compliments, or to appear vulnerable or something. I see through it. You don't have to do it."

"No, that's not it."

"Fine. What do you want me to say? You're great. You inspire me every day. Blah, blah, blah." She rolled her eyes and took another drink.

"No," Luc answered. "That's not what I mean. Listen. I mean I'm *really not* a detective at all."

She put her drink down. "What?"

"I'm not a detective."

"You're not a...?" She stammered.

"Not a detective. At all."

Their waitress approached the table. "You two good here?"

"Uh..." Luc tried, waiting for a sign of any reaction from Alaina.

The waitress replied, "In case you were interested today, our specials are— "

"Could you give us a second?" Luc asked her without taking his eyes off Alaina.

"Sure," the waitress said. "I'll be right back."

Moments more passed. Alaina squinted as she leered at Luc. She said nothing, but sipped her drink again, looking as though she was trying to solve a complicated math equation tattooed on the busboy's forehead. She fished a cigarette out of her purse without looking down.

"So..." Luc said.

"Are you serious?" Alaina whispered after taking another slow sip of her martini. "You're serious? Is that true? You're not a detective—at all?"

"No."

"Like, not even at all? You have never done police work or anything like that?" She asked.

"No."

Another few moments passed as Luc watched Alaina process the information. "So, I don't understand. How did you get here?" Alaina still hunched over her drink, her breath causing small ripples on the surface.

Luc sighed. "It's a long story. But, I was in a café, and this guy just sat down and offered me this job out of nowhere."

"De Mouton?" Alaina guessed.

"Yes. He thought I was the greatest detective of all time."

"And you're not?"

"No. Definitely not."

"So, why'd he think you are?" She asked.

"I'm not rich. I don't do anything that would suggest I'm a detective. I'm just a busboy in my parent's café." Luc wasn't thinking about any ramifications beyond talking to Alaina. He didn't think about what might happen if Alaina told anyone at the PPPPGGGCLC. The busboy was caught in the moment with a beautiful girl.

"Huh," she grunted as she leaned back and took another sip of her drink.

"So," Luc asked, "what do you think?"

A moment passed.

A smile crept onto Alaina's face as she answered, "That's *fucking awesome.*"

"Really?" Luc asked with a smile.

"Seriously. It's badass." She lit her cigarette and took a deep drag. No one had ever called Luc badass before.

"I can't think of anyone," Alaina continued, "who has ever given President Cravenmoore a bigger middle finger than this."

"So, you're not mad?" Luc asked.

"Mad? Are you kidding? This is hilarious."

"Hilarious? Why?"

"I don't know, you know? All these stuffy rich guys. You've got them thinking that you're the greatest detective of all time, or whatever. That's amazing."

"I know, right? My roommate, Charlie, can't believe it."

"I don't believe it either. But it's great," she said.

"So, you're not going to say anything?"

"Say anything? No, why would I?"

"I don't know? I just thought because you grew up there, maybe you'd not want me going in there and lying and all that stuff," Luc answered.

"Please. I've been lying to my parents and their friends my whole life. It's my thing. So, let me ask you a question."

"Sure," Luc said.

"Are those glasses real?"

"My glasses? Yes."

"Oh," Alaina said, leaning back in her chair with apparent disappointment.

"Why? Why would they be fake?" Luc took his glasses off and looked at them. They seemed normal to him.

"They're just a little over-the-top, that's all," Alaina answered with a smile. "It's okay, they look good on you."

"Over-the-top?"

"Forget it. It's nothing. I just thought they were part of your act for a second. But, it's cool. They work. Forget I said anything."

"Okay." Luc took a sip of his drink, wondering if he should get new frames.

"You know what you should do?" Alaina said.

"What?" Luc asked.

"You have to solve this thing."

"Are you serious?"

"Yes. Totally," she offered as small clouds of smoke billowed from her mouth.

"You're okay if we keep going?" Luc asked.

"Definitely. This makes it so much more fun for me."

"You weren't having fun?"

"No, I was. But imagine what I was asked to do." She reached for her drink and shook the ice in the glass. "Here I was supposed to show up and look like the perfect club ambassador. The perfect daughter to a lifelong club member. You know me enough by now to know that I hate that, right?"

"Yes, I get that."

"Exactly. Now, I get to be your partner. An imposter. I get to help you infiltrate the world built by assholes."

Luc's eyebrows rose as she spoke. "That sounds a lot like Dorian Thibault," he said. "Maybe Armande Marwane was just like you. He was someone who was disenchanted with the status quo of the club, and here comes Dorian Thibault, an outsider who's not afraid to walk into the club and act like one of them."

"Maybe," Alaina said.

"And from there, they meet Tag le Tier," Luc continued.

"And he likes the situation as much as Dorian and Armande," Alaina answered.

"Not to mention the fact that he idolizes the guys."

"I see the attraction," Alaina said, nodding.

With the word 'attraction,' Luc's heart gave him a good thump.

Their waitress approached the table again. "Did you two say 'Tag le Tier'?" She asked.

Luc was annoyed with the woman.

"Yes, we did," Alaina said, also bothered.

"Crazy, right?" the waitress asked.

"Yes," Luc said rolling his eyes. "He's been found. We're aware."

"Well yes, but they just said it on the news," the waitress said nodding back toward a TV in the bar. "He's escaped."

Chapter IX.

The next morning, Luc Martin spilled wine all over his shirt. That's one of the perils of being a busboy. He thought the bottle was empty after the people dining left the table. It wasn't. Luc collected the remnants of breakfast crepes in disgust.

Words rang in his ears from the night before. He couldn't believe that he'd told Alaina the truth—or that she'd received it so well. He felt a deeper connection with her.

After hearing that Tag le Tier had escaped, they both had many questions. Where did he go? Did he have help? Did he use martial arts to kick through a wall as he suggested he might? Did he go back to wherever he was hiding out in the first place? Would he try again to steal a re-venomized raccoon? What the hell was a re-venomized raccoon, anyway?

They finished drinks just as Luc was feeling too tipsy. Alaina only got more pretty, if that was possible, as Luc felt more drunk. He was counting the minutes until he saw her again that afternoon. Until then, he'd need to do his duty to his parents as a busboy. Alaina had promised to meet him at the PPPPGGGCLC to look through the archives in the librarium—the half library, half aquarium.

"Having a rough day?" Luc's mother asked him over his shoulder.

"No, I'm fine," he responded.

"Wine for breakfast. That's something, huh?" The woman whispered. There weren't many patrons in the café, and they were all out of earshot anyway.

"I guess," Luc answered.

"Look, Luc," his mother said as she pulled him into the kitchen. "I feel like I may have been a little hard on you the other day. I'm sorry for that."

"It's okay. Really." Luc wanted to leave the dirty dishes in the wash basin, but his mother was blocking his path.

"Well, your dad made me feel like I overstepped."

"No, it's okay," Luc repeated.

"No, really. I'd love to give you a little time off. But, there's something I want to discuss with you."

"Okay?" Luc answered.

"It's just that your father and I have been thinking about your role at the café—"

"Hi Luc," a familiar voice interrupted.

Luc turned around. He froze. "Janet? Hi."

"Hey. I've been trying to reach you."

"Oh Janet! How nice to meet you!" Luc's mom exclaimed. "Is it true that you have 17 little brothers? That's incredible. Your parents must be exhausted."

Luc and Janet just watched her.

"I'll give you a moment. Luc, let's chat soon," Luc's mother said as she left the pair alone. "Luc—to be continued."

"Sure, Mom," Luc said.

"Luc, what's wrong?" Janet asked once the busboy's mother left.

"What are you doing here?" Luc answered, escorting his supposed ex-girlfriend to a table in the corner, away from any guests.

"I just wanted to check in. I've called the apartment a few times, and Charlie said you haven't been home a lot."

"I've been working."

"Well, I thought we could go out tonight."

"Janet—"

"You know, just since it's been a few days since we've seen each other."

"I don't think that's a good idea, Janet."

"Why not?"

"Well," Luc muttered, "we broke up. Remember?"

"WHAT?!" Janet exclaimed. Every head in the restaurant turned.

"Let's go outside," Luc said as he reached for her and began to stand, but Janet tore her arm from his light grasp. She wasn't going anywhere.

"I mean," Luc repeated, "we broke up last week."

"Um… no. You said you wanted a to stay in for a few days. That's it," she hissed and pounded the table. A salt shaker tipped over, sending grains of salt over the tablecloth. Luc sighed at the mess as he felt the sweat on his palms start accumulating.

"No, there was more to it than that. Janet, please."

"So that's your idea? You just run off and not answer the phone in your apartment?"

"Not really."

"I'm surprised at Charlie," she said.

"At Charlie? Why?"

"Of the two of you, I at least would have thought

he'd have the crab apples to tell me you wanted out of this thing."

"Janet, please."

"Janet please, yourself. Have a great shift," she said, standing. "No. I mean, have a great life," she snapped and stormed out the front door.

All the restaurant guests returned to their meals. Luc felt his parents standing behind him. He didn't have to look to know they were there.

"You have a girlfriend?" His dad asked.

"No."

"Why don't you take the rest of the day off?" His mom suggested.

*   *   *

Luc and Alaina met at their usual spot near the two enormous double glass doors to the plouquette lawn. The light flooded through the glass behind her, softening her edges and darkening her face. But Luc could still see her smile when she saw him as Coat-check Carl ushered him beyond the foyer.

"Hi," Luc said.

"Hi."

"How are you?" He asked.

"I'm fine. Ready to hit the librarium?"

"Sure. Do you know what we're looking for?" Luc lowered his voice as they started walking. "I'm not sure I do."

"Anything, I suppose. This club keeps crazy records. Maybe we could find something about how Dorian Thibault became a member."

"Oh yeah. That's a good idea. I didn't realize we had access to that stuff."

"Well, that'll be the trick. We don't."

"But I thought any member could use the librarium?" Luc asked.

"Yes, the general sections for reference and recreational reading—plus the fighting starfish and deadly eel menagerie—are all open to everyone. But club records in the archives are a different story. Either way, I think I can get us in."

"That's great. How?"

"I don't know. My dad is a big deal around here. I'll just tell them he sent me or something."

"Okay. If you think that will work."

"Monsieur Pigeon!" A familiar voice exclaimed.

Luc turned to see President Cravenmoore approaching.

"Hard at work I see?" The President asked.

"Yes sir," Luc answered.

"How's our Alaina working out for you?"

"She's a big help. Thank you."

"Great to hear. Luc, I'm hoping you'll join me on my morning walk. Some fresh air could do me good, and I'd like a quick word."

"Of course," Luc replied. "Alaina, I'll meet you in the librarium if you want to get a head start."

"Sounds good," she answered before turning to leave.

"Right this way, Luc," the President said. The man

led Luc down the hall. As usual, Maurice de Mouton was in tow, several feet behind. "Tell me, have you ever enjoyed a Sweenish massage?"

"Sweenish massage?" Luc asked. "I've never heard of that. Do you mean a 'Swedish massage'?"

"No, no," the President said as they turned a corner. "Sweenish. It's half Swedish, half Finnish."

"I didn't realize there were Finnish massages. Are the techniques different from a Swedish massage?" Luc didn't know the techniques of a Swedish massage either.

"No, I'm sorry, you misunderstand," Cravenmoore explained. "It's not the technique of the massage. It's basically a massage given by someone of both Swedish and Finnish descent."

"Oh, okay."

"As far as technique, they use many oils to snare the senses—including mint jelly. Plus, the fingernails play a role. It's the perfect intersection of prodding and stabbing."

"Stabbing? What does that even mean?"

"Never you mind. It's for the elite."

"Okay. Did you say mint jelly?"

"Yes," Cravenmoore said as he walked.

"You mean, the stuff people eat on lamb or steak?" Luc asked.

"Sure," the President huffed, "if you're a poor person." The man threw his shock of white hair back as he laughed.

Gross, Luc thought, imagining the green substance all over someone getting a massage.

"Anyway," the President continued, "I hope you don't mind walking me to my morning massage. I like to go through the hornet farm, just to check in on them. It's on the way. Have you seen it yet?"

"I haven't."

"It's through here." Cravenmoore opened the door for Luc. Inside, the room was much bigger than Luc could have imagined. Rows and rows of wooden and glass cases held hornet hives. A loud hum made the room almost shake. There had to be a million hornets.

"Did these used to be book cases?" Luc asked. He nearly had to shout over the buzzing.

"Yes," Cravenmoore answered. "In fact, this was our old library, before we built the librarium upstairs."

A person walked by in full protective gear.

"Why does that person need a suit like that if all the hornet nests are behind glass?" Luc asked.

"Well, she does need to harvest them to sustain our restaurant. Most of the hornets are as tame as can be. We pride ourselves on the training program. But there are a few hundred 'bad eggs' in each nest. I'm always astonished at how viciously they attack the outside of the suit."

"That sounds awful."

"Let me tell you, Pigeon. The wild French hornet has an inherently good soul. But every now and then you'll find one that is afflicted with a severe personality disorder that makes him act like a true asshole."

"But didn't you say hundreds in each nest attack the person in the suit?"

"Yes. Only thing that stings worse than a hornet is my ex-wife! But seriously, it's a shame how few of these proud and intelligent animals embrace a healthy education in our hornet training program."

Luc noticed a large red button on the wall with a sign that read, "Do not press."

"What's that button?" Luc asked.

"Oh, you do NOT want to press that," Cravenmoore warned.

"What happens?" Luc asked.

"That drops all the glass on all the hornet nest cages."

"Wow, that sounds awful."

"I know," Cravenmoore agreed. "There's nothing worse than trying to wrangle a hornet who's gotten off his leash—let alone tens of thousands."

"Why would you even have a button like that?" Luc asked.

"Design oversight," Cravenmoore replied. "It was accidentally installed during construction. Someone pressed it once, just to see what would happen. It was nearly impossible to clear the courtyard. It took years to get the hornet population back. The restaurant had to serve veal and lobster, like some sort of fast food joint."

The person in the suit walked by again.

"Salut, Yvette!" The President called out. "How's it going today? Everything 'buzzing' along as normal?" Cravenmoore giggled.

"Production is up in nest number 81!"

"Horny little hornets!" The President exclaimed. "I make that joke every time," he whispered to Luc. "Thanks Yvette!"

"You got it," she answered, walking away.

"So, tell me, Pigeon." Cravenmoore began leading Luc as they passed rows of nests. "Before you get into the latest details on your findings, just give me a quick answer on something. How close are you to closing the case?"

"Well, we've interviewed some people, as you know. Hugo in the pro shop, Former Police Chief Flive Pompousselpeck."

"Yes, very good. So, you're close then?"

"Well, I wouldn't go that far. There are still a lot of unanswered questions."

"Of course. Would you say you're another day or so away from finishing, though?"

"Well, I don't know. I mean, it's important that we get this right. Right?" Luc asked. Even if he wasn't a real detective, he knew the case didn't feel close to a conclusion.

"Of course. Were you able to get anything useful out of that arrogant little snot of a lawn boy?"

"I'm sorry, who?"

"The lawn boy who thought he could ride Phyllis."

"I don't think that he thought he could ride that horse."

"Arrogant little snot," the President said again.

"Anyway, no. Do you think he had any information that could be helpful? No one has told me that he might be a valuable resource."

"Absolutely not. He wasn't even alive when all this happened."

Luc was confused. "Okay then."

"So, to ask my question again: how close are you to being finished?"

"Well, I'd say we're a good way from being done. We don't know where Tag has been for the last few years, and I'm not even sure if the trophy actually burned in the fire."

"I see," the President said as he stopped to admire a hornet pressing itself up against the glass, trying to attack the man's face as he leaned in. "There is something very important that I need you to remember."

"Okay. What's that?" Luc asked.

"We would love it if you could wrap this up. It makes our members nervous to know that there are maybe some people out there who wish us harm. For them to not know what happened to the trophy is unsettling."

"So, what would you like me to do?"

"Of course, you must do what's right to find the truth. But, it would be really great if you could come to your conclusions very quickly—and confirm the original report."

"How does that explain Tag, though?"

"Well, isn't that what you're finding out? I'm sure he just escaped the fire at the last second. But it would be great if you could confirm that as being truthful."

"I see."

"Now," the President continued. "I invite you to come upstairs and watch as four women, who will be among the most striking hunchbacks you've ever seen, work their magic on me."

"I think I have to go meet Alaina."

"You sure? I'll tell them to try not to get any mint jelly on you."

"No, I'm sure," Luc replied, horrified. "Thank you, though."

*   *   *

Alaina was already leaving the librarium as Luc approached.

"Hey," she greeted him.

Luc noticed her clutching a manila envelope. "Hey. Did you find anything?"

"Oh yeah. Let's walk." She led him back down the hall that bordered the courtyard.

"That's great. What is it?"

"First," she began, dropping her voice to a whisper, "all this stuff was under serious lock and key. I waited for the clerk to get called away, and I ran back into the archives."

"Wow. How'd you get out?"

"Well, it's all organized by year, so I went straight to the right time period, and I just pulled this out. But there's so much more that I left behind, so who knows what else is up there."

"So, what did you get?" Luc asked. "Do you know how Dorian got in here in the first place?"

"Well, no, not yet. In fact, there wasn't anything in this folder except for pictures."

"Oh, bummer."

"Yeah, but it's still not bad. Check this out." Alaina looked up and down the hall. They were alone. She stopped walking and opened the folder to the first picture. It was a happy group of people.

In the center of everyone, a beaming man held the Waterford Cup. He had dark thick hair that came to a point on the front of his forehead. A downright Shakespearean mustache and beard framed movie star-quality teeth.

"Is that Dorian Thibault?" Luc asked.

"Sure is."

"Wow. Now we know what he looks like."

"Sure do, but that's not the best part. Not by far."

"Oh yeah?"

"Look more closely."

Luc skimmed the photo. "Well, that looks like Cravenmoore at his side."

"It is, yes. Who else do you see?"

"Well, I see Yelly sulking in the background."

"Poor Yelly," Alaina added.

Luc looked at each face. One man was laughing into his bourbon. Another red-faced man doubled over, cackling. But a well-dressed black man standing just behind Dorian caught his eye. It was someone he'd seen recently. The busboy's adrenaline surged.

"That's Roman Lubin. I mean, we talked to that guy on his doorstep yesterday!"

"Yep. And here's even better news," Alaina added. "I don't think his name is Roman Lubin. According to the handwriting on the back of this photo, that's Armande Marwane."

*   *   *

Luc and Alaina ran down the sidewalk. They passed a metro station, but Luc was too excited to go beneath and wait for a train. When they finally stood on the stoop of Roman Lubin's apartment, the two frantically swallowed air to catch their breaths. This time, they knew to whom they would be speaking.

The door opened as it did before.

"You're back," he surrendered.

"Sorry to bother you again, Monsieur Lubin," Luc began.

"You're Armande Marwane," Alaina blurted out.

The man sighed. "I knew it wouldn't take you long to figure that out. Come on inside."

The inside of his townhouse was beautiful. Marble floors. Ornate gold chandeliers. Armande Marwane may have been keeping out of the public eye, but not out of business.

Armande led them through his entryway and invited them into the front room. Luc and Alaina gaped at the majesty of the den. The busboy only began to imagine what the rest of the property looked like.

"Please, have a seat. What were your names again?" Armande asked. He motioned to a couch that was worth more than Luc and Charlie's entire apartment. Luc and Alaina sat, and Armande fell into a massive leather chair opposite them.

"I'm Alaina Amandine."

"And I'm... uh..." Luc struggled. Should he introduce himself as the greatest detective of all time? That seemed ridiculous.

"You may call him Monsieur Pigeon," Alaina assisted.

"Excuse me? Pigeon?"

"That's his code name," Alaina explained. "He's the greatest detective of all time."

Well that takes care of that, Luc thought.

"I see. You're a cop?"

"I'm a private detective," Luc answered. "I've been hired by the Paris Publique Plouquette—"

"Right. Cravenmoore, huh?" Marwane asked.

"That's right," Luc answered.

"I should have known when you showed up on my doorstep in those white pants. Leave it to the PPPPGGGCLC to find me. How is Cravenmoore?" Armande asked, his perfect white teeth shining against his black skin. "I take it he's responsible for your ridiculous code name too?"

"Yes. He seems fine, I think. At least he seemed fine as I watched him head in for a Sweenish massage this morning."

"Ah yes, the Sweenish massage. Always kind of freaked me out. I do not miss those. Do they still use a strawberry mincemeat-based lubricant?"

"No, I heard they had to stop since they found traces of asbestos in that," Alaina answered.

"That explains a lot. What are they on to now?"

"Mint jelly," she said.

"Yuck," Marwane grumbled.

"You mean they don't offer the Sweenish massage at the Private?" Luc asked.

"I don't know. I'm a member there, but I don't show up. For obvious reasons, I don't go out in public often."

"So, if you don't mind," Luc started, "I have so many questions."

"Of course, you do. I'll answer what I can." Armande leaned back and settled into his chair.

"Where have you been?"

"I've been right here."

"What about the fire? How did you get out?"

"C'mon," Armande said. "Do you really care about the fire? It's Dorian you're looking for, isn't it?"

"Definitely. But I still want to know about the fire."

"But the fire shouldn't matter. If I know Cravenmoore, he doesn't care how Dorian did it. He just cares about where he is and what comes next."

Luc thought of his recent discussion in the hornet farm. "You're probably right. Do you know where Dorian Thibault is?"

"No. We haven't been in touch for years."

"So, Dorian Thibault is alive?"

"Surely, you must have guessed that by now."

Luc looked at Alaina. This was their first good solid clue that Dorian was still alive.

"When did you hear from him last?" Luc asked.

"I'm not sure. It's been years. We were close back

then. He was my best friend."

"Did you meet at the club?" Alaina asked.

"Yep."

"Do you know where he came from?" She asked.

"What do you mean? Like, where he grew up?" Armande asked.

"No, well, sure, but that's not what we meant," Luc answered. "More like how he got into the club in the first place."

"I don't know. He was a member for a while before we became friends. A few months probably. Once we started hanging out, I just assumed he was a rich guy like all the rest of us. Didn't need to validate it."

"But he wasn't," Alaina confirmed.

"Nope," Armande answered, smiling.

"When did you find out that he wasn't rich? That he snuck in?" Luc asked.

"We were in the bar one night, getting drunk. I had asked him to teach me how to play plouquette, but we wound up in the bar every time he tried to teach me anything. He must have felt comfortable with me, because that's the night he told me."

"And you didn't say anything to anyone?" Luc asked.

"Of course not. Like I said. He was my best friend. I thought it was kind of cool."

"So, did he ever teach you to play?" Alaina asked.

"Sort of," Armande answered.

"I wish someone would explain it to me," Luc added.

"Ah, you don't need someone to teach you. Just pick

up a book about it," Armande said.

"Those exist?" Luc asked.

"Sure. You just have to find the right bookstore," Armande answered.

"Let me guess, I need to go somewhere 'for the elite?'"

"Probably," Armande answered.

"So, did Dorian teach you to how to play or not?" Alaina asked.

"Well, yes and no. Teaching me plouquette was more a part of the deal later on," Armande answered.

"What do you mean?" Alaina asked.

"Well, I would help him steal the cup, and in exchange, he'd teach me how to play plouquette for real."

"That's all it took for him to convince you to help him?" Luc asked.

"And to fake your own death?" Alaina added. "That would have to be some friend."

"Well, of course, there's more to it than that," Armande said, smiling at Alaina. "I'd had it with Cravenmoore. He was selfish. Never did anything with the club's interest—or any member's interest, for that matter—in mind. He just wanted to be a name. And to be richer than he already was. It didn't take much for Dorian to convince me to screw Cravenmoore over. I was ready to get out of there anyway."

"What about the police?" Luc asked.

"Yeah," Alaina added. "Faking your own death is no small amount of fraud."

"I'm aware. But you two will learn as you grow up—rich people get away with a lot."

"So, I've noticed," Luc answered.

"So, tell me, how is Yelly Reardon?" Armande asked.

"Poor Yelly," Luc muttered instinctively.

"He's fine," Alaina said.

"He won one yet?"

"Not yet," she answered.

"Poor Yelly," Armande added. "He had always wanted so badly to do the impossibly-majestic-high-arc-rainbow-hammer-mallet throw."

"He still does," Alaina responded with a smirk.

"Saw him practicing for it the other day," Luc added.

"That's unsurprising. Best of luck to him," Armande noted.

"So," Luc continued. "Where is the cup?"

"No idea," Armande said with a small smile. "Dorian has it somewhere, obviously."

"So, it really did survive the fire?" Alaina asked.

"Yes."

"And you have no idea where Dorian is?" Luc asked.

"No."

"What happened after you stole the cup?" Luc continued. "How long did you stay in touch with Dorian?"

"Well, we stayed close for several years. My parents had a property far out in the country. We built a plouquette lawn out there, and spent most of the next few years after the heist there. Like I said, we were best friends."

"Was Tag with you?" Alaina asked.

"Only for a brief time. Tag wasn't one of us. He was a good guy, but he wasn't wealthy, and he couldn't handle the hiding."

"So where did he go?" Luc asked.

"I have no idea."

"Why was he caught breaking into a pet store?"

"I read," Armande answered, "that he was trying to steal a re-venomized raccoon. Is that right?"

"That's what we heard too," Alaina answered.

"I never even knew those were out there," Luc added.

"It's for the elite," Armande said.

"So, do you have any idea where Tag could be hiding out now?" Luc asked.

"Not a clue." Armande answered as his giant leather chair creaked under his weight.

"Could Dorian have broken him out?" Alaina asked.

"Not a clue," Armande repeated. "Like I said, we lost touch with Tag a long time ago. Plus, I haven't spoken to Dorian in years."

"I see," Luc said. "You never said why you lost touch with Dorian."

"Right," Armande said.

"So, did he ever teach you how to play plouquette?" Alaina added.

"Well, he started to. We played almost every day. It's not that I didn't know how to play, it's just that I wasn't any good."

"Okay," Alaina said.

"But every time we'd get going in the game,"

Armande continued, "we'd just get to talking, or drinking, and before you knew it, it'd be dark out and we'd have to head inside without me being too much better at anything other than standing around with a cocktail in my hand on a plouquette lawn."

"Sounds a lot like what goes on at the PPPPGGGCLC today," Luc said. "Based on what I've seen, at least."

"It's always been that way. It's a pretty social sport."

"Why does playing it even matter then?" Alaina asked.

"Oh, if you've never seen an impossibly-majestic-high-arc-rainbow-hammer-mallet throw end a three-day match with a couple million euros on the line, then you don't know the meaning of adrenaline," Armande answered.

"I'm sure," Luc answered.

"Anyway, after a couple of years of hiding, Dorian needed a change of scene," Armande concluded. "So, he left."

"Why didn't you go with him?" Alaina asked.

"Well, I was afraid to leave. We were well-hidden there. I didn't get stir crazy like Dorian did. I liked being settled. But Dorian has a much more restless heart than most people. He needed to be among the living."

"So that's it? Your best friend just took off, and left you no clue as to where he was going?" Luc asked.

"Yeah, that sounds fishy," Alaina retorted. "If you two were that close, there's no way he would have just ditched you."

"You're right," Armande said. "But we agreed that it was better if we didn't know what the other was up to.

Plausible deniability. In case either of us got caught somehow."

"I see," Luc answered.

"But of course, you were going to get caught," Alaina said. "I mean, you opened your door for us, and we're strangers to you."

"Good point," Armande answered. "I'm not accustomed to teenagers hunting me down."

"I'm not a teenager," Alaina said.

"I've just been laying low as Roman Lubin for so long, I guess I didn't expect you to show up. It's worked well so far if I just play the part of rich shut-in. No one has ever come looking for me here."

"What about Dorian Thibault," Luc asked. "Do you have any idea where is he hiding?"

"I like to imagine that he's off somewhere, maybe owning his own bookshop or something."

"Why's that?" Luc asked.

"He always said he might want to. I just hope he's doing what he loves. I always wanted the best for him."

* * *

Luc and Alaina sat at the bar at the Paris Publique Plouquette Pitch, Grounds, Gardens, Grass Court, and Lawn Club. Two dirty martinis rested on the dark wood in front of them.

"Where's Dolt today?" Luc asked.

"I'm not sure. He's around here somewhere," Alaina

answered. "Just may not be working the bar today."

Luc wondered if he could set up Dolt with Janet. That might end the bartender's relationship with Alaina, and it might keep Janet away from him. But that was a fantasy. He didn't know how to do it.

"So, what's the next step, detective?" Alaina asked.

"It's a good question. I'm not sure."

"I can't believe we found Armande Marwane."

"I know."

She lowered her voice. "Do you realize that actual police couldn't find the guy? You are like a real detective!"

Luc smiled. "Well, I didn't do it alone. You were there too. You are pretty good at this stuff. You ask good questions."

Alaina took a sip of her drink. "I'm just good at snooping around, that's all."

"Maybe there's more in the librarium for us to look at?" Luc suggested.

"Yeah, maybe. Could always sneak in there again. Do you think Marwane was telling us the truth?"

"About what?"

"Well," Alaina mused, "what if he had Tag stashed in his attic or something while we were talking to him?"

"I didn't think of that."

"What if he's tipping off Dorian that we're close? What if he's packing his stuff and skipping town right now?"

"I guess that's a possibility."

"I'm not sure I trust him," Alaina said.

"Why?" Luc asked.

"I don't know. He was just a little too friendly."

"Well, unfortunately, I think we *have* to trust him," Luc said. "At least until we get some new piece of information. Then, we can take whatever we find back to him and see if he'd be willing to help, or lend some new insight."

"Yeah, that's a good plan."

"Like a new photo from that envelope you got in the librarium," Luc continued.

"We already know what they all look like. Would a new picture do any good?"

"I don't know, I'm just thinking here."

"Well," Alaina answered, "if we do find something new and can take it back to him, we'll at least have a few answers about if he's telling the truth or not."

"How's that?"

"If he's still at his place, we'll know that he's at least not on the run having just been identified for the first time in twenty years."

"Yeah. When you say it like that, though," Luc added, "I'd be shocked if he was still there just waiting for us to turn him in to Cravenmoore."

"Or the police," Alaina added.

"Right."

They both took another drink as they pondered the next step.

"I guess," Luc continued, "our best shot is still the librarium."

"I guess so," Alaina agreed.

"Although, what about Zoo La La?" Luc asked.

"That pet place that Tag was trying to break into?"
"Yeah. Maybe it's worth looking at," he suggested.
"Why's that?" Alaina asked.
"I don't know. I'm just trying to be thorough. You never know where you might find a clue."
"Sure, if you want to."
"I mean, maybe the owners would recognize Tag as someone who cased the place before he tried to break in. And what if he wasn't alone during his visits? Could we find someone who was close to Tag during the two decades he was hiding? If so, could they tell us if Tag was in touch with Dorian?"
"Interesting. That's some real detective thinking there, Pigeon." Alaina sounded impressed.
"I know it's far-fetched. I'm just trying to cover everything."
Maurice de Mouton entered the bar, scanned the room, and approached Luc and Alaina.
"Mademoiselle Amandine," he said. The man looked down the length of his nose at her.
"Bonjour, Monsieur de Mouton."
"President Cravenmoore would like a word."
Alaina looked at Luc. "That's strange."
"Do you want me to wait here for you?" Luc asked.
"That won't be necessary," de Mouton answered.

Chapter X.

Luc waited for Alaina. An hour or so passed and she didn't return to the bar. It was getting late, so Luc walked back to his apartment.

The next morning was the busboy's scheduled day off from the café, so Luc stood staring at Zoo La La's storefront. A mannequin posed in the front window wearing a black and white striped bikini, implying frightening consequences for any inventory of pet zebras.

Luc had come alone. He called over to the club before he left, but Alaina wasn't in yet. Luc would catch her later since he was skeptical about finding anything at Zoo La La anyway.

If Luc hadn't heard that Zoo La La was an exotic pet store, he would never have known it based on the store's appearance. Nothing indicated that there could be a re-venomized raccoon inside, let alone a pygmy grizzly bear—and any other terrifying horrors.

The world's greatest fake detective was discouraged, though, to find out that the store only accepted shoppers by appointment. If it was truly "for the elite" as President Cravenmoore had asserted, Luc knew he shouldn't be surprised that he couldn't just walk right in.

Luc stalked around the block to the back alley. He found the back door with a small placard indicating the pet store's rear shipping entrance. The fake detective knew that he was standing in the exact spot where Tag must have been arrested, but there was no indication of any forceful entry.

Something else caught Luc's eye, though. Another door next to Zoo La La's rear entrance displayed a small placard simply reading, "books." Luc jogged back around to the front of the building. The shop next to Zoo La La was in fact a bookstore.

A bell above the door jingled as Luc entered. The busboy only went in because Armande had hoped that Dorian owned a bookshop somewhere. The chances that this was it were miniscule, Luc thought. But he didn't have any other lead to follow.

There was not another person in sight. Shelves of countless spines smelled like an attic. Luc took in the scene before a tall man with an armful of books peered around at him from behind a shelf.

"Good afternoon," the man greeted Luc.

"Good afternoon."

"May I help you find anything?"

Luc felt the color leave his face. The bookshop worker staring back at him had salt-and-pepper grey hair, but there was no mistaking the man in the picture holding the Waterford Cup: that thick hair that came to a point on the front of his forehead, the Shakespearean mustache and beard, the movie star-quality teeth. Whatever his name was now, Luc was sure that this man once was known as Dorian Thibault.

"I, uh, I," Luc stammered.

"Everything okay?" The man asked with a smile.

"Yes. Sorry."

"Well, let me know if I can help you find something."

Luc thought. *What do you say in a moment like this?*
The busboy considered confronting the man. Without Alaina, that felt wrong. Should he just browse for a few minutes to not arouse suspicion and then sprint back to the PPPPGGGCLC to tell the President that he found Dorian Thibault? Given all the facts of the case so far, that felt irresponsible. Was the man before him actually out of touch with Armande and Tag? Might this be Luc's only chance to confront this man before he was tipped off by the others and disappears forever—again? The busboy felt as though he knew what Alaina would do in this situation. It inspired him.

"Actually, maybe there is something you can help me find," Luc continued.

"Okay," the man answered as he placed his stack of books on the grey floorboards.

Luc thought fast. "I'm looking for a book on a sport called plouquette."

"Huh," the man said as he moved to the desktop computer behind the counter. "I've never heard of that."

"It's for the elite," Luc answered.

"As you can see," the man gestured at the interior of the bookshop, "I'm not that."

"Are you sure about that... Dorian?" Luc felt his neck hair rise as he said it. He'd never been more direct in his life. His glasses felt tight behind his ears, as if the sweat pushing out of his head was making his skull swell.

The man paused. "I'm sorry?"

"You're Dorian Thibault, aren't you?" Luc swallowed.

A smile crept on the man's face. "Who are you?"

"You're him, aren't you?" Luc repeated.

"Are you a cop?"

"No, I'm a private detective, hired by the Paris Publique Plouquette Pitch, Grounds, Gardens, Grass Court, and Lawn Club."

"Cravenmoore," the man whispered.

"I can't believe it. You're him."

"Who else knows?" Dorian sighed.

Luc was ecstatic. "I knew it! This is great!"

"Who else knows?" Dorian repeated.

"No one, I promise."

"No one knows you were coming to investigate the bookstore today?"

"The bookstore? No, that was an accident."

"An accident? What do you mean?" He asked.

"I came to check out Zoo La La next door."

"Okay." The man exhaled again.

Luc could tell he was lost in thought, trying to assess the situation.

"That's where Tag le Tier was arrested," Luc said.

"Right. Tag." Dorian's gaze wandered.

"What is it?" Luc asked, catching the man's change in expression. "Do you know where Tag is?"

"I don't. We haven't been in touch in many years."

"So, where's the cup?"

"Let me guess, Cravenmoore has offered you some incredible reward for it, hasn't he?"

"It didn't burn in the fire, did it?"

"No."

"How'd you all escape the fire?"

"We were never there. It was all part of our plan. Armande, Tag, and I hid all over town, just waiting for a distraction. Accidental death happens all the time. We eyed the news. As soon as the first reports rolled in that a fire was happening, we raced straight there and tipped the chief of police—"

"Pompousselpeck?"

"Yep, that's him. We tipped him on the way. We arrived in time to put part of the trophy in the fire and get away."

"So, in reality, the fire didn't have anything to do with you?"

"Not at all. It was our ticket out—but not our doing."

"And you planted Yelly's nameplate," Luc said.

"Poor Yelly. How is he?" Dorian asked.

"He's fine, I think."

"Still trying to perfect the impossibly-majestic-high-arc-rainbow-hammer-mallet throw?"

"He is," Luc confirmed.

"Obviously."

"So, where's the cup now?" Luc asked.

Dorian smiled. "Look, you seem like a nice guy. But, I'm not giving it to you."

"Then why are you talking to me at all?" Luc asked.

"C'mon. You found me. It's not a secret that I'm here, apparently. And if it is, I can't expect you to keep it for long."

"I met Armande Marwane."

"Good for you. How is he?"

"He's fine. He guessed that you'd own a bookshop."

"Armande knows me well," Dorian said. "He was my best friend. He always knew that I loved books. I feel like you could always find treasure in them."

"Let me ask you this," Luc said, "how did you get into the club in the first place?"

"What do you mean?" Dorian asked. "I mean, I walked in through the front door. Is Coat-check Catherine still there?"

"It's Coat-check Carl."

"Oh, that's a shame. I hope Coat-check Catherine got to retire before her side job as a lion rodeo clown killed her."

"That's terrible!" Luc exclaimed. "What's a lion rodeo?"

"It's exactly what it sounds like. It's for the elite."

"Right. So, how'd you do it? You weren't a member of Paris' elite society. You weren't rich. How'd it happen?"

"You know, I think I better keep that one to myself. A good magician never explains the trick."

Another person entered the shop. Dorian smiled at them.

"Would you mind continuing this discussion some other time?" Dorian asked Luc under his breath.

Luc eyed the other shopper. The busboy had many more questions and not a clue about what to do next. After he spoke with Dorian more, should he run to find Alaina? Should he go straight to Cravenmoore and collect his reward?

"Excuse me," the stranger asked Dorian.

"I'm looking for Moliere. Do you have any? It's for a class."

"Good question," Dorian answered with cheer. He began clicking away on his computer.

Luc wanted this customer to leave so he could continue his interrogation. Maybe he should run over to Armande Marwane's after meeting with Dorian. Could he use Dorian's old friend to try and convince the bookshop owner to come out of hiding?

"You know," Dorian replied to the customer. "Let me check in the back. I have several boxes that arrived last week that I haven't unpacked, and it might be in there." Dorian eyed Luc. "I'll be right back," he said with a small nod.

Dorian disappeared behind the shelves. Moments—then minutes—passed. The other shopper was getting annoyed, and left, grumbling about customer service. Fifteen minutes. Twenty. Finally, Luc poked his head around the corner behind the shelves. No Dorian in sight.

Gaining confidence, Luc entered the back room of the bookshop. The busboy checked every nook. Dorian had slipped out.

*   *   *

Luc sprinted back to the club. He had to see Alaina. She'd be impressed and would want to head right back out with Luc to go to the bookshop. But, when Luc arrived, he couldn't find her in any of her usual spots. The busboy finally tracked her down in the spa on the second floor, at the direction of the other lawn girls.

Alaina appeared from a massage room wearing elbow-high cleaning gloves. Her clothing was stained green from head to toe. Her red hair jutted from her head like dirty feathers.

"Oh no, what's the matter?" Luc asked.

Alaina glanced at the spa receptionist and led Luc out of earshot before she began whispering to him.

"I've been reassigned."

"What?"

"I'm on Sweenish massage cleanup."

"Oh no."

"Yep. Mint jelly everywhere."

Luc thought the mint smell was kind of cute on her. Then again, she could have smelled like anything, and Luc would have been okay with it.

"Why did you get reassigned? What happened when Cravenmoore called you in?" He asked.

"He found out that I'd been snooping in the librarium."

"So? You were there on club business. I approved of it."

"Doesn't matter. I wasn't supposed to be in that section."

"I'll talk to him. I'll tell him to reassign you to me."

"It won't matter. He won't care."

"I don't get it, though. You were helping the case. Why would he want to do anything to impede our progress?"

"Like I said, he doesn't care. He wants this thing over

regardless of the outcome. He'll try to block anything that makes the club look bad, or its members—like Pompousselpeck."

"That makes sense," Luc said, thinking back to his own meeting with Cravenmoore.

"So, they stuck me here, and I'm sure they'll give you someone else to watch over you."

"Well, I'm not looking forward to that."

"You have no idea how nauseating it is cleaning up after one of these massages. There's no way they only use one jar of this stuff per session. There's just too much of it everywhere when they're done."

"I'm sorry."

"I'm the one who feels bad for you," Alaina replied. "They're going to give you someone else, I'm sure. Someone way less cool than me." She smirked. It was cute.

"Well, they may not need to," Luc said.

"Why?"

"Because I just blew this thing wide open."

"What do you mean?" She asked.

"While you were getting yourself reassigned to Sweenish cleanup, I was busy, off finding Dorian Thibault."

"What?" Her brown eyes grew twice their size.

"I found him."

"Oh, my God!" She exclaimed in her loudest whisper. She drew a little closer to Luc, forcing his pounding heart into overdrive. "Where? Weren't you going to Zoo La La?"

"I was. But, remember what Marwane said? That Dorian would probably own a bookshop?"

"Yeah."

"Well, there was a bookshop right next door. And sure enough, who's inside? Dorian Thibault."

"Are you serious?" Alaina asked in disbelief. "That seems pretty convenient."

"Yeah, pretty lucky, I guess."

The receptionist in the Sweenish massage spa made a sound.

"Look, I have to go back in there," she said. "What are you going to do next?"

"I'm not sure. I haven't gotten that far."

"Did he have the Waterford Cup?"

"Well, it wasn't, like, sitting out on a shelf or anything, but he definitely has it."

"We've got to think this through. I'm sure he'll run out on us. We'll have to act fast," Alaina said.

"You're still going to help me?" Luc asked.

"Of course. What are you talking about? We're in this thing."

Luc was relieved. "Okay good. That's great."

"I just have to keep my distance while we're here at the club."

"Great. Thank you," Luc said.

"Let's meet first thing tomorrow morning. Somewhere that's not here."

"I do have the morning shift at the café tomorrow, but let's meet right after," Luc offered.

The spa receptionist cleared her throat again.

Chapter XI.

"Let me get this straight," Charlie said as he poured himself a bowl of cereal for dinner. "You confessed that you aren't a real detective, and she didn't care?"

"Yeah, pretty much," Luc answered as he sat at the kitchen table, eating a microwave meal.

"That doesn't make sense."

"Why not?" The busboy asked.

"Well, why would she help protect you?" Charlie asked with cereal in his mouth.

"I don't know, I get the feeling that she likes rebelling a little bit. She's been playing the 'good girl' role her whole life."

"Okay. Interesting."

"And maybe, there's a chance she likes me a little bit. I don't know."

Charlie stopped chewing his cereal. "You mean *like* you?"

"Yeah."

Charlie erupted in laughter. "Yeeeaaah right, man."

Luc furled his brow. "What? Seriously, why are you laughing like that?"

"You think she likes you," Charlie repeated, through laughter.

"Is that so impossible?"

"No, but look. Listen to how this sounds," Charlie continued, having caught his breath. "You sneak your way into this insane club for super rich people. They give you some impossible task for millions of euros, and somehow along the way you get this beautiful girl to fall in love with you."

"Well, I wouldn't say she's in love with me, but I think she might like me."

"Wait, wait, wait. Of everything in this story though, that's where it falls apart. Sneak into a club? Sure, why not? Solve some cold case? Sure, but that's not really solved all the way yet, and I'm guessing you never do get that cup back. Instant riches? Maybe. But get a billionaire's daughter to fall for you? *And* she's incredibly beautiful? That's the fantasy here."

"Wait. Why is *that* the fantasy?"

"Look, I'm sorry. I'm not meaning to be a jerk. You're a great guy. A great catch. But think about this for a second."

"I think about it pretty much every second," Luc admitted as he bit into his dinner.

"Once the excitement of this whole thing blows over, she's never going to stick with you. This is a summer camp situation. Once it's over, the thing will fizzle."

"I never went to summer camp."

"Of course not. What's going to happen when they don't let you in the club anymore?"

"Why wouldn't they let me into the club?"

"You actually think that they'll make you a member or something when this is over?" Charlie asked.

"They might if I solve the case."

"Okay, let's pretend for one second that you solve the case. How long will it take them to figure out that you're not rich?"

"If I solve the case, I will be rich."

"Come on, man," Charlie whined. "Why do you even want to be a member?"

"I don't know. Alaina's there?"

"But that life isn't you. Do you even know how to play the sport? Plou-pette or whatever it is?"

"It's plouquette. And no, I don't know how to play. But neither does anyone else around there it seems."

"Look, here's my two things about this, then I'll shut up," Charlie offered. "First, the way you've told the story, it's just a little tough to believe that Alaina is as perfect as you think she is and would be head over heels for you."

"I still don't understand why it seems so far-fetched to you that I might be able to get a girl like her," Luc said.

"Because you attract the 'Janets' of the world. You attract the crazies. Girls who need someone to emotionally dominate."

"Janet didn't emotionally dominate me!"

"Right."

"I wouldn't say Janet was crazy, either," Luc said.

"Really? You wouldn't? Because not only did it take multiple times to get her to understand that you broke up with her—which I kind of still don't blame her for—but did you know that two days ago, she left an envelope on our doorstep?"

"She did?"

"I mean, I assume it was her," Charlie continued, "because it had a stack of pictures of the both of you in it, except your head was cut out of each one."

"Ugh." Luc's shoulders dropped as a forkful of food froze halfway to his mouth.

"Then, she called the apartment like 10 times before I finally answered to say you weren't here, and all she did was cry and apologize for all the headless pictures and say you were the best thing that ever happened to her and she'd do anything to get you back."

"Wow. Sorry you had to handle all that," Luc said.

"I had some beers. It was fine. I left your headless pictures out on the coffee table, but you haven't even seen them. Do you know why?"

"Well, I just haven't been here to—"

"Exactly," Charlie continued. "That's my second point. You're off pretending you're someone you're not. And last time I checked, that's not a healthy thing to do."

Luc sighed and relaxed in his chair a little, resigning to Charlie's truth.

"You're Luc Martin," Charlie continued. "You are a nice person, with nice parents who own a nice little café. That should be good enough for you. You're not the world's greatest detective with some lame code name."

"I do hate the name, 'Pigeon.'"

Just then, Richard flew into the kitchen and landed on the table right in front of Luc.

"Ew, get out of here!" He yelled with a swat.

"Take it easy on Richard!" Charlie yelled.

"What is he still doing here?!"

"Actually, this one's on you. He heard you say the

word 'pigeon' and thought you were calling him in here."

"You taught him to come when he's called? Like a dog?"

"Please," Charlie said, stroking the top of Richard's head. "Don't insult him. Dogs are cretins. Pigeons are intellectuals."

*   *   *

The next morning, Luc carried a pile of dishes to the café's kitchen sink. His head was swirling under the weight of meeting Dorian Thibault, seeing Alaina reassigned, and then hearing Janet was going off the deep end because of him.

He placed each dish in the sink, one by one, and didn't hear his mother approach behind him.

"Luc. Everything okay?"

Luc dropped a dish. It shattered on the tiled floor. The busboy stooped to clean up his mess.

"Pull yourself together, sweetie," his mother whispered.

"Sorry."

"Look. Come into the office. Let's talk for a moment."

Luc followed his mother into the restaurant office while his father glared at the two of them from the kitchen. He'd have to clean up the broken dish—and wait tables—with both Luc and his mother off the job.

"Close the door behind you." His mother took a seat. The room was too small to have another chair, so Luc closed the door and leaned up against it on the inside of the tiny room.

"What's going on?" The busboy asked.

"Well, I just want to make sure you're okay."

"I'm fine. You just surprised me back there. No big deal."

"Don't worry about the dish. That's not what I'd like to talk to you about," she assured him.

"Okay."

"So, I'm guessing it's girl trouble, huh?"

Luc sighed. "Come on, mom. It's nothing."

"You've been so distracted lately. Up until about a week ago, you were the best busboy in Paris. This girl has messed you up."

"It's not Janet."

"Well, the way she showed up here, I would have guessed otherwise. You're a real stud, just like your dad."

"Come on, mom," Luc repeated. He hated this.

"Look, I know a breakup can be hard. Especially with your first girlfriend."

"She's not my first girlfriend."

"Okay," his mother paused. "I didn't know you had another one before."

"Well, I haven't per se, but that's not the point," Luc answered.

"Ah, I see. So, Janet's your first girlfriend. I get it."

"Whatever. The point is, I don't want to talk about it. We broke up. It's over."

"Right. So how can you explain how you've been

acting lately if it's not that? Something is on your mind," Luc's mother pressed.

Luc wanted to brag that he was doing a side job that would make him millions of euros, and somehow doing it pretty well, but he knew that he couldn't tell his mother. She'd never understand. The woman would chide Luc for lying.

"Truly, I've just been… tired," Luc tried.

"Luc, we're all tired. There's a time when we have to grow up, stop whining about things we can't fix in life, and just start succeeding. Now, your father and I have been talking, and we feel as though it's time to take the first step to you eventually taking over the café: becoming a waiter."

"Wait, what?"

His mother was grinning, and Luc realized that this was a big moment for her. Luc's mother believed that she was delivering great news to Luc.

"Luc, I'm saying it's time. It's time for you to move up. Take on more responsibility. Take your first steps to making something of yourself. I'm making you a waiter!"

His mother clapped her hands without making a sound.

"Look Mom—"

"Plus, this will be good for you. You can get your mind off the girl, maybe even impress a few new ones who come in here? Huh? You never know!"

"I don't know, mom."

"The only thing I'll need from you is a little more of a time commitment."

"Uh... you will?"

"Naturally. There's some training I'll get you going on, and your shifts will be a little longer. Plus, I think I'll put you on a little more often to give your father a rest every now and then."

"Um, thank you, but, honestly, I'm not sure."

"About what?"

"Well, I'm not sure that I... want to be a waiter." Luc braced himself for his mom's response.

"Honey, I understand that being a waiter looks hard. You have to talk directly to a lot of customers, you have to know the menu front-to-back. But I believe you can do it. You'll really have to, especially if you're going to own the café one day."

"I know, I get it, mom," Luc said. "But, I'm just not sure I need to own the café. Is that something you've wanted? Have we ever talked about that?"

Luc's mother was expressionless and silent for a full five seconds. The busboy didn't know how to read the reaction.

"You're not interested in taking over the café one day?"

"Well, I don't know—"

"Luc, I have built this place with my bare hands. I'm willing to just *give* you this. It's not just a place. It's an established business. A community. The people who come in here, the neighborhood, they are all relying on you to keep going someday. To keep this legacy alive. Luc, you have the chance to build this into something as big as le Consulat or la

Maison Rose. It could be an institution."

"I know, but I've just been wondering lately if it's for me or not."

"For you? What about for me? What about everything I've built? My legacy? Are you willing just to sell it down the road to just anybody? Why would you do that?"

"That's not what I'm saying."

"Do you have any idea how many people would kill for this opportunity?"

"To be a waiter?"

"Yes, well, no, but yes. The world just doesn't give opportunities away. It doesn't just give out successful, established businesses to just anyone. You have to work for them from the ground up. You have to sweat. You have to bleed. And guess what? I've done all that for you. You've found a golden goose. All you have to do is take it. All the hard work is already done!"

"You make it sound like it would be easy," Luc answered, finally gaining courage to provide a counterpoint. "Did you ever stop to ask yourself if I wanted to own a café someday?"

"I didn't think I needed to. I thought you loved and honored your father and me enough to do it for us. Let us retire in peace and happiness."

"I want you both to do that, mom, but what if owning a café isn't my path?"

"Your path? Your *path*? No one has a path. What are you even talking about? You're crazy. I'm giving you your path. It's an amazing path. You'll be great at it!"

"Well, it's not my path if I don't want it."

Luc's mother threw up her hands in disbelief. "How can you not want it? I don't get it."

"Look mom, I'll be a waiter if you want me to. If that helps."

"Get out of here," she snapped. "We'll talk about this later. Don't worry. I won't bother you to wait a table. If it's not on 'your path,' then I don't want you being led astray in life."

Luc opened the door, only to be greeted by his father's scowl. The busboy assumed that his dad didn't appreciate being left to serve every table in the small café, but there was also a chance that he'd been listening at the door. Either way, Luc was sorry to see him upset, too. He returned to his mundane work, regretting the entire exchange with his mother.

* * *

After his shift in the café, Luc ran home to change out of his busboy clothes. As soon as he walked through the door, the smell of stale potato chips hit him in the face. Charlie leapt off the couch.

"Where have you been?" Luc's roommate asked. The busboy noticed that Charlie had been sitting amongst several empty bags of chips.

"At work? You knew this. Are you okay?"

"You're late," Charlie said.

"Not by much. And what do you care? Was I

supposed to pick up some beer on the way home? Need more chips?"

"No. It's just that Janet's been here for, like, 40 minutes."

"What?" Luc asked. He looked around and didn't see anyone.

"Yeah, I tried to chat her up for a while, but I couldn't keep it up for long. She's waiting in your room."

"Oh," Luc said, as he looked at his bedroom door.

"Remember man, she's crazy," Charlie stated.

Luc walked to the door. Would his room be trashed? On fire? He opened it gingerly. As soon as she saw him, Janet stood. She'd been waiting on the corner of the bed. Not an item seemed to have been touched in his room.

"Hi Luc. Late breakfast day, huh?" She asked.

"Janet. What are you doing here?"

"I just thought I'd drop by to say I'm sorry. I brought you these." She offered him a bouquet of flowers.

"You brought me flowers?" Luc asked.

"Yep," she answered, with a look on her face that made it look like she thought she was the cutest girl in the world. "I was going to put them in water, but I couldn't find a vase. Do you have a vase?"

"I think my mom left one here once," Luc answered.

"Oh well. You can find it later. I'll just put them here for now." She laid them on the bed.

"What are you doing here?" Luc asked again.

"I just feel bad about the way we left things last time we saw each other. That's not the way I should be treating my boyfriend."

"But we broke up."

"C'mon Luc, it was just a fight. You have to relax. This is what people do. They fight."

"Do people send each other a stack of pictures with all the heads cut out?" Luc asked.

Janet pouted. "I'm sorry about that too. I was just… bleh… in a bad place that night."

"Obviously," Luc answered.

"C'mon, when you think about it, it was funny."

"Hmmm. I'm not sure about that," Luc answered.

"Luc, you have to put yourself in my position here. I've been a wreck. Imagine the dinner table at my house."

"Yeah, 17 little brothers. You've said it's huge."

"It is. And everyone's asking me, 'Janet, why are you sad? Be happy Janet!' What am I supposed to tell them? That the greatest guy ever and I are having trouble? C'mon, I miss you, Luc."

Luc stood in silence.

"C'mon." She paused, but Luc still didn't answer. "How about this," she said. "Let me take you out to dinner tonight. We'll have a date anywhere you want."

"I have a pretty busy afternoon."

"What? What's going on? Isn't your shift over for today?" She asked.

"Yes, it is. I just have other plans."

"What are you doing?" Janet asked.

"Nothing. I'm just doing a little work."

"For your mom?"

"No," Luc answered.

Janet shrugged. "What then?"

"I don't know. I'm just busy okay?"

She stared at him. Janet's scowl intensified. "What's her name?"

"What? Who?"

"There's another girl, isn't there? What's her name?"

"There's no other girl," Luc said.

"I bet it's 'Slutsy.'"

"Is that a name?" Luc asked.

"WHAT'S HER NAME?!"

"What? No? It's a job. It's not like that."

"Okay, so what job is it?"

"It's nothing, okay? Look. We broke up. I think you should go," Luc said as forcefully as he could.

"I get it," Janet replied. Her demeanor eased. "You got a job in another café."

"What? No."

"No, that's it. You found a better job. Maybe as a waiter or something, and you don't want your mom to know."

"That's not it."

"That's exactly it. You know how I know?" Janet asked. "Because I know you, Luc Martin. I know you better than anyone."

"We were only going out for a few months."

"So? Who knows you better than me? Charlie?"

"Maybe, yeah. And my parents," the busboy said.

Janet shook her head. "You're pathetic. Your parents. Well, I hope you like hanging out with your parents, because I think you're going to be doing it a lot throughout your thirties, forties, fifties, and forever."

"Okay," Luc said.

"You know what would be really horrible?"

"What?"

"If your precious mom found out about your second job. I'd hate to hear that someone told her before you had the chance to."

"Janet, if you're threatening to tell my mom that I got another job in a café, then be my guest. It's not true, so I'm sure I won't have too much of a problem calming her down."

Janet stomped her foot like a child. "Forget you, man. I'm leaving. Call me when you grow up."

Janet stormed into the small living room between Luc's bedroom and kitchen. Luc followed her, but didn't say anything. Charlie, still on the couch, gave him an eye when they entered.

"You know what else," she added as she violently turned towards him one last time.

"What?"

"You are such a complete loser. Who works for their own parents, anyway?!"

The pigeon flew from Charlie's room into the living room with a pencil in its mouth.

"Ew! What is that?!" Janet yelled.

"Thanks, Richard," Charlie said. He took the pencil from the bird and picked up a crossword puzzle from the coffee table. The pigeon bowed to acknowledge Charlie's gratitude before staring back at the couple.

"What's it look like?" Luc answered his horrified, ex-girlfriend. "That's a pigeon."

"Ew. It's on your coffee table," she said.

"I know," Luc answered expressionless.

"So, he's Charlie's pet or something?"

"Roommate," Charlie called out without looking up.

"That's disgusting," Janet said.

"I know," answered Luc.

The girl looked over Luc's shoulder at Charlie, still sitting on the living room sofa, undoubtedly listening in on the entire exchange but doing his best to seem like he wasn't.

"That's gross," Janet continued. "You know pigeons carry diseases, right?"

"Hey!" Luc said. "That *pigeon* has a name. It's Richard."

Charlie beamed at Luc.

"Okay, idiots," Janet said. "You know, Charlie, I thought you could teach Luc how not to be a loser, but I guess that's out the window now."

"Piss off," he yelled back at her.

Richard huffed.

Janet looked back at Luc. "Your roommate's a dick too," she added before she charged out the door and slammed it behind her.

Luc turned and made eye contact with Charlie. The busboy didn't say anything.

"I think there's a vase under the sink," his roommate said.

* * *

That afternoon, Luc was waiting on a bench in one of Paris' many small neighborhood parks. A distant accordion played on a street corner. The fake detective wondered why more Parisians didn't use the public parks. He almost always expected them to be more crowded than they were. If he shut his eyes, the sounds of birds and wind in the trees almost drowned out the white noise of the city. Almost.

Luc had been trying to forget the ugly altercation with Janet back in the apartment. He just wished she'd go away once and for all. But when Alaina arrived, he didn't care about anything else.

"Hey," Alaina greeted.

"Hey," Luc answered, excited to see her. "How was massage cleanup?"

"Ugh," she sighed as she collapsed on the bench next to Luc. "I don't want to talk about it."

"Okay. Sorry."

"I do want to hear about Dorian Thibault, though," she said.

"Yeah, he was nice enough. Didn't tell me a lot, other than confirming that they weren't in the fire. But then he took off on me."

"But you found him, and that's the important thing."

"That's true. One step closer to the cup," Luc said.

"When are you going to tell Cravenmoore?" Alaina asked, lightly kicking the small gravel on the walkway beneath the bench.

"Yeah, I'm not sure. What do you think?"

"What's stopping you?" Alaina asked.

"I don't know," Luc began. "I don't like how he just wants to see this thing end regardless of a fair outcome. I don't like it that he didn't tell us that Dorian wasn't rich and snuck his way into the club. It seems like Cravenmoore isn't willing to admit that part, he'd rather just try and pin a fake cheating accusation on Dorian and let the issue rest."

"Cravenmoore is shady. I've always thought so," Alaina said.

"Exactly. So that makes me feel like I shouldn't let him know what's going on until I figure it out. Until I can, like, regulate the situation a little bit."

"Here's a question for you," Alaina said. "If you found the cup today, would you turn it in?"

"Definitely. For two million euros, for sure."

"What would you do about Dorian? And Armande for that matter?"

"Well, that's just it. If I found the cup today, I would turn it in. But I don't think I'd say anything about Dorian. Why turn him in if I get what Cravenmoore is really looking for?"

"And you don't think vengeance against Dorian and Armande is what Cravenmoore is looking for?" Alaina asked.

"I guess not."

"So, you'd spare them?"

"I think so," Luc said. "I wouldn't want to make them my enemies. Plus, the way Cravenmoore talks, it makes me feel like he deserves to be screwed over a little bit." Luc squinted as a cloud moved to reveal the autumn sun.

"Totally," Alaina answered. "So, I have something that I think you'll love."

"Oh yeah?"

Alaina reached into her backpack, and pulled out a manila folder.

"What's that?" Luc continued. "Is that more from the librarium? Did you steal that?"

"I did."

"Jesus, Alaina." Luc thought that was hot.

"But even better, I found a clue."

"You did?"

"Yep. In more pictures. You were right to think about that. Look," she urged.

Luc opened the folder and fanned out the top several images. They were all various photos taken around the club.

"Recognize anyone?" Alaina asked.

"Well, yes, obviously. There's Dorian." It was the same picture of Dorian holding the cup. Luc glanced at the rest. "He's in every one."

"Yep, what else do you see?"

"Well, there's Marwane again too."

"Right, Armande is in some. What else?" Alaina asked.

"I'm not sure. I don't see Tag?"

"Well that doesn't surprise me. How many club members take the time to pose with the staff. Or even hang out with the staff?"

"Good point," Luc said.

"No, you're missing it. Look. The girl."

"What girl?" Luc asked.

"She's in almost every picture. And she's hanging on Dorian's arm in almost half of them."

Sure enough, the same girl appeared in each photo either next to Dorian, or somewhere in the background.

"Do you recognize her?" Alaina asked.

"I'm not sure. I don't know the club members as well as you do. I guess she looks a little familiar."

"Picture her about twenty years older. A few grey hairs. Some crow's feet. But that smile and throw-back-your-head laugh looks exactly the same."

"That's Marianne Merriweather!" Luc exclaimed.

"Yep. If these pictures are any indication, I'd bet you a hundred euros that she was Dorian's girlfriend," Alaina said.

"Just because she's in every picture?" Luc asked.

"Think about it. He was the center of attention and everyone loved him. So is she. They would have been a power pairing. The club's 'it' couple."

"We have to talk to her," Luc said.

"Definitely. But first, I have to go see the book shop with you."

"What do we say to Dorian?" Luc wondered aloud, "assuming he's there."

"I don't know. If anything, I just want to see that he's real."

"Sure. And who knows? Maybe he's thought it over a little and wants to turn over the cup?"

"I wouldn't count on that, but maybe he'll slip up

and give us a clue to where it is," Alaina hoped.

"Yeah, right."

"But, mainly, I just have to see him. We've been talking about him forever like he's a ghost."

*   *   *

But when Luc and Alaina arrived at the bookshop, they found the door locked, and the windows dark.

"Huh, that's funny. He should be open," Luc thought aloud, pressing his face to the glass.

"He ran. Not surprised," Alaina answered.

Luc grunted. "I'm not sure why, but I kind of expected him to still be here."

"Why? I figured he'd bolt. If the police find him, that's it," Alaina said.

"I wasn't going to turn him in, though. At least not yet."

"How would he have known that?" Alaina asked. "I'm surprised that Armande Marwane didn't take off after we turned up, too."

"Yeah. I don't know why he trusted that we wouldn't turn him in. I guess Dorian didn't share his faith."

"Guess not. Like I said, I'm not surprised." Alaina tapped on the glass of Zoo La La. "So, this is where Tag got arrested, huh?"

"Yep. Around back."

"Should we go check it out?"

"Honestly, I went back there. There's nothing there."

"I guess there's nothing left to do but go talk to Marianne," Alaina suggested.

The couple began heading back to the club. The day was perfect, and Luc loved walking the streets of his city with Alaina. At any moment, he could barely trust himself with not blurting out the way he felt about her. She was lovely, and he fought the temptation to tell her, only to protect himself from the inevitable heartbreak of a beautiful girl denying him.

Chapter XII.

As soon as the two walked through the front door of the Paris Publique Plouquette Pitch, Grounds, Gardens, Grass Court, and Lawn Club, Coat-check Carl glared at them.

"President wants to see you," the little old man grunted.

"For what?" Alaina asked.

"Not you. Him."

"Ah, okay," Luc acknowledged.

"Actually, Mademoiselle Amandine, your presence is requested upstairs in Sweenish massage room 71," the little man grunted.

"There are 71 massage rooms?" Luc asked.

"There are an even 148," Coat-check Carl answered.

Luc winced. "What makes that even? Why not 150? To have a true 'even' 150?"

"An even number is anything divisible by two, dumbass," Coat-check Carl grunted without making eye contact, closing the front door behind Luc and Alaina. "Why would anyone possibly need 150 massage rooms? It's too many."

"And 148 isn't?" Luc asked.

"C'mon," Alaina answered, pulling him away from the front foyer. "Don't bother with him. I'll meet you later on if you want."

"Definitely."

"Let me know what Cravenmoore has to say."

"Of course," Luc said, as he watched her walk away. Luc also wondered if Coat-check Carl was a member of parliament alongside Coat-check Chad. It didn't seem likely.

"Pigeon," Cravenmoore called from down the hall as he approached.

Luc waved.

"Come on in."

Inside the President's dark office, Maurice de Mouton lurked in the corner as usual. A dark haired, pale-skinned boy sat in one of the chairs facing the President's desk. Countless puzzle pieces lay strewn about the floor and Cravenmoore's desk.

"Pigeon, meet Evan Yanis. He'll be your new shadow. Please have a seat."

Luc shook hands with Evan, and the three men sat.

"Evan is one of our best lawn boys," Cravenmoore continued. "He has nearly no weaknesses, except for a lot of allergies. And big ears, I guess."

"If it's no trouble, sir," Luc began, "I really wouldn't mind continuing my work with Mademoiselle Amandine–"

"Out of the question, young man. We'd never give you someone so incompetent and skill-less."

"I wouldn't have said she was either of those," Luc argued.

"Trust me," Cravenmoore answered. "You don't want her involved in your business dealings. She's dishonest, disorganized, and more of a liability than anything else. I'm sure you noticed, having spent so much time with her on the case."

Luc found it interesting that Cravenmoore wasn't mentioning anything about firing Alaina from the case due to the folder she stole. The President was more interested in slandering her character than acknowledging she could have gotten a real lead in the case—even if she was somewhere that she wasn't supposed to be.

"Regardless, like I said, this is Evan. He'll assist you from here on out."

"Hello," Luc said with a smile.

Evan didn't smile back. "Hello, Pigeon."

"Evan, please," the President said, "show some decorum. It's Monsieur Pigeon."

"Of course, my apologies," Evan said, drilling a hole into Luc with his stare.

"Go ahead, Evan," Cravenmoore urged, "tell him about yourself."

"I'm Evan Yanis," the small man said with gravity. "I'm really looking forward to bringing these men to justice with you—and returning the Waterford Cup to its rightful place in our trophy cabinet, if it's still out there."

"Yes. If the cup still exists, I'm pleased to say that Evan is as passionate as I am about seeing the great Yelly Reardon's name rightfully seared into the gold on a new plaque for it, once it's returned."

"I see," Luc nodded. "Good."

"I chose Evan," the President continued, "because he is an uncompromising young man of honesty and morals. He's been one of my most loyal lawn boys for several years now, and I trust him to get you everything you need for this case—

anytime you need it."

"That's great," Luc deadpanned.

"Maybe you wouldn't mind catching Evan up with your progress," Cravenmoore suggested.

"In the case?" Luc asked, swallowing hard. Cue the palm sweat and glasses steam.

"Yes."

"Right now?"

"Yes. Just a quick version with your up-to-the-minute details," Cravenmoore said.

"Right now?" Luc asked again.

"Of course, yes."

Evan's stare was unwavering.

Luc scrambled to try and remember what he'd told Cravenmoore and what he hadn't. Obviously, the club President had no idea that Luc and Alaina had already located and spoken with both Dorian Thibault and Armande Marwane.

"Well, as you may have heard," Luc began, "about 20 years ago, there was this thing called the Waterford Cup."

"Of course," Evan Yanis said. "I'm familiar with that part of the story."

"Oh, okay good. Then you know that Tag le Tier was recently found alive," Luc confirmed, knowing full well Evan would have heard that. He was stalling, trying to think of a way out of this situation. He didn't want to say too much to Cravenmoore. And Evan Yanis was surely in the President's back pocket.

"I heard Tag was caught," Evan replied.

"Oh good. Well, we were able to speak with him in person."

"What did he say?" asked Evan.

"Well, not much. He told us about his relationship with Dorian Thibault and Armande Marwane."

"Which was?" Evan asked.

"Well, he looked up to them."

"I've heard that from everyone around here," Evan said. "Is that it?"

"Well, we've been interviewing club members. I talked to Hugo in the plouquette pro shop. And Flive Pompousselpeck."

"What did they say?" Evan asked.

"Well, Hugo loaned me these white pants, for starters," Luc said, itching his leg.

"I've been meaning to say," the President interjected. "They look really, really nice."

"Thank you," Luc answered.

"What did Hugo say about the case?" Evan asked.

"Well, he was the one that suggested I speak with Chief Pompousselpeck."

"Okay," Evan said, nodding.

"And *he* recommended that I speak with his wife at the Paris Private Plouquette Conglomerate."

"Bunch of grade-A dong-kickers over there," the President grunted.

"And was the chief's wife helpful?" Evan asked.

Luc thought for a moment. "Dead end," he lied.

"They're behind this for sure," Cravenmoore said.

"Well to be honest," Luc said, "I have no reason to believe their club had anything to do with it. I talked to a few people there, and it didn't seem as though the club was involved."

"Of course, they were involved," the President said. "They are our rival club. I bet the Waterford Cup is sitting over there in their trophy case as we speak."

"So, what comes next?" Evan asked. "How do we expose those douche kits over at the Private?"

"Well, Alaina did notice something important just yesterday," Luc answered. "When we were looking at old pictures, we saw that a current member here is in almost all of them."

The President shifted at the mention of Alaina's misdeeds. He fiddled with a puzzle piece on his desk.

"We think," Luc continued, "that Marianne Merriweather may have known Dorian Thibault well. Maybe even dated or something. I thought we could talk to her."

"I know her," Evan replied. "I've been a lawn boy for many of her plouquette games. We should find her immediately."

"Well, I see that you two have much more to do together," the President said with confidence. "Good luck to you both. If you need anything from me, I am of course available to you as I work on this 18,000-piece puzzle of a satellite-view of my own house, complete with me in the side yard flogging an old tire last Bastille Day."

"Classy, sir," de Mouton said.

"I already did the puzzle a few months ago, but I just

can't resist a second go. I'm doing it again. It's more difficult to manage than even my ex-wife!"

De Mouton and Cravenmoore erupted into laughter again, as if the joke was brand new.

"Maurice," Cravenmoore managed between wheezes, "please, show them out."

De Mouton opened the door, and the bright daylight of the corridor flooded the President's dark office. Evan walked ahead of Luc.

"Follow me, Pigeon," Evan said, "I know exactly where Madame Merriweather will be."

All Luc could think about was what Alaina was doing at that very moment. He wished they were together.

* * *

Evan and Luc arrived in the bar moments later. The clinking sounds of glassware as Dolt shined champagne flutes seemed louder with a near empty dining room. The bartender worked so quickly that Luc thought the cleaning could not have been thorough.

Luc and Evan saw Marianne Merriweather across the room, holding court as usual, but the bartender called the men over to the bar before they could reach Marianne.

"Hi Dolt," Luc managed.

"Hey boys," the bartender greeted. "Have I mentioned lately that you look great in white pants, Pigeon?"

"No."

"How are you liking your new job, Evan?" Dolt

asked.

"Shove it, Dolt," the lawn boy-turned-detective-shadow spat.

"Take it easy, Yanis. Just 'because *you* can't get the girl and I can doesn't mean you have to be a jerk about it."

Luc snapped his head at his new companion. Evan remained silently hateful of Dolt.

"What's that about?" Luc asked.

"This little guy is in love with Alaina," Dolt answered, motioning to Evan.

"You are?!" Luc asked Evan.

Evan didn't acknowledge him.

"No, he's not," Luc guessed, looking at a silent Evan.

"Are you kidding me?!" Dolt exclaimed at Luc. "He's super in love with her. But he embarrassed himself when he professed his love and tried to win her over."

"That's not true," Evan replied.

"C'mon man, it's okay. That's just how it goes sometimes. Calm down." Dolt hung a glass from the ceiling rack. A few drips fell from the upside-down piece of glassware, evidence of his shoddy cleaning job.

"Look Dolt," Luc interrupted. "We're in the middle of something. What's up?"

The bartender continued cleaning a glass. "Nothing. Just wanted to see if you guys saw some poor sap out on the lawn just now get bucked off Phyllis." He let out a short, cutting laugh. "It was ridiculous."

"We must have missed it," Luc answered.

"Well, he got on her. It was a lawn boy. I think one of

the members made him. And next thing you know, he was flying through the air."

"Does this happen often?" Luc asked.

"Almost every day," Evan confirmed.

"Pigeon, you have to try it," Dolt suggested.

"No thanks."

"I'm allergic to horses," Evan confessed.

"What aren't you allergic to?" Dolt asked.

"We have to go," Evan said, still making a face at Dolt.

"See you around, Yanis," Dolt said.

"Asshole," Evan said under his breath.

"Sorry about him, man," Luc said, trying to be nice to Evan despite a pretty cold shoulder so far.

"Mind your own business, Pigeon."

Luc turned to Marianne's table. The group went silent as they approached.

"Yes, maybe mind your own business Monsieur Pigeon," a stranger at the table said.

"Now, now Pierre," Marianne chided. "That's not very hospitable. Monsieur Pigeon, what may I do for you?"

"Well Madame Merriweather," I was hoping I could have a word with you.

"We. We would like a word," Evan interrupted without looking at Luc.

"Of course, gentlemen," she replied. "I thought you might come looking for me at some point." She turned to the other guests at her table. "If you all wouldn't be so kind, I'd like a few moments alone with Messieurs Pigeon and Yanis.

I'll meet you all out on the lawn in a little while."

The table cleared, with more than a few stares at Luc.

"You'll have to excuse my friends," Marianne began. "When it comes to sensitive subjects, they are particularly prickly."

"And what sensitive subject would they be upset with that has to do with me?" Luc asked.

"Don't be naïve, detective," she answered.

"I'm here to find the cup," Luc replied. "Do they have a problem with that?

"You're here to find Dorian," she corrected him.

"Well, yes, that too."

"And the trail has inevitably led you to me, hasn't it?" She asked.

"It has."

"Can't say I'm surprised. No one talks about it anymore, so I knew you wouldn't come to me immediately. But, everyone knows about it."

"You're referring to your relationship with Dorian?"

Marianne lit a cigarette. "That's right." She turned to the bartender. "Dolt! Another please," she stated as she tapped the edge of her glass with her fingernail.

"So, you two were close?" Evan asked.

"Monsieur Yanis, if you don't mind," Marianne said. "I would like a few moments alone with Monsieur Pigeon. After all, he's the detective here. You are not."

"I'm sorry," Evan answered, not smiling. "But I am the President's eyes and ears…"

"Exactly," Marianne interrupted him. "Cravenmoore

and I don't agree on things, and I would appreciate it if his eyes—and his ears for that matter—weren't around here. Have Monsieur Pigeon fill you in when I'm finished talking with him, but I want the time alone."

"But—"

"Thank you, Evan," Marianne stated, settling in her chair. She inhaled smoke as if to put a period on her dismissal.

Evan grimaced again—he never smiled anyway—before moving to a table near the door.

"What was that all about?" Luc asked Marianne.

"Nothing. I just hate that little weasel."

"Why is he a weasel?" Luc asked.

"He's Cravenmoore's favorite lawn boy. Always at his side. He doesn't do anything that he thinks won't impress the President."

"I see."

"Anyway, on to bigger things," the woman said.

"Yes," Luc answered.

"So? Have you found him?"

"Dorian?" Luc swallowed. He still wasn't sure about how much to tell people at the club. "No, I haven't," he lied.

"What did Tag say? Is Dorian alive out there?" Marianne asked.

"Tag said he was dead."

"Tag doesn't know. He's not too bright. Never has been. Sweet guy, though. Very nice person," Marianne conceded.

"That's about what everybody has been telling me."

"I never wanted to admit it, but I think Dorian is out

there," she ventured.

"You do?" Luc asked. He wondered if she noticed his leg jittering under the crisp white tablecloth.

"Think about it, Monsieur Pigeon. I was in love with him."

"I thought that much," Luc answered.

"Imagine how it must feel for me. The man of my dreams, the center of my life, running away and playing dead. I mourned him. I mourned him for years."

"Did you know about the plan ahead of time?" Luc asked.

"I knew he wanted to take the trophy back after Cravenmoore took it away."

"But he didn't say anything to you in advance about a fire or anything?"

"No. Once he was on the run, I didn't hear from him. But that was only a few days. The police were all over me. Watching my house, listening to my phone calls. It didn't bother me that he was out of touch with me. I assumed he'd show up on a dark night and whisk me away. The only thing was, before I knew it, everyone was saying he was dead."

"I'm sorry."

"And now you're here, and Tag was caught, so this whole thing is back. And it really feels like Dorian has been out there—for twenty plus years, not even trying to get in touch with me."

"If you don't mind me asking," Luc answered, "did you ever get married?"

"I didn't. Dorian was the love of my life. I've seen

other men from time to time, but nothing matched the spark that there was between Dorian and me." She took a drag on her cigarette. When she inhaled, her crow's feet deepened.

"Here's a question. Where did he come from?"

"What do you mean? He's a Parisian. Always lived in Paris."

"I mean, how did he get in the club?"

"He had a member sponsor, just like anyone would."

"Do you remember who it was?"

"I didn't start seeing him until he'd been here for a few months, and by then, he told me his sponsor was gone."

"I see. Do you have any idea where he might have hidden the cup—that is if he's still out there, in hiding himself?"

Marianne put out her cigarette. The woman grimaced. "He always would say cryptic things like, 'if anything were ever to happen, I'd find my way back to you,' all that kind thing. So, I believed he'd show up again one day. But that died a long time ago, and it was just easier for me to mourn his passing."

Luc noticed that she hadn't answered his question. But then again, here was someone who was affected by Dorian and his actions, and the amount of scrutinizing, self-doubt, and heartbreak that she'd suffered throughout the years was showing. The busboy could see it, especially now that her friends weren't around.

"I never let anyone get too close," she continued. "I always try to keep myself among people, having a good time, though. There's a lot of natural Novocain in that."

Luc was beginning to feel bad for even asking her about Dorian. He looked back at Evan, who greeted Luc's gaze with an angry stare.

"Watch out for him." Marianne nodded towards Yanis. "I can't stand that little shit."

"I got that message."

"Don't think for one second that anything you tell him won't find its way back to Cravenmoore—and fast."

Luc felt something for Marianne. He envied her popularity, felt remorse for her heartache, and appreciated her opinion of Evan—something that Luc was feeling even without a great deal of experience with the lawn boy so far.

The busboy thought for a moment. Should he mention the truth about Dorian to Marianne? Would it break her even further and push away a potentially powerful ally? Or would it bring her one step closer to the closure she'd need? Could he arrange a meeting with Dorian somehow?

"Madame Merriweather," Luc said, lowering his voice so Evan could not eavesdrop from across the room. "What would you say to Dorian if you saw him again?"

Marianne lit a second cigarette. She said nothing.

"I mean," Luc persisted, "if he were alive."

The look in Marianne's eyes was intense. "I don't know what you're playing at, kid, but you've got some nerve asking me that."

"Okay, I'm sorry," Luc said.

"What Dorian and I had was like nothing I've ever experienced, and I'm keenly aware that it's not over. From the first moment we spoke to each other, I felt something powerful. There was energy there. And then after he left, there was a time when he could have ridden in here on a golden steed, and I would have forgiven everything and left with him again. He was an incredible man. Maybe the perfect man."

"Wow."

"But don't mistake my feelings. If he walked in here today, it would be like he was walking right out of a grave, and back into the living world. A ghost, out of place and certainly out of favor, particularly with me."

Luc didn't answer.

"If I saw him right now," she continued, "I'd kill him—for real this time."

* * *

Luc left Marianne fuming into her dirty martini. As soon as Evan saw Luc rise to exit, he rose as well.

"Well, what happened?" The lawn boy chirped.

Luc noticed tiny beads of sweat forming on Evan's forehead. Whereas Luc always sweat from nerves, he felt as though the lawn boy sweat from anger.

"Nothing. She doesn't know where he is."

"Sure, she does. He's dead. I heard she sits alone in the park on the Seine where they held a memorial for him."

"She didn't mention that."

"Well, what did she say then?"

"Look, I need time to think," Luc stated as they left the restaurant and started down a hallway.

"Great. That's what I'm here to do. Tell me

everything."

When Luc didn't say anything for a moment, Evan grabbed his arm and pulled him into an empty conference room off the main hallway. No one out on the plouquette court saw it happen.

"Ow!" Luc squealed as he felt Yanis' grip.

"Listen, Pigeon," the shadow hissed. "I don't care how you handled this with Alaina, but let me tell you how this is going to go."

"Let go of me," Luc complained.

Evan released him and shut the conference room door behind them. Luc noticed a coat closet behind the lawn boy.

"I don't care how much they're paying you, and I don't care that you got Alaina to do some stupid illegal stuff for you, but—"

"Wait, what?" Luc exclaimed.

"I know she stole that folder from archives. And I know that it was probably you who put her up to it."

"I never said I did… and… I… uh… I never said I didn't," Luc managed, not trying to implicate Alaina any more than she already had herself.

"You got her to do all your dirty work, and she had to take the fall. Well guess what. I'm not going to be your little bitch."

"Take it easy, Evan."

"Look, if you ask me, you haven't been honest about this case at all. Cravenmoore likes you, but I have no clue why. You reek of lies. Greatest detective of all time? I doubt it.

We'll see."

"I'm not sure what you want from me," Luc pleaded. "Let's just get going so we can find the cup, okay?"

"Hang on a sec," Evan stated. "First things first. Tell me everything Marianne just said to you."

Evan could feel his blood heating up. "She doesn't like you. How's that for starters?" Luc eyed the closet behind Evan.

"Of course, she doesn't," Evan stated. "That lady has been flirting around here forever without a care for anyone else. Just because I'm a lawn boy and have to do everything every member says doesn't mean I have to like it. I see through her and she knows it."

"Look." Luc tried to control his adrenaline. "I'm not sure what you're getting at here, but we need to figure out what the next step is." The busboy knew exactly what he wanted the next step to be. Dorian was gone, but he thought there was a chance Armande would still be holed up in his millionaire's townhome. Maybe Dorian ran to him, or at least Luc wanted to tell Marwane that he found Dorian at the bookstore.

And then there was Alaina. It killed Luc that she was upstairs somewhere, elbow-deep in green steak garnish that had been all over some old fat guy's naked skin. It also killed him that this guy Evan apparently was in love with her, but not in any caring way. With Evan Yanis, it felt like he wanted ownership of Alaina.

"Start talking," Yanis grunted.

For the first time, Luc noticed that he was taller than

Evan. He looked down at the man's red, deep-set little eyes. He thought Evan might weigh a little more than he, but it was a risk he was willing to take.

Without thinking, Luc leapt at the shadow. He drove Evan into the coat closet. He heard the hangers clang against one another as the lawn boy stumbled into the back wall. Luc slammed the closet door closed, and wedged the doorknob of the outer door so the closet would stay shut.

He could hear Yanis pounding from the inside, screaming for help. Luc stepped into the bright hallway. No one was around to hear the lawn boy, and no one out on the plouquette grounds seemed to be able to hear the small man through the large panes of glass.

Luc knew he had to continue this case without Cravenmoore breathing down on the back of his neck. He was off to Armande Marwane's.

Chapter XIII.

When Luc found Armande Marwane's house dark and locked up, the busboy felt as though Dorian's accomplice was gone for good. There was only one more place that the fake detective thought he could go. It was a long shot, but he thought to try to meet Flova Pompousselpeck again.

The wife of the former chief of police had been friendly and helpful, and she'd even hinted that she would be available to Luc and Alaina had they needed her. But would the Paris Private Plouquette Conglomerate turn him away if he showed up uninvited?

Luc ran through Paris' neighborhoods, sprinting through streets too narrow for cars. Rows upon rows of balconies moved above him as he sprinted by sweet-smelling flower boxes.

Out of breath, Luc knocked at the Paris Private Plouquette Conglomerate. Coat-check Chad peered down at Luc.

"Look who's back," the man said.

"Bonjour," Luc panted. "Is Madame Pompousselpeck available?"

"Are you aware that nearly 15 of our public servants per year are accused of sleeping with a parliamentary intern?" Coat-check Chad stated.

"What?" Luc asked, holding himself up on the doorframe as he caught his breath. "What does that have to do with anything?"

"Well, it must be stopped."

"Sure… it's improper, I guess…"

"No," the man objected. "I mean, these accusations. We need legislations in place to help the interns keep these secrets. They derail progress and distract the media and public—which is why I'm running for another term. Can I count on your support?"

"Sure, whatever. Is Madame Pompousselpeck available?" Luc said, catching his breath.

"Thank you! If I could just get your email address, I'd be happy to add you to my newsletter. Plus, for a five-euro donation, I can give you a bumper sticker."

"Please, I really need to speak with Madame Pompousselpeck," Luc said for a third time.

"Wait here. I'll see if she's available for guests," Coat-check Chad said as he closed the door.

Minutes passed. Luc worried this had been a bad idea. He looked for patterns in the wood grain of the door though, unwilling to turn himself away.

Finally, the door reopened and the man escorted the busboy to the terrace café at the Private, where the wife of the former chief of police was waiting to meet them.

"Madame Pompousselpeck, thank you for agreeing to see me," Luc said as he approached. Coat-check Chad returned to his post.

"Of course. Please, have a seat." The woman pushed an empty wrought-iron chair away from the small table with her foot. The chair's legs grunted as they ribbed the stone surface beneath.

"What can I do for you?" She asked as Luc sat.

"Did you know," Luc said as he dropped his voice, "that the man we went to see after we came to visit you at the Private was Armande Marwane himself?"

The police chief's wife carefully set her coffee cup down. "He was?"

"After we visited him, we found a picture of him at the Publique. It's the same man. Roman Lubin *is* Armande Marwane."

"I don't believe it," the woman said as she gasped.

"It's true," Luc said, nodding.

"So, he's been hiding right here in Paris the whole time?"

Luc nodded again.

"I've never met the man myself. If you'll recall, it was Snippy's recommendation that you visit him."

"Right. Well, I just went to go find him again, and he's gone."

"Well that's not surprising."

"Maybe he just didn't answer his door. But I suspect he's taken off."

"I would have if I were him," she commented. The woman stirred her coffee with a small spoon.

"But we visited him twice. The first time was after the barber here—"

"Please, he has a name. 'Snippy.'"

"Sorry. Snippy. Anyway, the first time, we didn't recognize Marwane and he was short with us. Then, we came across some pictures, and it turns out, he was in a couple of them, and that's how we discovered that it was him."

"Interesting," Madame Pompousselpeck replied. "And was he helpful when you went back to see him?"

"Actually, he was, which was a surprise."

"Well," the woman answered, "maybe he's just ready for this thing to be over."

"But there's more to it," Luc added.

"Okay?"

"Well," Luc lowered his voice again, "I found Dorian."

A waitress approached. "Good evening Monsieur and Madame…"

"Not now!" Madame Pompousselpeck chirped as she waved the young woman off. Flova leaned in. "You found Dorian Thibault?"

"Yep," Luc confirmed. "I saw him with my own eyes. And I talked to him."

"You talked to him? Incredible."

"It was."

"And was he helpful?" She asked, leaning on the café table with her elbows. The wrought-iron piece of outdoor furniture teetered on the cobblestone.

"I mean, kind of," Luc answered. "He didn't hand over the Waterford Cup or anything, though."

"Have you tried going back to talk to him?" Flova asked.

"Yes. Alaina and I went back, but he was gone too. He took off faster than Armande did."

"I'm not surprised. He's probably been ready for that

for years."

"Yeah, that's what I'm thinking," Luc answered.

"Was there anything either of them said about where they might be going? What they might be doing? Are they still in Paris, do you think?" Madame Pompousselpeck asked.

"I have no idea."

"They didn't give you a clue of any kind?"

"Not that I'm aware of. Why?"

"I don't know," the woman thought aloud. "It just seems like Snippy thought these guys were pranksters. Along those lines, what if they liked to set traps? You should be careful, Monsieur Pigeon."

"I will, thank you. But nothing so far has made be believe they would hurt anyone."

"That's true. I'm just trying to look out for you. After hearing all that though, I can't imagine how much new information I could give you."

The woman's spoon made small 'tinks' each time she stirred her coffee.

"I know. I just need someone to discuss this with," Luc said. "They gave me a new assistant at the club, and he isn't as helpful as he is just really aggressive. They have Alaina on Sweenish massage cleanup —"

"That's the worst," Madame Pompousselpeck sighed.

"So, I've heard."

"I think your next step is to recall everything you can about your conversations with Dorian and Armande. Who knows? Maybe they let on more than they meant to."

"What about Tag?" Luc asked.

"From what it sounds like everyone has said, it doesn't sound like Tag is bright enough to have dropped you a hint."

"But something's been bothering me," Luc mentioned as he shifted in his chair.

"What's that?" Madame Pompousselpeck asked.

"Well, it couldn't have been a coincidence that Tag was trying to break into a pet store right next to Dorian's bookshop."

"So?"

"So," Luc continued, "what if he wasn't looking for a re-venomized raccoon. "What if he was actually looking for Dorian?"

"That seems like a stretch."

"I know, but I'm looking for anything here. What if Tag and Dorian really weren't in touch?"

"But why would Tag not just walk in then to the shop and look for Dorian when it was open?" Madame Pompousselpeck asked.

"Wait," Luc answered. "Maybe he wasn't looking for Dorian. Maybe he wanted to go in the shop without Dorian there. Maybe he was looking for the cup."

"That's interesting," the woman said as she sipped her coffee.

"That would make more sense," Luc said. "After all, it was Armande who sent me off in the direction of the bookshop in the first place. Maybe they all want me to get the cup away from Dorian for some reason."

"Maybe you should go back to the bookshop,"

Madame Pompousselpeck suggested.

*   *   *

Luc fell into a small office. His palms swelled with redness. His digits throbbed and cracked. The busboy felt as though it had taken an hour to hoist himself to the second-floor window in the back of the bookshop. But in truth, it had only been a few painful minutes.

He lay motionless on the desk. He felt papers beneath him, a stapler. He'd knocked over a desk lamp but now sat in silence. Had anyone seen him break in? He waited. Listened. He heard no sirens.

It took Luc nearly all afternoon to decide to break into the bookshop. He walked around the block six times before he gathered the courage to do it. He stopped in a bar and took a shot, and that had helped. But, he regretted that move as he struggled his way up the drainpipe.

Luc looked back out the window as he finally found the strength to lift himself off the desk. As far as he could tell, no prying eyes were watching him from other windows in the alley. No one stood below.

Luc leapt up with renewed energy. He began searching the office. He was looking for anything: the trophy, some note with an address on it, anything that might tell him where Dorian, Armande, or Tag had gone. Surely if Dorian had ever been keeping the actual trophy there, it was long gone by now.

The office turned up empty. Luc descended the

narrow wooden staircase, moved beyond the "employees only" sign, and arrived in the bookshop itself downstairs. Outside the front window, he could see people pass on the sidewalk. He hoped no one would stop to peer into the blackness of the shop.

Luc looked under the front counter. Nothing. He looked in each box that was stacked by the locked back door. Nothing. The busboy even checked the trash bins. Nothing.

Almost at his wit's end, Luc returned to the main front room. He stared out at the neighborhood. Was the shop a dead end? Almost despondent, he happened to look back at the bookshelf.

There, on the top level, a thick, green-spined book stood out to the busboy. In large letters, one word said it all: "Plouquette."

Luc asked Dorian for a book about the sport during his first visit. The man had said that he didn't have one. But there it was. The busboy grabbed a nearby ladder, and rolled it to the spot of the book. Luc rose to the top shelf.

Still on the ladder, the busboy flipped through the pages. There were diagrams of the equipment, an entire chapter on the proper in-game attire, but nothing that indicated how to play.

Luc looked back at the shelf to see if any of the spines next to the book on plouquette also addressed the subject. But there in the darkness of the empty space left by the book he'd removed, something caught his eye: a hint of gold.

And then it all made sense: Armande's suggestion that Luc pick up a book about plouquette, Dorian's phrase that treasure could be found in books. Whether the men meant it or not, they *were* clues. In his amazement, the busboy forgot he was holding the book on plouquette. It fell all the way to the floor, landing with a thud.

Luc tore the other titles off the shelf. Pages fluttered as each fell to the hardwood floors below. And behind the space where the row of books had rested, there it was. The Sir Larabee Waterford Cup.

Luc reached into the blackness and dragged the cup to the edge of the shelf. He could tell it was heavy. The shelf had been built with this hiding place in mind. The books had hidden a perfectly shaped compartment for the trophy. Luc examined his find. It was aged and still bore the spot where Yelly's name had once rested on a small plate. Poor Yelly.

As he lifted it off the shelf and into his arms, Luc realized he'd misjudged the object's weight. He fell backwards and went crashing to the floor. It hurt. Luc didn't know how long he lay on the ground, but he didn't get up immediately.

When he finally did, he wondered how he hadn't broken his back. The fall had to have been more than four feet. It didn't matter, though. He had the cup. But what now?

Should he just walk it right over to the club? Did he take it to his apartment and wait until he decided whether or not to tell the police about Dorian and Armande? Should he take the cup to the police? If he did that, it might be impounded as evidence. If the cup weren't returned to the club, would he get the reward?

With more gusto and preparation than before, Luc lifted the trophy into his arms. Just walking with it hurt. How was he going to take it anywhere? He'd never survive the trip out the second-story window with the cup. Luc knew he would have to exit through the back door. He'd have to risk someone seeing him in the alley either way.

Luc unlocked the back door and swung it open with his hip. He hunched over the weight of the trophy. Much to the busboy's surprise, Evan Yanis stood waiting on the other side.

"Bonjour, Pigeon," the little lawn boy greeted with disdain.

"Evan," Luc blurted out. "Uh... where did you come from?"

"I've been following you the whole time."

"You have?"

"I figured the Private was behind all this. The President will be pleased to hear that he was right all along."

"They're not behind anything," Luc said, already panting under the weight of the trophy.

"Then why did you go there and then come straight here to get the cup?"

"They didn't tell me anything about where it was. I figured it out."

"Well, we'll see if Cravenmoore believes you," Evan said.

Luc's knees buckled under the weight of the heavy trophy. He lowered it to the ground as gently as he could.

"Look, I'm sorry about—"

"Putting me in a closet?" Evan said. "Yeah, you should be. If President Cravenmoore knew, he'd eat you for lunch."

"You haven't told him yet?" Luc asked as he raised his eyebrows. He tried massaging the pain out of his forearms.

"I've been too busy following you all over town."

"Look. I'm sorry about locking you in there," Luc began, mustering the courage to truly confront Evan. "I didn't want to do that, but you were being a jerk back there. I didn't feel like I had a choice."

"Your assignment is to let me shadow you. I am supposed to report back to the President. It's as simple as that."

"My assignment was to find the Waterford Cup. Which I did. Go report on that."

"No need," Evan snapped as he puffed out his chest, "because I'm waltzing in there with this thing. I'll be a hero."

"Like hell you are. I found it. I'm the one being paid to search."

"Yeah, but you couldn't get the job done. They put me on the case with you, and within a day the trophy turns up. President Cravenmoore will have no choice but to recognize that I was the brain you needed for the job."

"Please. You were locked in a closet."

"Go ahead. Tell him yourself that you locked me in there. I'm sure that will go over well," Evan answered.

"Look, let's just take a breath here. The important thing is, we've got the cup. We're all good," Luc said. He figured he could work out Cravenmoore when he got there.

"Good idea," Evan replied. "Go ahead. Take a rest. I'm taking the cup back."

"Be my guest," Luc answered.

Evan bent, but could barely get the Waterford Cup off the ground. After a few tries and some grunting, he finally looked at Luc with resignation in his eyes.

"Yeah, that's what I thought. We'll each take a side," Luc suggested.

Chapter XIV.

When the big glass doors to the playing surface at the Paris Publique Plouquette Pitch, Grounds, Gardens, Grass Court, and Lawn Club swung open, every player froze to see Luc and Evan limp in with the Waterford Cup. The crowd gasped.

Emerging from a fog of people, President Cravenmoore floated toward them in astonishment. He dropped his mallet on the short, wiry grass. Everyone else stood like art in a statue garden.

"Gentlemen," he gasped, unable to take his eyes off the cup. "Look at this."

"Here you go, sir," Luc began. "The Waterford Cup, as promised."

"What a sight," the President murmured as he gazed at the prize.

The crowd hummed with enthusiastic murmurs.

"Couldn't have done it without me, sir," Evan added.

But the President wasn't listening.

"Madames and Messieurs!" Cravenmoore exclaimed as he turned around. "I am pleased to present to you, for the first time in over two decades, the Sir Larabee Waterford Cup!"

The crowd of plouquette players erupted into cheers. Yelly Reardon came rushing to the front of the group with tears in his eyes.

"Ah my dear Yelly," the President continued.

Luc swore he could hear a barely-audible response

from the entire crowd, "poor Yelly."

"Let it be known to all," Cravenmoore went on, "that we will have Monsieur Reardon's name rightfully branded on this piece of hardware as soon as possible. A new nameplate for a truly deserving champion!"

The crowd clapped. Yelly turned, waving. Luc thought he'd probably been waiting for this moment ever since the original heist. A part of him thought Yelly might even deserve it, even if Dorian won fairly.

"And another note," the President continued his impromptu speech. "None of this would have been possible without the greatest detective in the whole world—and I'm not exaggerating when I say that, we checked, and he is—Monsieur Pigeon!"

Luc smiled sheepishly. He'd never been announced in front of a crowd before. He waved. Evan made a face. Phyllis the horse whinnied.

It was then that Luc noticed Marianne Merriweather in the crowd. She looked on with interest. She didn't smile. He'd never seen her not smile when around friends.

"Maurice," the President called to his right-hand man. "Please see to it that this gets placed in the trophy cabinet where it belongs. Let's maybe put an extra lock on it this time," he said with a chuckle. The crowd was amused as well. "As my ex-wife always said, 'I'll leave you if you don't lock me down.'" Cravenmoore laughed, but few others did.

"One of your weaker ones, sir," Maurice de Mouton whispered to him.

Cravenmoore composed himself. "Let us all head to

the bar," he continued, undeterred, "to celebrate the return of the great Sir Larabee Waterford Cup with free drinks for the next hour!"

The crowd erupted again and started to disperse.

Cravenmoore turned to Luc and Evan. "Nice job, gentlemen. Let's go to my office."

*   *   *

Luc and Evan sat facing Cravenmoore's desk in the dark office. They didn't say a word to each other. Luc felt uneasy. He enjoyed being celebrated, but he didn't like that he felt like the bad guys had won.

"Well, this calls for a drink. Scotch?" Cravenmoore offered.

"Yes, thank you," Evan replied.

"No thank you," Luc answered.

"What's the matter, Pigeon? You won!" The President reminded him.

"I know."

A clock struck. A mechanical pterodactyl shot from a small door near the minute hand. It shrieked. Cravenmoore looked up.

"What do you think of my new time piece, gentlemen?"

"It's really nice," Evan answered.

"I love it," Cravenmoore went on as he poured drinks. "It was a gift from our resident woodworker. He's also a member of the Pterodactyl Remembrance Society. Makes beautiful clocks. The mechanism of this one is lubricated with hornet blood from our farm, so you know it's good."

Gross, Luc thought.

"Pigeon," the President continued, "did you know we use *every part* of the hornet?"

"So, you've mentioned."

"Ah. Good. We're proud of it. We do love the glorious hornet around here. I call them 'God's misunderstood beast.' Would you like one? As I said earlier, we'd be happy to give you one as a pet. As part of your reward?"

"No thanks," Luc answered, grimacing.

"Suit yourself. They are loyal as hell and great with kids. Anyway, your reward will be on the way shortly. I'll have Maurice get the funds transfer started as soon as you give me your bank details."

"I'll get them to you," Luc replied. He thought of Alaina. She was being punished, but it had been her discoveries that ultimately led to the cup.

As Cravenmoore handed drinks to Evan and Luc, ice cubes lightly knocked on the inside of the glass. Apparently, the President hadn't listened when Luc declined the beverage.

"Let me ask you this," Cravenmoore went on, "what about Dorian Thibault and Armande Marwane?"

"What about them?" Luc shrugged.

"Did you ever find them?"

"No, I didn't," Luc lied.

"Well, where was the cup?"

"We found the cup in an old bookstore," Evan answered.

"Thank you, Yanis," Cravenmoore answered through his teeth. "But I was asking Monsieur Pigeon. Listen to what he has to say. You could learn something from this man."

Evan squirmed.

"An old bookstore?" The President continued. "What led you there?"

Luc thought fast. "Well, I didn't have very many leads. But, I knew that Tag was caught trying to break into Zoo La La."

"To steal a re-venomized raccoon, yes," the President answered.

"Right," Luc confirmed. "Well, this bookshop was next door. And it occurred to me that maybe Tag was trying to break in there instead of Zoo La La, because, well, who really needs a re-venomized raccoon?"

"Everyone?" The President asked. "I mean. They are a real delight. Great for home security, and obedient with leash work. But it's no hornet."

"Okay," Luc said. "But what I meant was, I had a hunch that he was looking for the cup maybe. So, I got into the bookstore, had a look around, and there it was."

"Hell of a hunch," Evan stated under his breath.

"You see, Evan?" The President replied. "This is what makes him the greatest detective of all time. What might be a fleeting idea for you and me, that we might just dismiss out of hand too easily, is something that leads him to his goal. He uses his instincts and he wins. Not unlike plouquette itself. Wow. Sometimes I can't believe how deep that game really is."

"I wouldn't know," Luc muttered.

"Well congratulations again, Monsieur Pigeon," the President said as Maurice de Mouton entered. "As I said before, I'll have Maurice get to work on the transfer right away. Maurice, my good man, is the trophy in its rightful spot?"

"We're going to have to reinforce the shelf. It's heavy and our trophy case has aged."

"I see. Well, I trust you to get it done," Cravenmoore said.

"Did you notice, sir," Evan interrupted, "that when you assigned me to the case, everything immediately worked itself—"

"Please Evan," the President cut him off. "You can debrief me later. I'm still speaking with Monsieur Pigeon."

Evan's face became red. Luc couldn't tell if he was embarrassed or furious.

"I'd like to make a deal with you, Monsieur Pigeon," the President continued.

"Okay," Luc replied.

"How about for another million, you find me the men who did this."

"Wasn't that part of his original assignment?" Evan asked.

"Absolutely," Cravenmoore answered. "But now, I *really* want them found."

Evan sat back, still displeased. He wasn't finding a way to derail Luc.

"You don't think they're dead anymore?" Luc asked.

"Of course not," the President said. "But you'll never hear me say that in public. But if the cup was out there, I believe Dorian Thibault and Armande Marwane are out there too. I believe they're running the streets of Paris, cursing my name—not unlike my ex-wife."

"Good one, sir," Maurice said from his corner. "You're back in rhythm."

"Can you do it for me, Pigeon? Can you find them for me?"

"For another million?" Luc asked.

"That's right."

Without thinking about Dorian, Armande, Tag, or even how he would go about doing it, Luc blurted out, "sure."

"Excellent. I'll make sure you have a couple of tickets to the upcoming Waterford Cup tournament, as well."

"That's great, thanks."

"It's the least we can do. Now, gentlemen, if you don't mind, you'll have to excuse me." The President stood and began walking out. "I have my weekly one-ball juggling lesson this afternoon with Pierre Pantsuit. I don't want to be late."

"President Cravenmoore," Evan interjected, "When may I have a little time, one on one, to debrief you on the case?"

"I'll find you later," the President replied, halfway to the door.

"Yes, of course," Evan responded, jumping up after him. "But I thought we could do it today."

"I'm not too worried about it, Yanis," Cravenmoore

said. "We'll talk sometime."

The President was gone, leaving Evan, Luc, and Maurice de Mouton in the President's office.

"This isn't over," Evan said as he wheeled around to face Luc. "I bet you're proud of yourself."

*   *   *

Luc joined the raucous club members in the bar. He'd never seen it so crowded. Complete strangers were patting him on his back, spilling his drink with every "congratulations!"

"How's it feel to be the hero of the Paris Publique Plouquette Pitch, Grounds, Gardens, Grass Court, and Lawn Club?" one woman asked.

"It's great," Luc lied. He wondered how Alaina would react to his fame.

"Really, you must tell us how you did it! You are a magnificent creature!" The woman hawed.

"I don't know," Luc answered. He didn't consider the idea that he'd be famous in the club if he'd succeeded. He looked around the room as he searched for an appropriate answer for the woman. He saw Marianne Merriweather looking at him, still not smiling.

"You're too modest, Monsieur Pigeon," the woman continued.

Luc felt a soft hand on his forearm. "May I speak with him?" A familiar voice asked.

The busboy looked up. "Alaina!"

"Hey."

The woman left the two alone.

"Dolt looks like he has his hands full," Luc started.

"Sure does. He and I haven't gotten to hang out as much lately. He's trying to perfect the impossibly-majestic-high-arc-rainbow-hammer-mallet throw."

"He is? Does he even play plouquette?"

"Not that I'm aware of."

"Weird," Luc said.

"That's Dolt, though. Never willing to put the time in on the basics. Always trying to shoot the moon before he learns to shoot a tin can off a fence post."

"Everything okay with you guys?"

"Never mind," Alaina answered.

Luc sensed the obvious tension, but decided to drop it. "Anyway, how are you?! It feels like I haven't seen you in forever."

"Fine. I mean, massage duty. Whatever. But you. You did it," she said, smiling. "You found the cup."

"Sure did."

She lowered her voice in the crowd. "How long did it take you to decide to bring it in here?"

"I didn't have a choice," Luc answered quietly as numerous shoulders brushed up against him. "I thought I'd ditched Evan here at the club, but he wound up following me back to the bookstore. He made me bring it back immediately."

"It was in the bookstore?"

"Yep," Luc whispered. "I got to thinking, and just

realized that I'd have the freedom to look around if Dorian wasn't in there. And sure enough, the cup was hidden behind the books."

"Pretty cool."

"How's massage duty?" Luc asked.

"Ugh. It's nasty," she complained. "But I need to know more. Did you ever find Dorian and Armande again? Or Tag?"

"No. I have no clue where to look. But Cravenmoore offered me more money to find them now that the cup is back."

"Are you going to take it?"

"I said I would," Luc answered.

"Any idea where to start looking?"

"Not really. I did go back and talk to the wife of the former chief of police again, Madame Pompousselpeck."

"Oh yeah? And she was helpful?"

"A little. Just support when I needed it. I'm not sure why she's so kind," Luc mentioned. "But, she seems to have a real sense that this should be handled the right way. Not her husband's way."

"I see."

"Listen," Luc said, mustering some courage. "I'd love to keep talking to you about the case, but we can't do it here comfortably."

"We could meet in a park tomorrow?" She suggested.

Chapter XV.

Luc's mother sat at a table, waiting near the bar in their family café. Soft yellow light made the space look welcoming, although Luc didn't want to be there.

"You're late," she said. "Everything okay?"

The busboy hadn't been able to fall asleep the night before. Luc couldn't keep his mind off the case—or Alaina. He was operating on low energy.

"Yes, I'm fine."

"Look, before things get busy around here, we need to talk."

"Okay," Luc answered.

"Let me see that apron of yours."

Luc hadn't put it on yet, so he handed it to her. She invited Luc to sit across from her.

"I have a new one for you," the café owner said.

"What's wrong with my apron?"

"Nothing. It's just that it's a busboy's. I got you a new one. It's for a waiter."

"C'mon, Mom," Luc whined.

"I know, I know. Just do this for me. Give it a shot. I bet you'll like the money," she sang.

Luc held his tongue. He wanted to tell his mother that he was expecting a two-million-euro payment any moment. In fact, now that he had headspace to consider it, Luc planned on gently telling his mother that he'd leave the café as soon as it came through.

"What's the matter?" She asked. "And don't say you don't want the café. Put it out of your head. I don't want you to feel any pressure. Just take this one step for me."

"I don't know, mom," Luc said. He didn't want the added responsibility anyway. He never had.

"Just take the apron, please. This will make your father and me very happy. He serves every single table in this place. Give him a hand."

Luc took the apron.

"Great. Thank you. And hey, there's something else."

"What's that?" Luc asked.

"Your girlfriend was in here this morning," his mother said.

"My girlfriend?"

"Janet."

"This morning? Janet was here?" Luc stammered.

"Yes."

"She's not my girlfriend."

"She seemed upset," Luc's mother said with a shrug. "When I asked her if I could give you a message, she just said that she'd brought a box of all your stuff."

"Oh, okay," Luc said.

"But when I offered to carry it in, she simply stood at the front door on the sidewalk, dropped a match in, and set it all on fire."

"Oh."

"I hope it wasn't anything important," his mother said.

Luc couldn't even remember what any of it was. "I'm

sure it was fine."

"Luc," his mother warned. "I'm just not sure she's a good fit for you."

"That was the understatement of the year," Luc said. "But don't worry about it, Mom. We broke up."

"I'm just saying, your father and I are concerned. We don't want her to burn the café down."

"She's not going to burn down the café. I promise."

"How do you know?" Luc's mother said.

"If I put on the apron and wait tables today, will you stop talking about Janet?"

Luc's mother threw her hands in the air, a silent confirmation that she'd drop the subject. "Sure, of course. You got it. And thank you, by the way. For starting to serve tables."

"Sure."

The shift went impossibly slow for Luc. He got several orders wrong. He dropped a tray of drinks. "You'll get better," his mother assured him, but Luc knew he didn't want to get better. Plus, he was now counting the minutes until he quit the café. The only question was how to let his mother down lightly.

* * *

In another quiet city park in Paris, Luc Martin waited for Alaina. He sat in his busboy—now waiter—clothes. A weeping willow drooped over his wooden bench, the reflection of which could be seen upside down from the other side of the pond.

The weathered bench bent under his weight. Luc stared at the wood. He was so sleep-deprived that it looked like the paint was peeling as he stared at it.

"Hey," Alaina said as she approached, snapping Luc out of his daydream.

"Oh, hey," Luc answered.

Alaina was out of her typical club clothes. She was dressed casually, and her hair was tied up above her head. Luc thought she was maybe more beautiful than he'd ever seen her.

"So, how have you been doing?"

"I've been pretty good," Luc answered.

"Good."

"How about you?" He asked.

"Yeah, me too," she replied as she sat down next to Luc.

"Still on massage cleanup duty?"

"Yep. I imagine they'll have me on that for a while. Until I 'learn my lesson,' they say. Whatever."

"Sorry about that, again."

"It's my fault," she said as she watched ducks paddle in the green water. "I should have been more careful up in the librarium."

"No, come on. You were doing the right thing."

"That's what I'm wondering, though," she said as she looked down at the gravel dust of the park walkway beneath her feet.

"What's that?" Luc asked.

"Is it really the right thing?" She said without looking at him.

"Well, solving the case? Using all the evidence you could find to get the cup back? That sounds like the right thing to me."

"Well, yeah," Alaina said. "But that's not the stuff that matters. Think about it. We've still got a couple of people out there missing, and the bunch of assholes that run the PPPPGGGCLC have pretty much won."

"Well, it's what they paid me for."

"Oh, congratulations," Alaina answered. "You got paid to help the bad guys."

"C'mon, Alaina. I mean, I saw an opportunity and I took it. What's wrong with that?"

"Listen to yourself, man," she said, leaning back on the bench. "Why not stick it to these guys somehow? I thought that's what you were doing when you were pretending to be a detective, but so far, all you've done is help them win."

Luc thought for a moment. "Maybe you're right."

"Of course, I'm right. I'm always right. And don't think this is just about Armande, Tag, and Dorian either."

"Okay?"

"Think about it. Marianne Merriweather? This affects her too."

"Yeah, I get that," Luc nodded as he sighed. "I can't help but think that she's just been walking around with a broken heart for a few decades."

"Exactly," Alaina answered. "She is just good at

developing the mechanisms it takes to hide it, or at least suppress it."

"You want to know something else? I saw Dolt the other day," Luc noted, returning to Alaina's boyfriend.

"Don't change the subject."

"Apparently, he doesn't get along with Evan Yanis."

"Yeah, Dolt is the worst to him. But, Evan is also the worst in his own way, so there's not much you can do about that."

"Can I ask you something?" Luc said. "What do you see in Dolt, anyway?"

Alaina shifted. She diverted eye contact. "I don't know. He's a popular guy. People like him. I said I don't want to talk about it."

"Aren't all bartenders popular?" Luc asked as he pressed on.

"I suppose so," she answered, moving her amber hair behind her ear.

"Look, I hope you don't mind me saying it— "

"Luc, don't—"

He had to go for it. Luc had been searching for a way to say it each night as he lay in bed. "I just feel like you deserve to be with someone who really cares about you. Someone who knows what they have when they have you." Luc could feel his heart hammering away.

"Luc, come on."

"I'm just saying, what about m— "

"Monsieur Pigeon," a voice came from behind.

Luc and Alaina both turned.

"Or do you prefer that I call you Luc Martin?" Dorian Thibault asked as he approached from the shade beneath the willow overhead.

The blood drained from both Luc and Alaina's faces.

"You're... you're Dorian Thibault," Alaina stammered.

"You got it. Is there room on that bench for me?" He asked as he sat. He wore a blindingly white polo, the sleeves of which were perfectly fitted around shapely arms. His hair was parted in a straighter-than-straight line, but his eyes made it look as though he hadn't slept in days. The only other difference between this and the last time Luc saw him, was that he was unshaven. But Luc thought he looked more like a celebrity than ever.

Luc and Alaina both scooted themselves to one side, and Dorian sat down on the end next to Alaina, who couldn't hide her astonishment.

"How did you find us?" Luc asked.

"I've been following you for a while now," Dorian told Luc.

"You have?" Luc asked.

"Yep. To and from the club. To your apartment. To the café where you work—which is owned by your parents."

Luc couldn't talk.

"Don't look so surprised," the man answered smiling. "You don't fake your own death and sneak around for 22 years without figuring out how not to be noticed." Dorian looked at Alaina. "Hi, I don't think we've met."

"Alaina Amandine," she greeted. The lawn girl

couldn't find a way to close her mouth.

"You're a beautiful girl. Luc's a lucky guy."

"Oh, we're not together," Luc replied as quickly as he could just so he didn't have to hear Alaina say it herself.

"Oh, sorry. My mistake," Dorian said. "Anyway, I see you paid a visit to my bookstore."

Luc looked away.

"Are you planning on returning to put my desk upstairs back in order?" Dorian asked.

"Well, I…" Luc stammered.

"I also noticed something was missing. Something pretty valuable," Dorian said. "Meant a lot to me."

"I'm sorry. I did what I was hired to do," Luc said, still avoiding eye contact.

"Sure. I get it," Dorian said as he sat back, surveying the scene in the park.

"Look," Luc reasoned. "I know you won it fair and square, but—"

"Stop it," Dorian interrupted him. "I didn't come here to give you a hard time about the cup."

"You didn't?"

"No, give me a break. It's just a cup. The item itself lost its meaning to me years ago. Let Yelly have it for all I care."

"Poor Yelly," Alaina whispered.

"So why did you come here?" Luc asked. "Why have you been following me?"

"C'mon, you're a smart guy. You know. I need to hear you say that you won't turn me in."

"What if he does?" Alaina asked.

"Interesting. Do you usually do the talking for both of you?" Dorian asked Alaina.

"No, she doesn't," Luc interjected. "But still. What if I did turn you in? I'm not saying that I'm going to, but what if I did?"

"You won't," Dorian guessed.

"Why not?" Alaina asked.

"Because Alaina, how do you think they'd react if they discovered Luc here wasn't the greatest detective of all time?"

"You know?" Alaina asked.

"Of course. And apparently, so do you," Dorian offered.

"Yeah," Alaina answered, looking back at Luc. "He told me a while back."

"Interesting," Dorian thought aloud. "I didn't think you had the marbles to come clean to her, kid."

"How do you know so much about me?" Luc asked.

"Like I said, I've been watching you, 'Monsieur Pigeon.'" The man emphasized the quotation marks with his fingers.

"So, what?" Luc said.

"So, my point is," Dorian continued. "If you turn me in, I turn on you. Cravenmoore will know the truth about you so fast, you won't know what happened."

Luc looked to the ground again.

"Picture it," Dorian offered. "Whatever they've agreed to pay you, that'll be gone for sure. You can't lie to these people and expect them to understand it. I should know."

"He has a good point," Alaina noted, looking towards Luc.

"Plus, what do you think the chances are that you two would ever see each other again?" the man suggested.

Luc looked at Alaina, but this time she was looking at Dorian.

"Just think about it," Dorian went on. "If you're never let in the club again, when will you see each other? Sure, maybe once or twice early on in a café, but not like it is now. It's not like you two go to the same grocery store or anything."

"What's a grocery store?" Alaina asked.

"Exactly," Dorian answered. "Rich people, am I right Luc?"

"I have a question for you," Alaina interrupted. "If you were following him, why'd you even let him get to the cup? Or better yet, why'd you even leave it behind at the bookstore in the first place?"

"It's like I told you," Dorian answered. "I haven't cared about that thing in years. It's Cravenmoore who wants it. Once Tag slipped up and got caught, I knew Cravenmoore would start searching for me again. I knew he wouldn't give up, either, until he got the Waterford Cup back. So, I figured I'd end the whole cat-and-mouse game before it got too close for me."

Luc snickered.

"What?" Dorian asked.

"Shows what you know," the busboy answered. "They still asked me to come after you, even after they got the cup back."

Dorian looked vexed for the first time in the conversation. "Huh. I didn't expect that. Why?"

"I don't know," Luc said with a shrug. "Sounds like Cravenmoore cares about more than just the cup. Might have revenge on the mind."

"Never mind that, then," Dorian answered. "I've been hiding for years. I won't stop now."

"What about Marianne?" Alaina asked.

Dorian paused. "What about Marianne?"

"Don't you think she's affected by all this?" Luc answered.

Dorian took a deep breath. "Mademoiselle Merriweather can take care of herself."

"Of course, she can," Alaina stated.

"But there's been a notable change in her since the cup came back. Really since Tag was discovered," Luc added.

"You're letting this distract you, Luc," Dorian replied. "Don't forget what this is about."

"And what's it really about?" Alaina asked. "She doesn't matter to you?"

"Of course, she does," Dorian answered. "But she doesn't matter to the situation at hand. At least not anymore."

"I'd say she's an important part of it," Luc countered. "Can you imagine how she's felt about this for the last 22 years? It's shaped everything about who she is."

"You're not going to convince me that she's a broken

woman or anything," Dorian stated.

"She's not," Luc answered. "But she has let it define her. She is a social leader at the club, but it's not because she wanted to be. It's her defense."

"But don't think for a second," Alaina continued, "that she'll let that down if she saw you. It's rewired her. Every single guy at the club has tried to take her out, and she's impossible. They all fall in love with her, believing she's the one, but she'll never give herself over that far."

"Like I said," Dorian restated, staring out at the pond, "she can take care of herself."

Luc thought for a moment. "Are you taking care of yourself?"

"What?" He asked.

"Luc's right," Alaina added, picking up on Dorian's change in mood since he sat down. "What if you're the broken one? Not Marianne."

"I'm not saying he's broken," Luc corrected Alaina. "But, what if I tried to get Marianne here to talk? Dorian, would you like to see her again?"

"What good would that do?" Alaina asked under her breath.

"Good question," Dorian answered.

In the end, Luc still didn't know if he'd turn Dorian and Armande in. They just didn't seem like the bad guys in the situation. But, the busboy did sense that it would help both Dorian and Marianne if they saw each other.

"Look," Luc explained, nodding at Alaina. "She accused me earlier of helping the bad guy—Cravenmoore. If anything, I figured he'd hate the idea of a secret meeting between you two—Dorian and Marianne—and that's enough to convince me to try and make it happen. So, what do you think? Do you want to see her?"

Dorian thought for a moment. "Okay," he agreed. "If you can make that happen, I won't leak your secret about being a fraud to Cravenmoore."

"And I won't tell Cravenmoore that I've found you," Luc answered.

"Deal," Dorian said.

Chapter XVI.

Luc and Alaina began their walk all the way back to the Paris Publique Plouquette Pitch, Grounds, Gardens, Grass Court, and Lawn Club. Luc hadn't forgotten about the conversation they were having before Dorian appeared. He wanted to tell Alaina how he felt about her—even if he felt as though he could predict her negative reaction—but the moment when courage was with him had passed.

The couple strode alongside large stone walls. Every so often, they'd pass colorful graffiti, something that distracted Alaina and gave Luc a chance to look at a spot on her neck just below her ear. He thought it was a perfect spot.

"What exactly is your plan here?" Alaina asked as they walked.

"I'm sorry? What plan?" Luc was still thinking about how to tell Alaina how he felt.

"You agreed with Cravenmoore that you'd go after Dorian and Armande. Are you still?"

"No, I don't think so."

"Is that the kind of 'no, I don't think so' that becomes a 'yes, I changed my mind' at some point?"

"No… I don't know… Probably not," Luc answered.

"Listen to yourself." Alaina scoffed at the busboy. "These are real people here. Aren't you already getting, like, millions of euros for this? Are you sure you need more just to ruin their lives?"

"I'm not out to ruin anyone's life."

"Right, but that's what you'd be doing if you turned them in. Dorian and Armande will go to jail."

"Well, I'm trying to dream up a way to let Cravenmoore know I found them—without actually turning them into the police," Luc thought aloud.

"That's stupid."

"I don't know," Luc said, watching his feet walk to the sound of a street-corner accordion player. "Just a thought."

"First of all, you haven't found them at all. Dorian chose to find *you* just now. You have no idea where he's holed up in the city. Plus, you have no clue if he's hiding somewhere with Armande, or if Armande is off somewhere crazy, like Iceland—or America. You just don't know."

"True. But how great would it be if I could find a way to get Cravenmoore's money without turning the guys in?"

"I don't know what you're still fighting for," Alaina said. "We've already won. Sure, it's bad enough that you returned the cup, but Dorian and Armande are still free out there, and that really bugs Cravenmoore. Why can't you just leave it? You're being paid already, aren't you? Don't get greedy about it," Alaina continued.

* * *

Once back at the club, Coat-check Carl was his usual charming self. After loudly noticing some wear and tear on Luc's white pants, the man pointed the busboy in the direction of Marianne Merriweather. Alaina scuttled back off to

Sweenish massage duty.

"Madame Merriweather," Luc greeted as he approached her on the lawn.

The woman turned, cigarette in holder in hand. It was the first time Luc had ever seen her alone. She held a plouquette mallet in her other hand. She didn't say anything to Luc as he approached.

"Trying to perfect the impossibly-majestic-high-arc-rainbow-hammer-mallet throw?" Luc offered, hoping to get her to smile.

"Good afternoon, Pigeon," she replied stone-faced. It looked to Luc as if she'd aged in just the last week. She was still beautiful, but wearier.

"Good afternoon," Luc answered.

"What can I do for you this time?" She asked.

"Well, I'm not sure how to put this—"

"Let's see," the woman guessed. "I've heard through rumors that Cravenmoore asked you to find Dorian Thibault. Is that true?"

"Yes, Mademoiselle. It's why I came to you today."

Marianne Merriweather rolled her eyes. "Let me save you the trouble, at the risk of sounding repetitive: I don't know where he is, okay?"

"I know."

"I realize you're doing your job, but as I said, he has never reached out. If that's all you need to hear, then I would appreciate the opportunity to be left alone."

"Are you okay, Mademoiselle Merriweather? You are... different."

The woman sighed and nudged a plouquette ball with the toe of her heeled boot. "Have you ever lost someone close to you, Pigeon?" She asked.

"Well, my grandparents died, I guess that's—"

"I'm sorry to hear that," she interrupted him. "But imagine it was someone your age. Someone you intimately cared about. Someone you loved passionately. Have you ever been in love, Pigeon?"

"I had a girlfriend. We actually just broke up recently."

"That's not what I asked."

Luc sighed. "No, I admit I haven't ever lost anyone close to me." But the idea of losing Alaina was fresh in his mind, and it made his chest hurt.

"I won't try and explain what it feels like—to have loved someone, and had them taken away." She took a deep drag on her cigarette. "But now, in my case, every day I believe more and more that maybe Dorian wasn't taken away. It's becoming clear that he left. Now, I'm dealing with something new, knowing that the man whose loss hurt me the most, who supposedly died and was buried 22 years ago, might actually still be out there. Hiding. It makes all that pain of the loss feel as fresh as if it happened yesterday. Only now, it's mixed with anger. Confusion. Hate. I don't know."

"Well, I'm sorry."

"So, is that everything you need? Like I said, I came out here to be alone today."

"One last thing," Luc tried. "I know how difficult this whole thing has been for you. But, what if I told you that we could do something—rather go somewhere—that might help you with some of those feelings."

"I'm not going to therapy with you, kid."

"No, that's not what I meant. Actually, it might be a little like that, come to think of it. But no, I'm not suggesting we go to a doctor or anything. I just have something with the case that might help you bring closure."

"Where is it?"

Luc thought. "I can't tell you, yet."

"Then I'm not going."

"I know, but please. Just trust me. Have I given you a reason not to trust me yet?" Luc offered.

"I guess not."

"I'll tell you what. It's not far, and you can leave at any time."

Marianne took another drag on her cigarette as she thought.

"If you don't come with me," Luc continued, "all that pain will just sit. I'm offering something that might help."

The woman looked around the grounds as she debated with herself. "Fine," she managed. "But I want to be back for happy hour."

* * *

Luc checked his watch as he sat on the peeling park bench under the willow with Marianne. Dorian was late. Marianne hadn't said more than a few words the entire way there, let alone in the few minutes they'd been waiting on the park bench.

"Sorry to keep you waiting, Mademoiselle Merriweather," Luc said.

"It's Dorian, isn't it? That's why we're here. You've found him."

"Well—"

"You're not good at keeping secrets."

If she only knew, Luc thought.

"Your naïve little face betrayed you from the moment you walked up to me back at the club," she continued. Marianne hadn't stopped smoking the entire time Luc had been with her that day. She ground a butt out with her foot.

"Should I have told you?" Luc asked.

"No. If you'd said it out loud, I wouldn't have come with you," she answered as she lifted another cigarette out of a small tin case. "But let's get on with it. No use waiting. Where is he?"

"I'm here," a shaky voice said from behind them.

Luc swiveled to see Dorian approach, but Marianne didn't turn around. She shut her eyes, suppressing tears. Then, Luc saw the unmistakable vacant flash of rage when she opened them again.

"Marianne, I'm sorry," Dorian said as he circled the bench to face the seated pair.

Marianne still didn't answer or look at him.

Luc's impulse was to greet the man, but he reminded himself that this meeting wasn't for him.

Finally, Marianne spoke.

"I'm surprised you showed, after all this time. I half

expected you to send Armande."

"Marianne, please," Dorian pleaded.

"No. This was a bad idea," she said as she stood. She moved as if she was going to walk away, but Dorian put his hand on hers. She yanked it away.

"Absolutely not," she said. "You may not charm me."

"Please, I've waited so long to look at you again," Dorian tried.

"You've waited?!" She spat, staring him down. "*You've* waited?!"

"You're right, I know."

"You left, Dorian. That was your choice. You could have had me forever. I was just a kid, but I would have stuck by you."

"I was just a kid, too."

"So that's your excuse? You were a kid, and you made a dumb decision? You left me, and now you expect a hug and a 'how are you?'"

"Not exactly."

"What do you want then? What was the purpose of this?" She asked.

"Well, I knew you would hear about Tag. Plus, this kid here found the cup. I assumed you'd guess that I was alive."

"Part of me deep down always suspected you were out there somewhere," she answered. "I let myself live the lie for a long time because it was just easier that way, but if I searched myself, I could say I believed you were out here all along. But to see you now, it feels hollow."

"Marianne, please," Dorian tried again. He looked like he wanted to say something, but his famous charisma was finally failing him.

"So, I'll ask you again," Marianne stated. "What do you want from me?"

Dorian didn't say anything. He looked at the ground.

"Are you here to apologize?" She pressed.

"Yes, of course. I'm very sorry."

"For what? Was it hard for you to stay hidden?"

"Yes, definitely."

"Yeah, I bet it was," she said.

"Marianne."

"Did it ever occur to you that I might have gone with you?"

"No, you wouldn't have," he answered.

"I would have back then. Absolutely."

"You were too much into the social scene. I have lived a lonely existence since I left. I had to keep hidden."

"That's a sad song you're singing. Who cares? You chose it," Marianne said.

Dorian paused, looking at the face of the woman he'd left years earlier. "It was not a life you would have enjoyed."

"I'm telling you Dorian, I was deeply in love with you. There's no way around that. You can't deny it."

"I loved you too." He paused to take a deep breath. "And sometimes, I think I still do."

Luc noticed that look of rage flash in Marianne's eyes again. He was nervous about witnessing the exchange, but thought that if he just stayed quiet, sitting on the bench as they stood and fought, they wouldn't ask him to leave. To Luc, it felt as though they'd forgotten he was there.

"You do? I mean, of course you do." She spat. "Of course. That's such an easy thing for you to say. Why not?"

"Please, I'm serious," Dorian answered.

"I bet you *think* you are serious."

"No, I am. Countless times I've thought of you. There hasn't been anyone else since."

"Is that supposed to make me feel better somehow?"

"Please. I'm sure every single guy in Paris was all over you once I was gone."

"How dare you?" She snapped. "I've taken care of my heart ever since you gave up the job. Never relied on anyone to do it for me since."

Dorian looked around the park and took a deep breath. "Maybe we shouldn't have met like this," Dorian wondered.

"Maybe you should have actually died 22 years ago," Marianne said.

"You don't mean that," Dorian stated.

"Would have been a lot easier," she answered. "And a whole lot more sincere of you."

Dorian sighed.

Luc felt like the entire exchange had in fact *not* helped either party.

Dorian looked at the busboy. "Thanks for the meeting, Luc. I'll hold up my end of the deal still if you hold up yours."

Dorian didn't wait for Luc to answer. He took a last,

lingering look at Marianne's wild eyes. Luc watched the man turn and head down the path.

"What deal?" Marianne asked as she watched him disappear around a corner.

"Never mind. Just something I said I'd do to get him here."

"Well, don't worry about honoring whatever deal you made with him. Do whatever is best for you, period. That's what he'd do."

Chapter XVII.

The next morning, Luc arrived at work feeling much more energized than the day before. The dark café would soon be hopping with patrons. Sugar cubes diving into coffees. Steam bleeding out of croissants.

"You're here early." His mother greeted him while counting money in the cramped office off the kitchen.

"I know, I needed to talk to you," Luc answered.

"Let me guess, you don't want to be a waiter today."

"No, that's not it."

Luc's mother looked up at her son. "Where's your apron? Did you forget it again?"

"No, mom. Just listen."

"Okay." She placed the money on the table and gave Luc her undivided attention. "What's up? Is it that arsonist Janet?"

"No—"

"Because I'm great at giving advice about girls, but I'm horrible with giving advice about arsonists." Luc's mother smiled.

"She wasn't an arsonist," Luc insisted.

"She set a box of your stuff on fire. That's a criminal act. Look up arson, because I'm sure that's what it means."

"No, it is, but that's not why I'm here."

"Okay, sorry. We can stop talking about Janet," Luc's mother said.

"Please, stop saying her name. I have too much to

think about."

"Okay." She threw her hands in the air. "Okay."

Luc's stomach was upset with nerves. He felt his breath grow shorter. "I... I... came in early today to tell you that I'm quitting." He couldn't look her in the eye.

"You're quitting?" His mother asked after a short pause. "You're quitting what?"

"The café. I'm not going to work here anymore."

"Do you just need a break? Let's not be brash. Do you need a few days off? I'm sorry I didn't take you more seriously when you asked the other day. Are you doing that weekend trip on the train or something?"

"No, I'm not doing that. I really do want to leave the café for good," Luc answered.

The woman took a deep breath. "Why? What are you going to do?"

"Well," Luc said. "I have something else lined up. Something really good. For a lot of money."

"What is it?"

"I'm not ready to go into yet," Luc went on with some hesitation, "but I am getting paid on it soon. And it's a lot."

"Look, I understand if you found something that pays well. But you should think this through. Is this because I tried to make you wait tables when you didn't want to? You must grow up about that."

"It's not that."

"And the café? Who's going to run it when I can't anymore? Luc, we've talked about this. It's irresponsible to just leave us. Just take a break. Relax for a few days."

"No mom, it's more than that," Luc answered, gaining courage. He could feel his hands shaking in his pockets, though. "I don't feel like you listen to me. You're so concerned with running this place, and who's going to take over when you're gone, you forgot to listen to me. You forgot that I might not want this for myself."

"Luc, it's a good job. Those are hard to find," his mother reasoned.

"But I did find one, and it's really good. In fact, it's so good that I may not ever have to worry about money again," Luc pleaded.

"Sounds too good to be true. You're describing it like you won the lottery. Life is not like that."

"I know that you think that, mom, but you are going to have to let me figure that out for myself. Now, I'm going to work today because I don't want you and dad to have to do everything yourselves—"

"Which is exactly what you're suggesting by quitting," she interrupted him.

"…But you should put up the 'help wanted' sign, because I'm leaving. That's my final decision," Luc stated.

The busboy noticed his mother looking despondent for the first time ever. She looked like a woman that was finally accepting her son's desire to leave.

"This will break your father's heart."

"It's not like I'm quitting the family," Luc answered.

"It feels like you are. We always saw this as something we could share with you."

"I know," Luc replied. He felt the pangs of guilt that come with letting a parent down, but he also felt the shot of adrenaline that came with standing up for himself for maybe the first time in his life. Charlie would be proud.

*   *   *

Luc arrived at his apartment after his shift with more energy than ever. He threw his keys onto the small table crowded with mail and change near the front door, and Richard was right there to pick them up and fly off into the bedroom.

"Hey!" Luc yelled. "Charlie, the pigeon has my keys."

"Yeah, he'll do that," Charlie yelled from the other room. "He thinks it's hilarious."

"Does he do that often?" Luc called back as he gazed out their dormitory window at the tops of Parisian trees.

"Yep," Charlie answered, emerging from his bedroom. "But it only seems to be your stuff. There's a chance he was trained as a homing pigeon, but he appears to have a real sense of humor about it."

"I'm glad he finds it funny," Luc remarked. "Hey, let's get a beer."

"You serious?" Charlie answered. "But it's 11:30 in the morning. That's not your style."

"You're right, it's yours. But I'm celebrating."

"What's the occasion?" Charlie asked as he headed to the fridge.

Richard flew back in from the bedroom, delivering a

bottle opener to Charlie as he pulled a couple of beers out of the fridge.

"The wire transfer should hit any day from the club since I found the cup, and I just told my mom I'm leaving the café."

"Really?! Wow. That's big news," Charlie said, his voice low.

"Why don't you sound happy?"

"I don't know. What are you going to do now?" Beer mist exploded from the tops of two bottles as Charlie opened them. They clinked against one another has he held both in one hand, extending one in the busboy's direction.

"I don't know," Luc said, accepting the beer and collapsing on the couch.

"So, you're just leaving your family?" Luc's roommate wasn't smiling.

"Charlie, are you serious?" Luc asked. "If anyone understood this, I thought it would be you."

"I don't know. Just seems like you need to have a job," Charlie replied. He stepped over a pile of jeans and shoes he'd left on the floor to fall onto the other end of the couch.

"Are you serious?" Luc repeated. "*You* don't have a job."

"Yeah, but I'm me. And you're you. I'm glad you took your risk and got out of your comfort zone, but this is really going into the deep end, isn't it?"

Luc couldn't believe what he was hearing out of Charlie.

"So what?" Charlie continued between sips of beer.

"Are you going to be a full-time detective now? A real one?"

"No. I mean, I don't know."

"This is crazy. You did solve the case, I guess," Charlie thought aloud.

"Yeah, they want me to go after the guys now," Luc added.

"This Dorian Thibault guy you've mentioned, and whoever else?"

"Right."

"Are you going to do it?"

"No, I don't think so. I have no idea where they are, although Dorian trusts me enough to meet with me. I never know where he goes afterwards or anything."

"This sounds like a bad idea—to try and find them," Charlie replied as someone knocked on their door.

Luc sat on the couch and sipped his beer. Charlie rose and worked his way to the door.

"Is Luc here?" The voice was familiar. It took Luc to his feet.

"Alaina. Hi," Luc said as he turned to see the beautiful, red-headed girl standing a foot or two inside his front door.

"Hey," she answered with a small wave.

Charlie stood stunned.

"Uh... what are you doing here? How did you find my apartment?" Luc asked.

"I followed you this morning."

"Hi, I'm Charlie," Luc's roommate said, clearly taken with Alaina's beauty. He extended his hand.

"Hi," she answered, accepting the handshake without enthusiasm.

"Can we talk, Luc?" She asked.

"Sure," he answered. "Do you want a beer?"

"We're celebrating," Charlie said, looking for any reason to be included in a conversation with the beautiful girl.

"Let's go in the kitchen," Luc suggested.

"Why is there a pigeon on your coffee table?" Alaina asked.

"Don't mind him," Charlie answered. "That's our roommate. He's a pigeon. Or she. We have no idea. But I named him Richard. Isn't that hilarious?"

"Hilarious," Alaina answered with raised eyebrows.

"Let's go in the kitchen," Luc repeated. "Can you give us a minute, Charlie?" Luc asked.

"I'll be in my room if you need me," Luc's roommate answered. Charlie snapped his fingers and Richard followed him as he withdrew to his bedroom.

"I'll take that beer," Alaina said as they walked.

"Great."

"What are you celebrating?" She asked.

"You know," Luc said. "The case being about over. The money hitting my account any minute. I quit my mom's café. That stuff."

"That's a lot," Alaina said, not sounding thrilled. She sat down at the kitchen table, and Luc put a beer in front of her. "Thanks. I didn't realize you were going to quit the café so soon."

"I sure did."

"Good for you. I know you didn't like it," she replied. "So, this is where you live, huh? Looks about right for a busboy." She looked around the tiny space as she sipped beer.

"Thanks, I guess. And not a busboy anymore. Soon to be a millionaire," he corrected her.

"Right." She looked around a little. "Charlie seems like a piece of work."

"He's okay, yeah," Luc answered.

"Doesn't know how to talk to girls."

"Yeah, well, neither do I, so…"

"I think you do okay," she said, still looking around.

Luc's heart started racing again. It was getting to be a familiar feeling around Alaina.

"So," he asked, "what are you up to today?"

"I wanted to talk to you about everything," she answered, focusing on Luc finally.

"Sure, go ahead."

"Well," Alaina started after a sip from her beer, "I've been thinking about this for a while. But I think we have to right a wrong."

"If you're worried I'm going to turn in Dorian, then don't. I'm not going to do it," Luc said.

"No, that's not it," she answered, "but I'm glad you're not. If I really believed you'd do that, I'd try to talk you out of that for sure."

"So, what's the wrong to right? Dorian, Armande, and Tag are all on the run again. I even got Marianne and Dorian to meet."

"How'd that go?" She asked as she raised her

eyebrows again.

"Not that great. As you might expect for a couple that has gone through what they've gone through."

"How'd it end?" She asked.

"Not good. He ran off. She was fighting back tears of pure hate. At least that's what it looked like to me."

"I'm not surprised."

"So, to your point about righting a wrong, I'm not sure there's a real wrong left," Luc ventured.

"No, there's one."

"What's that? Sweenish massage duty? They can't keep you on that forever, can they?"

"No that's not it, although they could, but I'm not worried about it," she said as she took another sip. "No, I'm talking about the Sir Larabee Waterford Cup."

"What about it?"

"Well, it doesn't belong sitting in the case with Yelly's name on it. It's Dorian's. He won it fair and square."

"C'mon. I don't disagree, but the trophy is so..." Luc searched for the right word. "...meaningless in this all, don't you think?"

"Must not be to Dorian," Alaina answered. "He threw away his whole life to keep it."

"That's true." Luc nodded. "But he said he didn't care. So, what are you suggesting?"

Alaina leaned in a little and lowered her voice, even though they were in the confines of Luc's kitchen. "I think we should steal the cup back."

Luc stopped mid-drink. "You're kidding."

"I'm not."

"Why? He said he didn't care about it anymore," Luc repeated.

"I told you," she answered. "To right a wrong."

"I'm in," Charlie announced as he appeared in the doorway to the small kitchen. He'd been eavesdropping the entire time. Richard stood on his shoulder.

"What? Charlie, no," Luc protested.

"Okay, great," Alaina answered.

"What?! No," Luc repeated.

"Great!" Charlie answered, not listening to Luc.

"No, this is not happening, man," Luc snorted. "You were against all this just a second ago."

"No, I was against you quitting the café," he answered as he entered the kitchen and pulled another beer out of the refrigerator. "I'm all for stealing the cup back," the roommate replied.

"Great," Alaina said again. "Luc, are you coming with us?"

"Didn't you just open a beer?" Luc asked.

"Yeah, I finished it."

"Nice," Alaina answered with a smirk.

"Wait, Alaina. Seriously," Luc said, shifting his focus. "Charlie can't go. He doesn't know anything about this case, the people, everything."

"We're stealing the cup," Charlie said. "I got it. What more is there to know?"

"We're not stealing the cup," Luc answered.

"Luc," Alaina said. "Think about it. If we leave

everything as it is right now, Cravenmoore has won."

"I'm not going to search for—and turn in—Dorian. You said yourself, we're ahead now," Luc countered.

"I've thought it through some more," Alaina said. "Don't you want more? Don't you want to screw Cravenmoore?"

"I do. Definitely, I do," Charlie answered. "Hate that guy."

"You don't know him," Luc snapped. "You have no idea what we're talking about."

"C'mon, man. Let me steal something with you. The 'new you' would let me do this," Charlie said.

"Look man, may I have a few minutes alone with Alaina? Like, really alone? Without you hovering right here at the doorway?"

"Sure, whatever you need," Charlie answered. "But don't forget." He looked at Alaina. "I'm in. If this is going down, I'm in."

"Thanks, I'll keep that in mind," she answered.

Charlie went back in his room and closed the door.

"Sorry about that," Luc said.

"At least someone around here wants to do what's right," Alaina answered.

"He doesn't know anything," Luc said. "Sorry about him."

"So, you're really not going to help me steal this thing or what?" Alaina asked.

"Are you going to do it without me? Even if I don't agree to help?" Luc asked.

"I don't know," she answered. "It feels like I've been living at the club my whole life, and I just don't feel like it's really me. Everyone is so superficial. Cravenmoore is such a creepy bastard, and no one even cares about anyone else. So yeah, I'm really thinking about doing this."

Luc couldn't help but get distracted by her. Her beauty. Her sheer guts. Alaina wasn't afraid of anything, and Luc loved it. The busboy took a deep breath to slow his heartbeat.

"Alaina, I'm in love with you." *Finally*, he thought. He said it out loud. That wasn't even something that he'd dared to do when he was alone.

She scoffed. "C'mon, Luc." She avoided eye contact. "What are you doing?"

"I've been trying to get the courage to say it, and if this whole thing has taught me anything, it's that I should just say what I want to say, when I want to say it."

She shook her head.

"So, I'm saying it now," he continued. "I think you're amazing. Smart. Beautiful. Everything."

"You're not in love with me," she answered as she took another sip of beer.

"Yes I am."

"No, stop it. You're in love with the idea that you're about to be a millionaire."

"That's not it. I felt this for you since the moment we first met in Cravenmoore's office. There was something between us even then."

"I have a boyfriend," Alaina reminded him.

"I know."

"So, don't say that you love me. It's not cool."

"You having a boyfriend doesn't make me feel it any less."

"Yeah, but you don't say it out loud," she said.

Luc sat back in his chair and felt the hard kitchen wall behind him. "This hasn't been fun for you?" Luc asked her. "Working on this together?"

"No, it has," she said. "That's why I'm saying you have got to help me steal this cup back."

Luc shifted in his chair. "C'mon, I just can't do that. Stealing. That is the stuff that puts you in jail. I don't want to do anything illegal."

"Huh," Alaina grunted. "Aren't you the busboy who's defrauding the Paris Publique Plouquette Pitch, Grounds, Gardens, Grass Court, and Lawn Club for two million euros right now?"

"That's not the point," Luc answered.

"It could land you in jail, too."

Luc didn't answer. He knew what he was doing was wrong, but he didn't consider the consequences until that moment.

"So, take the extra step with me, and let's get things back to normal—where the cup is missing, and Dorian, Armande, and Tag are still out on the loose and no one knows where any of them are."

Luc thought. He wanted a chance with Alaina, but he wasn't ready to break into the trophy case for her. He'd done enough out of his comfort zone as it was.

"I'm sorry," he answered. "I just can't do it."

"C'mon Luc," she pleaded. "You won't do it for me?"

Luc's head swirled. "I just blurted out that I love you. Now you're going to flirt your way into making me do something I don't want to do, just after you basically said you didn't feel the same way for me?"

She took a swig from her beer.

"I guess I should go," she said, pushing the bottle away from her on the table.

"I mean, you could stay, and we could go get a drink or a bite?" Luc tried.

"Sorry," she answered.

Luc followed her to the door. The walk could not have gone too slowly for Luc, as he searched his mind for ways to get her to stay, just to talk to him. He needed to be around her, and he was suddenly fearful that he might never be again after his amorous admission and simultaneous refusal to help her commit larceny.

"Bye," she said as she left, shutting the door behind her. Luc wondered if that could have gone any worse.

Charlie's bedroom door opened at the sound of the front door closing.

"So, what's the plan?" Charlie asked, jogging into the living room. "Let's steal some shit!"

Chapter XVIII.

The next day, Luc Martin couldn't help but smile as he arrived at the Paris Publique Plouquette Pitch, Grounds, Gardens, Grass Court, and Lawn Club. For all he knew, he was already a millionaire. The former busboy had decided to tell Cravenmoore that he wouldn't be hunting down Dorian Thibault, Armande Marwane, and Tag le Tier. Luc was prepared to lie and say the trail had gone cold. He was ready to leave those white pants behind.

Luc had no plans to help Alaina steal the trophy. In fact, he didn't believe that she was going to do it anyway. With Cravenmoore on high alert, it wasn't going to be an easy heist, and Luc just assumed that Alaina was riled up about the subject. As time passed, she'd probably let go.

The busboy assumed he'd walk into the club, give Cravenmoore the news, maybe grab a Bloody Mary at the bar, and then find Alaina. Assuming she wasn't busy getting covered head-to-toe in mint jelly, he'd apologize for what he'd said the afternoon before, and start the road to forgetting the awkward conversation all together. He still loved her, but he knew he'd have to tread lightly on the subject from then on if they were going to stay friends. Luc wanted that. At least that way, she stayed in his life. Who knows? Maybe he'd be able to win her over again later.

Luc was greeted by Coat-check Carl as the heavy wooden door swung inwards at the PPPPGGGCLC.

Coat-check Carl grimaced. "It's you."

"Yes sir," Luc said with cheer. "Here to see President Cravenmoore."

"You know, I never liked you."

Luc furled his brow. "I... I'm sorry," he managed. Even for Coat-check Carl, that seemed cold.

"I could tell from the beginning that you weren't meant to wear white pants."

"*I* could have told you that," Luc answered.

"President's out on the lawn, but he'll want to see you."

As soon as Luc walked into the hallway near the tall, ornate double glass doors to the plouquette lawn, he saw Maurice de Mouton. It was as if the President's man was almost waiting for him.

"Right this way, Pigeon," de Mouton said without separating his teeth. Luc noticed the President himself walking in from the lawn when the busboy felt the hand of Maurice de Mouton on his shoulder. It felt like a brick. No one at the club had ever touched him. He didn't like it.

De Mouton led him into the President's office and offered him a chair. The dark room seemed even darker somehow. It couldn't have been more than a minute, but Luc waited with de Mouton in silence.

"Monsieur Pigeon," the President said as he entered the office and closed the door behind him.

"Mr. President, good morning," Luc answered.

"Sure."

"I wanted to come by this morning—"

"Hold that thought, Pigeon," the President

interrupted.

"Okay."

Cravenmoore sat in his chair. "Maybe you can tell me something."

"Sure," Luc replied.

"Why have you been secretly meeting with Dorian Thibault?"

Stunned, Luc couldn't answer.

"Hmm?" The President asked leaning in. "How much have you kept from me during this case?"

"I... I'm sorry, I..."

"Is it because you are just a busboy at a shitty little café?" Cravenmoore snapped.

Luc felt his breathing stop. "How... how do you know that?"

"It turns out that your friend Alaina is a terrible shadow. But Evan Yanis isn't."

Evan stepped out of the darkness behind Luc. The former busboy hadn't even noticed he was back there.

Luc must have looked as confused as he felt.

"That's right, Pigeon. Evan has seen it all," the President remarked.

The busboy turned to his shadow. "You followed me?" Luc asked.

"Of course," Evan answered.

"Did you think you could lock him in the closet and still earn his trust?" The President asked.

"No, well, I..." Luc managed.

"I was with you all over town," Evan replied. "I saw

you come and go from that café. I saw you talking to Dorian in the park. I saw you come and go from your terrible little top floor apartment. And I saw you with Alaina."

The last sentence sounded extra biting. Knowing how Evan felt about Alaina, Luc sensed that this was the part that was the worst for his shadow.

"Anything to say for yourself?" Cravenmoore asked.

"Well, I... I found the cup, didn't I?"

"You did," the President acknowledged. "Would you have even brought it to me if Evan hadn't confronted you in the alley?"

"Of course, sir," Luc answered.

"Yeah, right," Evan countered. "I doubt it."

"I would have!" Luc exclaimed.

"I suppose we'll never know," the President guessed. "Monsieur Pigeon, you can't blame me for doubting it. When were you planning on turning in Dorian Thibault?"

"I don't know where he's hiding. Truly, I don't. Evan will tell you, sir. He only ever found me. I never found him."

Evan said nothing.

"Did you ever make an attempt to follow him?" The President asked.

Luc didn't answer.

"Did you ever ask where he was hiding?" Cravenmoore continued.

"Why would he tell me that?" Luc answered.

"I don't know. You two seem to be best friends now."

"Well, we're not. I also don't even have a clue where Armande or Tag are."

"You didn't ask Dorian that either?" Cravenmoore asked.

"No."

"Well, when you really look at it, I'm embarrassed that I didn't see it sooner," the President stated.

"See what?" Luc asked.

"You're obviously not the greatest detective of all time. You're nothing," Cravenmoore answered.

"Look," Luc answered, finally getting defensive, "who cares if I'm not? I got farther in this thing than any of you did 22 years ago. I got a hell of a lot farther than Pompousselpeck when he was the chief of police. You got your trophy back. Wasn't that what you were paying me for?"

"Paying you? You have to be kidding me," the President scoffed with a smirk and a sigh. "If you think for one second that I'm giving you a dime, you're crazy. I put a stop on the payment this morning."

Luc sunk back in his chair.

"In fact," Cravenmoore noted, "you're lucky I don't march out onto the plouquette lawn right now and turn you over to Pompousselpeck for your lies. He may be retired, but he'll have his contemporaries over here so quick that you won't know what hit you."

"Why don't you do it, sir?" Maurice de Mouton asked from behind Luc.

"Turn him in?" Cravenmoore answered. "I'd love to, but we all know that it's the all-you-can-eat knockwurst-stuffed-crab meat day, and no one would forgive me around here if I ruined the year's biggest holiday by causing a distraction when this kid got arrested. Every member would be crankier than my ex-wife!"

"Good thinking, sir," de Mouton answered.

The President stood. "No, just this will have to do. Monsieur Pigeon..."

"His name is Luc Martin," Evan said, staring down the former busboy.

"Ah, thank you, Yanis," Cravenmoore answered. "Monsieur Luc Martin, you are hereby forever banished from the Paris Publique Plouquette Pitch, Grounds, Gardens, Grass Court, and Lawn Club, effective this moment forward. Any attempt to return will be met with a show of forceful removal, possible arrest, and sure no-quarter harassment from our in-house security team and their intern, Coat-check Carl Kaminski-Reynolds. I think you're familiar with him."

"Coat-check Carl is an intern?" Luc asked

"De Mouton will show you out," Cravenmoore answered.

*   *   *

Luc found himself back at his kitchen table. He sat alone drinking a beer. Afternoon light cast a green beer bottle prism shadow on the white kitchen table.

The weight of knowing he may never see Alaina again crushed the busboy. He almost didn't care that he was so close to becoming a millionaire earlier that day. Almost.

"So, when are you going to take those ridiculous pants off?" Charlie asked from the doorway.

Luc shrugged. "I hated them at first, but now they're kind of comfortable."

"What's wrong?"

"They found out," Luc sighed.

"Of course, they did," Charlie said as he entered and sat down with a beer of his own. "Did you really think that you'd be able to fool them forever?"

"I don't know."

"I mean, c'mon, man. No matter how much you wanted to be, you aren't the greatest detective of all time."

"I know."

"Did you get to say goodbye to Alaina?" Charlie asked.

"No."

"She's hot, man."

"Shut up," Luc said. He hadn't looked up from the top of his beer bottle once.

"Look on the bright side," Charlie said as he put his feet up on an empty kitchen table chair. "You just spent the last two weeks in the lap of luxury. You were treated like a king. A hot girl followed you around everywhere. You got to do exciting things, there was intrigue, riddles, whatever. You know how many people would love an experience like that?"

"Yeah."

"I mean, some of those ultra-rich guys that you met probably pay for experiences like that. Role-playing stuff. And you did it in real life. That's amazing."

Luc shrugged again as Charlie's pep talk continued.

"In fact, I was wrong about you. I thought you'd

never take a risk. But here you were, proving me wrong in the biggest way possible. I'm impressed, man. Who would have guessed that you would have found this Waterman trophy, or whatever it's called?"

"The Sir Larabee Waterford Cup," Luc corrected his roommate.

"Right, that thing. I mean, did you carry it, like, across Paris, or something? Think of the image. That's amazing. It's like you won the trophy yourself."

"It was crazy heavy. Not a good experience."

"Well hey, you might not have won it in a game, but holding that thing puts you in elite company. Like that guy Dorian that you admire so much."

"I did like the way it felt when I walked in the club with that thing," Luc admitted. "Hoisting it up for everyone to see, just like Dorian in that old picture."

Wait. The picture.

"Wait!" Luc exclaimed. "Something's wrong."

"What?" Charlie asked, mid drink of his beer.

"The picture."

"What picture?"

"There was a picture of Dorian when he won the cup. It's the first picture we ever found of him. It was also one of the ones that made Alaina recognize Marianne."

"So?" Charlie asked.

"There was something else. Something else I didn't notice until now. Something else I wouldn't have seen unless I had held the cup, which I hadn't done yet when I first saw the picture."

"What's that?"

"It's insanely heavy. I couldn't lift it to save my life. I had to drag it out of the bookshop."

"But you said you carried it back to the club."

"Yeah, with Evan Yanis' help. And even then, both he and I struggled the whole way. We couldn't get it above our waist."

"So?" Charlie asked. I still don't get it.

"In the picture," Luc continued, getting excited. "In the picture, Dorian is holding it up effortlessly."

"So? Is he ripped?"

"No. He's a normal person. And he was about my age when he was doing that."

"I'm still not following," Luc's roommate said as he took another sip.

"Don't you see? Something's changed. It's either not the real cup, or something's been added. Something really heavy. De Mouton even said the shelf wouldn't support it. It's not that the shelf has gotten weak at all. It's that the trophy has gotten heavy."

Charlie nodded, trying to piece together what was happening.

"It makes total sense now," Luc continued. "Why would Dorian leave the cup behind in the bookshop? If he was really on the run, why not just take it with him if he didn't want the cup to be found?"

"Why would he want the cup to be found?" Charlie asked, watching Luc pace in the tiny spot in front of their refrigerator.

"I don't know, but the bookshop was too easy. It was even Armande who gave us the clues that got us there. Why would he give us those? There's more to this."

"Are you sure you're not reading into this too much, my friend?" Charlie asked. "I mean, don't you just think it's time for this thing to be over? Time to go back to the café maybe? I know you're disappointed, but are you sure about all this?"

"No, I am. Think about it. Things just don't get heavier over time. I think they put something in the base of the trophy, or they made a replica that doesn't weigh the same, or something. Either way, it's not over. Something is still going on here."

Charlie took a deep breath. "Look, you remember what I said the other day. I'm in. I'm down to help however you want. But, what else is there to do? I mean, they found out about you, right? They're not just going to let you walk back in the door."

"That's true. But I'll think of something," Luc said, his mind speeding. "I've got to."

Chapter XIX.

Luc Martin washed a dish. The suds mixed with breadcrumbs and a smear of strawberry jam. Hot water stung his hands.

When Luc asked for his job back, his mother had answered with one word: "wash," and she handed the young man a dirty plate. That's how Luc spent his entire morning.

And now the busboy felt like he was back in the abyss. Only this time, his fear was gone. But no Alaina. No plouquette club. No purpose. He'd seen a taste of excitement, and he wanted more.

Dish done. Luc grabbed another off a bottomless stack.

There was more excitement out there. He was sure of it. The dramatic change in weight of the trophy left him hypothesizing all morning long. Just when he'd decide that the trophy must have been switched out for a decoy, he'd remind himself that he was only guessing. There could be other reasons it became heavier. Perhaps it had been tampered with. Luc kept thinking. Dish done.

Was there someone he could run to? It occurred to Luc that he didn't even know where Alaina lived. Surely, he couldn't go back anywhere near the club, though.

There were few others that he trusted there. Hugo, the pro shop manager was friendly, but Luc knew even less about him than he did Alaina. Dolt didn't seem like the kind of person who would be willing to help. And Marianne Merriweather was dealing with her own struggle. Luc knew he couldn't burden her any more than he'd already had. Dish done.

Then, it dawned on him. Flova Pompousselpeck. She was removed from the situation. She sympathized. He wasn't sure how, but he knew he had to see her. Would she agree to see him yet again? Would Coat-check Chad even open the door to talk to him? Could Luc stomach putting on the white pants just one more time? Dish done.

*   *   *

"I'm surprised you're here," Madame Pompousselpeck said as she sat across from Luc in the house café at the Paris Private Plouquette Conglomerate. All the silverware was gold, and Luc swore he recognized the person a few tables away as a French TV star.

"You heard what happened?" Luc asked.

"That you were fired, yeah."

"Have you heard why?"

"I heard parts, but I don't believe it."

"Well, it's true, I'm just a busboy at a café. I'm not the world's greatest detective," Luc admitted.

Madame Pompousselpeck shifted in her seat. "That's not what my husband told me."

"What did he say?"

"He said that Cravenmoore told him that you were caught stealing white pants from the pro shop…"

"That's not true! I hate white pants!"

"…Then trying to sell them to a roving band of

singer/songwriters..."

"What? No!"

"...And then using the proceeds to pay a lawn boy hush money..."

"What?"

"...Because you were caught trying to have relations with their club steed."

"My God. None of that is true," Luc said. "Why would he make all that up? And why singer/songwriters?"

"Cravenmoore hates singer/songwriters."

"Who doesn't?" Luc answered. "And I'm sorry, but I wouldn't go anywhere near Phyllis. For any reason. She scares the hell out of me."

"Who's Phyllis?"

"The club steed."

"She sounds more like a mare," Flova said.

"Well, I didn't do any of that."

"Look. Forget about all this," she advised. "Did you say that you are a busboy at a café, and that you're not the world's greatest detective of all time?"

"Yep."

"Wow."

"I faked the whole thing," Luc confirmed.

"Wow," she managed again, leaning back in her chair. "That's amazing. How did you get away with that?"

"One morning I was working in my parents' café, and some guy mistook me for the greatest detective of all time. And that guy was Maurice de Mouton. He works for Cravenmoore."

"I see. Impressive that you kept it up as long as you did."

"I guess."

"In fact, really impressive that you found Dorian Thibault, and recovered the cup. My husband was jealous."

That made Luc happy, but he tried not to show it. Sitting up higher in his chair, he stated, "I came here about the case."

"Well, don't you think it's over? Haven't you just gone back to being a... what was it that you said you did? Waited tables?"

"No. I'm a busboy. And dropping the case and returning to that job is exactly what my roommate says I should do. But, there's something up. And I'm not sure how you can help me, but I'm just looking for anyone to talk to about this stuff."

"Sure, go ahead," she said as she stirred her coffee.

"There's something going on with the cup itself."

"What do you mean?" Madame Pompousselpeck asked.

"Well, it's different. It's changed somehow."

"Well, it's been 22 years. I'm sure it could use a shine or something."

"Believe me, I'd give up if all I was just talking about was weathering or discoloration or something. But it somehow got really heavy over time. That's just weird. That doesn't happen on its own."

"That *is* strange."

"I'm not sure if it's a replica, or if the base has been

changed out, but I have a funny feeling that Dorian Thibault, Armande Marwane, and Tag le Tier still have something else up their sleeves."

"Hmm," Madame Pompousselpeck thought. "How do you know how much it weighed before? It's not like you were at the club back then to try and lift it."

"Yeah, but I've seen pictures. Dorian was able to pick that thing up, hold it above his head, cradle it with one arm, stuff like that. I just don't think you could do that now."

"Interesting. So, what do you do next? If you ask me, it sounds like you're out of options."

"Well, I am, really. I'd like to see Dorian or Armande again. But I have no idea where to find them. Plus, I'd love to see Alaina again and see what she says. I would never have been able to do any of this whole thing without her. Some of our best ideas were hers."

"You're in love with her, aren't you?"

"I… uh…"

"It's obvious," Madame Pompousselpeck urged. She sipped her coffee, pleased with herself.

Luc's face turned red.

"I guess. I don't know," he confirmed.

"Well, I do."

Luc thought for a moment. "Can I ask you a question?"

"Sure."

"It's not about Alaina or anything. It's something else."

"Sure, go ahead," the woman repeated.

"When you took us to meet the barber here..."

"Snippy, yes. Shaved your arm hair pretty well."

"...That he did. When you took us to meet him, did you know that he would send us off to meet Armande Marwane?"

"Haven't you asked me that once already?"

"I guess. I'm just looking for any answers."

"I see. Well, I just thought it would be nice for you to talk to someone who was around when everything happened back then—someone who might be more forthcoming than a current PPPPGGGCLC club member," Flova said. "That's why I introduced you to Snippy. No other reason."

"Right."

"I'm not even sure if Snippy knew that his friend Roman Lubin was Armande Marwane."

"I see," Luc answered. "Sorry to grill you a little. That had just been nagging at me a little bit as I thought through the case."

"No problem. You know, I think I may have something that can help you."

"You do?" Luc asked.

"Yep. If you want to go back to the club one last time, I can make it work," Madame Pompousselpeck said.

"You can?"

"Who knows? Maybe you'll be able to catch Alaina before you're seen by Cravenmoore or any of his cronies."

"Wait. Let me get this straight. We're talking about the PPPPGGGCLC here, right? Not this club, the Private?"

"Right."

"But you're not a member," Luc said.

"Obviously not," she answered. "But as you know, my husband is. And at the end of this week, I'll be there for the Sir Larabee Waterford Cup Annual Tournament."

"Oh right! That's this week!" Luc exclaimed. "But how will I get by Coat-check Carl?"

"Leave Coat-check Carl to me. Just meet me at quarter 'til four at the corner of Rue d'Ananas and Rue des Bananes."

"I'll do it," Luc said with confidence.

"Great. But you must make me one promise," Flova said with seriousness.

"Anything."

"Please, you can't make a scene. If you get noticed, there is no doubt that they will trace your presence back to me. And I know I've been good-natured with you, but the fact remains: my husband is Flive Pompousselpeck. He's a respected member of that club, plus he was close to the investigation that you just finished conducting. I don't want any shame to come to him, although I sympathize with you on several different aspects of your situation. Either way, are we understood?"

"Yes, definitely."

"Great. See you on Saturday at quarter 'til four."

"See you there," Luc said as he stood. "And thank you."

As Luc left the Paris Private Plouquette Conglomerate, it was all he could do to keep himself from skipping. Perhaps he let his elation distract him, for he thought he saw Janet watching him from down the block as he bid farewell to Coat-check Chad, but when he did a double-take, no one was there. He chose to ignore the notion that his crazy ex-girlfriend might have been following him.

Chapter XX.

The Sir Larabee Waterford Cup Tournament flags wagged in the air above the plouquette lawn. Ladies wore enormous hats. The men all wore their best suits.

Trying to calm his nerves, Luc adjusted the cuff of this shirt. In combination with his loaner white pants from the pro shop, Luc was wearing the most expensive and fancy outfit he owned. Still, the busboy was glad that his presence was unnoticed so far.

From his vantage point—a window overlooking the courtyard in the empty third-floor librarium—Luc could see the beads of sweat mounting on Yelly Reardon's brow as he fixated on his next move. Still, there was an awful lot of socializing happening where Luc thought he might see some plouquette action. He didn't recognize any of the players, except of course Yelly. While everyone threw his or her heads back with laughter, Yelly buckled down.

But Luc was having trouble concentrating on the tournament. He didn't see Alaina anywhere.

Luc was aware that this might be his only shot to see her one last time. He wasn't even sure what he was supposed to say. All Luc knew was that if he didn't see her or get to say goodbye, her memory would eat away at him for the rest of his life.

According to an elaborate scoreboard, almost one hundred players had now decreased to just a handful, including Yelly Reardon. As the tournament dragged on, the busboy knew that he had a diminishing window of opportunity to find and speak with Alaina.

With the outcome of the tournament close at hand, Luc wasn't surprised when he saw the Sir Larabee Waterford Cup wheeled out on a cart. As two grown men struggled to lift it to its position on the dais, Luc couldn't help but smirk.

*   *   *

The final bell rang. Yelly Reardon lifted his arms in triumph and dropped to his knees. The crowd on the plouquette court and in a smattering of windows above erupted into ecstatic applause. Yelly began to weep.

Luc watched as the officials shook the hands of the finalists. Yelly rose and began hugging everyone within arms' reach. On the dais, Luc watched as Cravenmoore stood observing, pleased with the outcome. De Mouton was busy, scrambling with a sound system before placing a microphone in front of Cravenmoore.

"Good afternoon Paris Publique Plouquette Pitch, Grounds, Gardens, Grass Court, and Lawn Club!" The President's voice boomed.

The crowd applauded. Having made his way through the crowd, Yelly climbed the stairs to join Cravenmoore on the platform.

"This day has been a long time coming for one man," President Cravenmoore continued.

Yelly blushed and wiped tears of happiness from his face.

"But," the President went on, "we'll get to that in a moment. I have a few prepared remarks."

Luc watched as the man shifted a few papers and cleared his throat. The busboy was still scanning the crowd for Alaina, but she was still nowhere to be seen. Should he take this opportunity to run down to the bar and risk seeing Dolt? Surely the bartender wouldn't turn him in. Or would he? Luc knew everyone of importance was in the courtyard. Still, he didn't want to put Madame Pompousselpeck's reputation in danger.

"It is on this auspicious occasion," President Cravenmoore launched into his prepared remarks, "that we celebrate more than just a sport. It brings together all types of people: those who have earned their wealth through inheritance—*and* the extremely privileged. It is no surprise then, that this sport in all its unity of spirit, should unite our spirit, the spirit of the elite, to band together in one semi-diverse community. And for that, we can be proud."

The crowd erupted.

"The man who proved triumphant in today's tournament is no stranger to you or the sport in general. In fact, the man holds the record for the most consecutive second-place finishes of all time, at 22, a record that will stand now for eternity, with his first-place finish today."

The crowd clapped again.

"Fun side note," the President continued, "the old record for most-consecutive second place finishes was 14, by Yann Frederick St. Sebastian Leibowitz, way back in 1646. He was, of course as everyone knows, beheaded for mediocrity in the tournament. It's a good thing our country's laws have changed since then, Yelly old boy, wouldn't you say?"

The crowd laughed and clapped vigorously again. Yelly sustained many slaps on the back as he began weeping joyful tears once more.

"Lucky for you," the President continued, "my ex-wife isn't running the show! She'd probably cut off more than your head for such a performance through the years!"

The crowd, and Yelly, laughed even harder.

"No, but seriously folks," the President continued. "The man who won today has quite literally devoted his entire adult life to the pursuit of plouquette excellence. And it's with great pleasure and pride that I award the Sir Larabee Waterford Cup—that's Sir Larabee Waterford, a proud sponsor of the Paris Publique Plouquette Pitch, Grounds, Gardens, Grass Court, and Lawn Club. Sir Larabee Waterford, making the finest fountain pens and also some ashtrays since 1882, that's Sir Larabee Waterford, where your signature is our signature—the Sir Larabee Waterford Cup... to Monsieur Yelly Reardon!"

The crowd exploded. Maurice de Mouton peeled back the paper on a new nameplate on the front of the cup.

"Yelly, old boy!" Cravenmoore yelled. "Get over here! Come see your name on this beauty! Claim your pri—"

"Hold on a minute, Keveen," a voice shouted from a second story balcony at one end of the pitch.

Every head in the courtyard turned. The crowd hushed. Luc knew the voice before he even looked over.

"Oh my God," Cravenmoore was heard saying in the

microphone. "It's Dorian Thibault. Back from the dead."

The crowd gasped.

"No. Please no," Yelly gasped.

"What the hell is going on here?" Cravenmoore asked. "How are you alive? How'd you even get in here?"

"Never mind," Dorian announced to the crowd. "I see many familiar faces here. You are all looking beautiful."

"Oh no you don't," Cravenmoore shouted, waving a finger. "I see what's going on here, but your famous Dorian Thibault charm won't work here. Someone get up there! Call the police! Get him out of here!"

No one moved.

"Where's Maurice?" the President yelled. "Pompousselpeck! Do something!"

"Chief Pompousselpeck?!" Dorian asked. "He's here? Where?"

"I'm here, Dorian," Flive answered as he moved to go inside. "As soon as I get up there, I'm taking you in!"

"I thought you were retired, my old friend," Dorian shouted back.

"Well, I'm back today!" The man exclaimed. "If you're coming out of retirement, so am I!"

"Go get him, Flive!" The President yelled.

The former chief of police squared off his stance, puffed his chest and saluted the President. "Skeeeerawwwww!" He shouted before lumbering toward the door. Luc remembered the pterodactyl salute.

"I hope it's not another 22 years before you get up here," Dorian answered. "You seem to have lost a spring in your step!"

Pompousselpeck went for a doorway, but Cravenmoore called out to him.

"Don't bother, Flive. We both know that you haven't been able to make it up a full flight of stairs in under an hour in years. What's the meaning of this, Thibault?" Cravenmoore shouted, no longer using the microphone. "If you hadn't noticed, Yelly just won the Sir Larabee Waterford Cup, and I was about to present it to him!"

Dorian started laughing. "Sure, you were."

"What's so funny, thief?!" Cravenmoore shouted back.

Luc couldn't keep his mouth shut. Forgetting his nerves, seeing Dorian standing on the balcony just to the busboy's right, Luc was energized.

"He's laughing because it's not the real cup!" Luc exploded. As every head turned on the plouquette court, Luc felt his face go white with fear as he remembered Madame Pompousselpeck's warning.

"Pigeon?! What are you doing here?" Cravenmoore yelled out.

Luc didn't know how to answer. "Hello," he said, with an awkward wave as he backed away from the window, hoping everyone might forget what just happened.

"Wait?! Pigeon!" Cravenmoore called after him. "Did you say it's not the real cup?"

"Bravo, Luc!" Dorian shouted.

The busboy took a step closer to the window.

"Ladies and gentlemen," Dorian Thibault announced

from his balcony at the north end of the courtyard, "let me properly introduce to you the man you've been indignantly referring to as 'Pigeon' for the last few weeks. Meet Luc Martin. Not the greatest detective of all time, but actually not the worst either."

Luc watched every face look between him, Dorian, and Cravenmoore in confusion.

"Sure, maybe we fed him some clues along the way, but Luc found me," Dorian continued to the crowd, "as well as Armande Marwane, and obviously, the Sir Larabee Waterford Cup—or so he thought at least."

"What do you mean by that, Dorian?" Cravenmoore shouted. "The cup is right here!" The President gestured at the trophy behind him on the table.

"Is it, Keveen?" Dorian answered, raising his hand in the air. He held a small remote device. The crowd watched as he pressed a button, and the cup burst into flame with a sudden pop—new nameplate and all.

"NOOOOOOOO!" Yelly screamed, once again falling to his knees.

"The cup!" Cravenmoore shouted. He threw his jacket over the flames, but it was too late. The cup was already melting into a distorted mess. The President's coat caught fire.

"Cravenmoore, calm down!" Dorian yelled above the murmurs of the crowd. "Just take it easy. I would never blow up the real cup."

"I knew it!" Luc shouted, feeling satisfied. But no one was paying attention to him.

"Even still," Cravenmoore shouted back. "Look what

you've done to Yelly!"

"Poor Yelly," Dorian muttered, along with most of the crowd.

"He's a fragile little butterfly!" The President continued. "You must have known that this would kill him. To finally win the cup, only to have it taken away once again—by you!"

Yelly continued to sob on his knees.

"Please," Dorian answered. "I would never do anything to harm poor Yelly. How I was supposed to know that he was going to win today? I mean he's good, but he's not the best."

"I suppose you're about to tell us that you are," Cravenmoore grumbled loudly.

"Precisely—which is why I would never blow up the real cup."

"So, where is it?!" Cravenmoore asked.

Dorian laughed again. "You can't possibly think that I am going to tell you that, can you? I wouldn't do that any more than I would have let Luc Martin leave my bookshop with the real cup."

Cravenmoore turned to Luc's window. "How long have you known, boy?"

"Known what?" Luc answered.

"Known that the cup was a fake."

"Not long."

"And why didn't you say anything?" Cravenmoore asked.

"He did!" Dorian interrupted. "Just now, and he's not

a moment too soon. I have to tell you, Luc, I've been very impressed by you."

"Ah, good to hear, Dorian," Cravenmoore exclaimed. "Thank goodness he has *your* seal of approval!"

"Don't listen to him, Luc," Dorian answered from his perch on the balcony. "You and I are so alike. Think about it. We were outsiders who lied our way into this circle. We were celebrated, almost felt like we'd earned our spot in this society legitimately. But, we couldn't make it last. We became too good for them to handle, so they let us go. They'd rather we be cast away instead of accepted on merit. That's what's wrong with these sorts of people."

"How dare you!" Cravenmoore yelled up at Dorian. "We're a club, not people!"

"So, why'd you come back?" Luc yelled from his window to Dorian. For some reason, his palms weren't sweating. "If the cup is still gone, why did you return?"

"Good question, my friend," Dorian answered with a smile. "I imagine I'm here for the same reason you're here."

"I'm here because I thought the cup was fake. And I was right!" Luc shouted.

"You were," Dorian acknowledged. "But, we both know that's not why you're really here. You're here for the girl."

Luc felt his face flush. He scanned the crowd again, unable to hide his embarrassment. Still no Alaina. Thank goodness she hadn't heard the accusation.

"And you know what?" Dorian asked, after Luc didn't answer. "I'm here for a girl too."

The crowd gasped, and all eyes moved to Marianne Merriweather, standing in the throng of people.

"Marianne," Dorian began.

She didn't answer. She didn't move.

"I can't tell you how sorry I am that we now find ourselves in this situation. Seeing you has broken my heart. You have deserved better than this."

She remained expressionless.

"I know it's not what you want to hear, but I'm still in love with—"

CLICK. A gun cocked. Dorian froze mid-sentence. Maurice de Mouton appeared behind him with a gun pointed at the back of his head. The crowd gasped again, and Marianne put a hand over her mouth in surprise.

"Whoa, whoa, whoa," Dorian managed, raising his empty hands. "Take it easy back there."

De Mouton moved forward to address the crowd.

"This has gone on long enough!" He shouted.

"Well done, Maurice!" Cravenmoore shouted back. "Bring the scoundrel down here so he can be brought to justice!"

"Don't touch me," Dorian grunted.

"Oh, I don't think you're in a position to be giving direction, right now, Thibault," de Mouton said, before he turned his head to address Luc. "I guess I'll be doing what you couldn't, Pigeon. I told Cravenmoore from the start, you weren't too much of anything. He should have just given me the job."

Luc grimaced.

"I've been waiting for today for a long time," de Mouton said to Dorian.

"Me too. Can't we just talk this out, Maurice?" Dorian retorted.

"Save it. Let's go, Thibault. I've dreamt of this momen—"

CRACK.

A plouquette mallet struck the man from behind. As de Mouton fell to the floor of the balcony, Madame Pompousselpeck emerged from behind him. The crowd gasped yet again. Luc was confused. Why was she on the balcony with Dorian and Maurice de Mouton?

"Oh, thank God," Dorian said. "What took you so long, Flova?"

"Flova?!" Cravenmoore yelled out in shock. "What the hell are you doing here?"

"Hello, Keveen. Nice to see you as always."

"Bite me, hag," the President snapped.

"Hey watch it!" Flive Pompousselpeck yelled out. "That's my wife, Cravenmoore."

The club President shook his head. "We've been duped, Pompousselpeck. She may be your wife now, but she and I were married first."

"*That's* your ex-wife?!" Flive yelled back at Cravenmoore.

The crowd gasped.

"Are you telling me that you didn't know?!" the President answered.

"Of course, I didn't know!"

"Well, I didn't know my ex went off and married you!" The President shouted back at the former chief of police.

"Why would I have married your ex-wife? Everyone says she's the worst!" Flive exclaimed.

"She *is*! And she's proving it right now!" Cravenmoore exclaimed. "On the day of the tournament, she found a way to come back and somehow stab me in the back. I told you she was terrible! She probably was behind this from the start!"

"For once, you're right, Keveen," Flova said. "Dorian is my protégé. I've been with him every step of the way, ever since you tossed me aside and sullied my reputation, I swore I'd have my revenge. And here I am."

"*You* were Dorian's help on the inside?!" The former Chief of Police Pompousselpeck yelled up at his wife. "I don't understand! We investigated every avenue!"

"Sure, you did, sweetheart. You didn't look hard enough, obviously. In fact, I've been operating under your nose the whole time."

It all made sense to Luc now. Flova had enough motivation to take down Cravenmoore and orchestrate the entire plot—over the course of 22 years. She was a woman on a mission.

"You *are* the worst!" Flive shouted at Flova.

"Calm down, Flivey honey. None of this is your fault."

"Did you just marry me to spite President Cravenmoore?"

"Yes. I'm sorry. You were very nice. But this was all

worth it. Look at Keveen's stupid face."

"You hag!" Cravenmoore yelled again.

"Tsk, tsk, no need to get petty," she answered.

"What do you want from us?! You've already destroyed so much!" The President called out.

"Oh, I've already gotten everything I want," Flova said. "I was fine to never come back here again. We have your cup. We've made a fool out of you for years. This has ended perfectly—for me. It's Dorian who has unfinished business."

Cravenmoore rolled his eyes, but everyone else looked to Marianne yet again.

"Marianne, my love, as I was saying. I hope you can find it in your heart to forgive me," Dorian shouted with passion.

Marianne still didn't say anything, but sighed as if she was allowing herself to process the situation.

"Let's pretend for one second that you can get Marianne to agree to leave with you," Cravenmoore yelled, "which she won't do, by the way, because she's a club member for life, and would never do anything to hurt the image of the club, I bet. Right Marianne?"

Marianne remained silent.

"As I was saying," Cravenmoore continued. "Your nice little speech for Marianne doesn't matter. What makes you think you're getting out of here? We're not going to let you leave. You are both going to jail!"

"I wouldn't count on it. We have a bargaining chip," Flova said with a smile.

"Oh yeah?! What's that?" Cravenmoore yelled.

"Armande!" She yelled.

In that moment, the doors below the balcony opened, and out from the bar area, Armande and Alaina entered. They pulled Evan between them, bound at his hands and mouth.

Luc felt all the blood leave his face again. Alaina had joined them? Was she trying to recruit him on behalf of Madame Pompousselpeck and Dorian when she visited him the other day?

"You can rest assured, Keveen, we took real pleasure in capturing this little runt," Flova boasted.

"Evan!" Cravenmoore yelled. "Be brave, sweet boy!"

Yanis rolled his eyes. He didn't look injured—just captured.

"And Alaina!" Cravenmoore screamed. "I should have known, you little delinquent. You should never have been trusted with any part of this. Let me guess, Pigeon is in on it too?"

"No, no, no," Flova corrected him, looking in Luc's direction. "Pigeon was practically working for us all along, but I wouldn't say he was in on it. I don't think he realized how much help he was to us. After Tag got caught, we knew it was a matter of time. So, we nudged him along to help him solve the case—only I don't think he knew it. In many ways, he was being true to you the whole time."

"He lied, though!" Cravenmoore countered. "He didn't tell me that he'd found Dorian—not to mention he lied about being the greatest detective of all time!"

"Well, I didn't lie—technically," Luc shouted. "I just didn't mention that I *wasn't* the greatest—"

"Shut up, Pigeon!" Cravenmoore yelled.

"Quit while you're ahead, Luc," Dorian noted from his balcony.

"Don't let yourself get distracted, Keveen," Flova yelled. "You haven't heard my exit strategy yet. Evan here played right into our hands. And if you let us go safely, we'll leave him behind."

"That's a dumb plan," Cravenmoore whined. "Because you will all be arrested, and we'll still get him back. Either way we win."

"No, we're leaving. You can just agree to do this the easy way, or the hard way. If you let us go peacefully, then you can have Evan Yanis back. But if you resist us, we'll just have to take him with us, and there's a good chance you'll never see him again."

"You wouldn't!" Cravenmoore yelled.

"Wouldn't what?" Flova answered. "Kill him? Of course not. That's not our business. But disappearance is. The only way Luc found us in the first place was because we wanted to be found."

"You always were a hook-nosed she-witch!" Cravenmoore yelled. "But you have forgotten one thing."

"What's that, Keveen?"

"You've forgotten about the Paris Publique Plouquette Pitch, Grounds, Gardens, Grass Court, and Lawn Club Secret Action Services Combat Squad!"

"The PPPPGGGCLCSASCS?" Flova answered. She looked around. "That's funny. I don't see them anywhere."

Cravenmoore went white. He looked at others on the

dais. "Wait, has anyone called the secret action services combat squad yet?"

As soon as he said it, tens of soldiers dressed in full combat garb rushed onto the plouquette pitch from inside the club. They covered every exit and surrounded everyone on the ground.

"Maurice de Mouton called us, sir," one soldier reported from underneath his blast shield.

"Oh, thank God," Cravenmoore sighed.

For the first time, Flova didn't look confident.

"What took you so long?" Cravenmoore asked.

"We had to get dressed, and some of the guys wanted a ciggie."

"At a time like this?!"

"Sorry, sir," the man said.

"No matter." Cravenmoore looked back up at Flova Pompousselpeck. "Well, now what? You didn't expect all these billionaires at the club to not have their own secret action services combat squad?"

From his window in the librarium, Luc heard Flova lower her voice and address Dorian.

"Any bright ideas, Thibault?" She asked.

Dorian was still locked in a stare with Marianne. "The combat squad has grown a lot since I was last here," he whispered.

"This makes it a lot harder to get to the river," she answered.

The river? What did that mean? Luc thought.

Luc knew he didn't want to aid the bad guys any

longer. The busboy needed to help Dorian, Armande, and now Flova Pompousselpeck and Alaina escape.

He could think of only one solution, but it would be painful. Luc backed away from the window, and sprinted for the flight of stairs. After hurling himself down one floor, he burst into the buzzing hornet farm. Luc ran the length of the room, speeding by rows of wood and glass that kept the noble hornets imprisoned.

He thought of what Cravenmoore told him. Someone had released the hornets once. The President said they'd flooded the courtyard. If Luc could do it again, maybe it would provide enough distraction to buy Alaina and the group some time to get out.

At last, the busboy arrived at the large "do not press" red button. Without hesitation, he punched it with his palm.

The glass in front of each hornet's nest dropped, and the room became a dark fog of pain-inflicting insects. Luc dashed for another stairwell, closing the door behind him just in time. He hoped those evil little minions of hate would find their way to the courtyard quickly.

Luc thought of Alaina as he raced back up the stairs to the librarium. How could he let her know he helped? Would she be able to get out of the courtyard before a thousand hornets stung her? Luc had to find a way to get to her, but he wasn't about to run into the courtyard. The busboy would have to watch her and follow her out of the building. A hornet appeared in the stairwell as he ran. Another. And then another.

Luc arrived back to his window upstairs in the

librarium. He kept one eye on the opposite door, knowing he might have to run for it if the hornets started pouring in. Cravenmoore stood below on the platform, laughing.

"And that's when I said," Luc heard Cravenmoore yell at Flova Pompousselpeck, "Maurice, the only thing that could ruin today would be if my ex-wife showed up! But it turns out, you being here is going to *make* my day! Because I'm taking you down after all these years!" The man bellowed with laughter.

"If we're going down, Keveen, then we're taking you with us," Flova announced.

"This ought to be good," the President answered. "How do you plan to do that?"

"I'm sorry to announce: I lied," she yelled.

"When you said you married me for my looks?!" Cravenmoore yelled.

C'mon hornets. Get here. Luc thought.

"Well, yes, but that's not what I meant. I meant just now. I lied when I said we came back to support Dorian. I have one more surprise that I've saved just for you."

"And what's that?!"

Flova smiled a wide, toothy, almost hideous grin. "TAAAAAAAAAAGGGG!" She called.

A man in the crowd thrust off his jacket and removed his top hat with a flourish. It was Tag le Tier. The people gasped, and backed away from him. He reached into the top hat with ceremony, and produced a small, furry animal.

"Oh no," Cravenmoore gasped. "Is that a... re-venomized raccoon?!"

Before anyone could answer, Tag dropped to one knee and held the beast out over the ground. "Sick 'em, Rainbow!" Tag yelled and dropped the raccoon on the grass.

As soon as the animal landed, it was sprinting straight for Cravenmoore. The crowd let out a shriek. A clear path to the President opened as people ran in all directions, but the raccoon wound up rocketing past Cravenmoore—and leapt at the throat of the unlucky bartender, Dolt D'Ormando. The young man screamed as he fell backwards.

The President looked dazed, as if he'd looked death right in the face. Two of the PPPPGGGCLC secret action services combat squad members rushed to Dolt's side. Amid raccoon shrieks and hisses, they pried Rainbow from the bartender's face. The animal clawed at the air as one of the soldiers held him. Dolt managed to stand with the help of the other squad member.

"You will pay for that, Flova," Cravenmoore hissed. "SQUAD," the man yelled. "Take her down. Take them all down!"

But no one moved. In fact, no one was listening to the club President. Instead, they were paying attention to a growing hum.

"What is that noise?" Someone asked.

It sounded like a hundred kazoos.

"It's getting louder."

A black cloud of hornets poured into the courtyard in tens of thousands. They came from everywhere: vents, windows, drainpipes. Each one flew with vengeful purpose and a scowl on its hornet face.

The crowd erupted fear. Billionaires ran in every direction. Entire platoons of hornets picked one human to chase, determined to inject poison into every square centimeter of exposed skin.

"Hornets!" Cravenmoore yelled into the microphone. "Who could ever have guessed that they would have turned against us so willingly?! Run!"

Luc looked at the balcony where Flova had been, but she had disappeared. Alaina and Armande Marwane were gone too. A few squad members were freeing Evan. The busboy noticed another squad member being violently attacked by Rainbow, who must have turned the tables on her opponent.

Luc looked up to see Dorian still on the balcony, locked in a stare with Marianne, who remained the only person in the crowd not screaming or running around. Marianne finally smiled. It was small, but Luc was sure it was there.

Without warning, Dorian let out a whistle, and amazingly, Phyllis, the club steed, galloped to a position beneath him under the balcony. Dorian swung his legs over the edge, landing on the horse. Phyllis reared in triumph, her mane flowing in hornet wing wind. Dorian gave her a playful slap on her thigh, and she galloped to Marianne's side. Luc was impressed.

The busboy saw Dorian lean over and whisper something to Marianne. The man extended his hand to her. She looked at him and remained motionless for only a second, before smiling back and accepting his hand. Dorian easily hoisted her onto the horse.

Phyllis reared back again as if to celebrate the pair's union, before taking off across the pitch towards the double glass doors at full speed. Dorian nabbed a plouquette mallet from a running billionaire as Phyllis sprinted through the crowd. He cocked his arm, and launched the mallet at the sky.

There it was.

The impossibly-majestic-high-arc-rainbow-hammer-mallet throw.

And it was perfect.

Luc squinted as he almost lost the image of the spinning mallet in the sun, before it returned to earth many slow moments later, shattering the giant double glass doors. Shards of glass rained on the chaos. Dorian and Marianne rode Phyllis through it all, directly into the building, and heading in the direction of the front door.

Luc took off through the librarium as fast as he could, but he stopped dead when he reached the door.

"Hey, Pigeon," Evan Yanis hissed. His arms and face were covered in small puffy hornet sting bumps.

"Evan. I don't have time for this, I have to go."

Evan pushed his sleeves up. "I've been waiting a long time for this."

"F-f-for what?" Luc stammered.

"I'm going to beat you until you can't even say your own name. Then, I'm going to lock you in a closet."

Even though Yanis was shorter than Luc, the busboy was still worried.

"Listen, Evan, I'm sorry about that, but you and I were never enemies here."

"Sure, Pigeon. I'll try to remember that next time you lie your way to a two million-euro paycheck."

"No, seriously, I have to run," Luc tried, backing away. "Can we talk about this some other time?"

"Where are you going in such a hurry? Afraid the police will arrest you when they don't catch Dorian and the rest of them? Because you should be. They'll take you down for fraud, assault, embezzlement, I don't know. And I can't wait to see it. But first, I'm going to make sure you go to jail with some bruises."

"I-I-I'm not running from the police," Luc stammered.

"Well maybe you should be," Evan suggested, advancing.

"I have to catch up with Alaina!" Luc blurted out.

Evan stopped.

"Surely you understand that," Luc pleaded. "You have to let me out of here."

"Why on Earth would I let you leave just to go talk to Alaina? She doesn't like you."

"So, what? Do you think she's in love with *you*?"

"I don't know," Evan answered, raising his voice.

"Look, man, I know her well enough by now to know that she doesn't care about you. Besides, she just had you gagged and tied up."

"She's been coerced by these thieves."

"Please, she's been looking for a chance to give this place the middle finger forever," Luc yelled above a growing hornet buzz.

Evan rushed at Luc and shoved him to the ground. The wooden floorboards of the librarium made a cracking sound under Luc's weight.

"Please, Evan, she's getting away," Luc pleaded as he crawled backwards.

"Time to even the score, Pigeon."

"Hold up," a familiar voice called.

Both Evan and Luc looked toward the door as a young black man walked in with a pigeon on his shoulder.

"Charlie?!" Luc exclaimed. "What are you doing here?"

"Who the hell are you?" Yanis spat. "And why is there a bird on your shoulder?"

"He has a name. And it's Richard!" Charlie grunted through his teeth.

"Whose name is Richard?" Evan asked.

"He's the pigeon," Charlie said as he rolled his eyes.

"No, *he's* the pigeon," Evan clarified, pointing at Luc.

"Don't call me Pigeon," Luc hissed as he stood. He wiped floorboard dust from his white pants. "Charlie, what are you doing here, man?"

"I told you I was going to help."

"I don't understand," Luc answered. "How have you been helping?"

"They assigned me to you," Charlie revealed. "Alaina, Flova, Dorian. Alaina called after she left the other day. She knew I wanted to help. So, they gave me a task—to make sure that you didn't get into trouble."

"I'm fine," Luc stated.

"You don't seem fine to me, Pigeon," Evan said. "I'm about to kick your ass. This guy and his bird can watch."

"STOP CALLING ME THAT!" Luc erupted. He didn't have time to notice if he was nervous or if his palms were sweating. In fact, his hands were clenched in fists for the first time in his life. "I'm Luc Martin! And I'm the *greatest fucking detective of all time!*"

Luc rushed at Evan. The little lawn boy shrieked as the busboy knocked him down. In less than one second, Luc had both feet planted on Evan's chest.

"My heart!" Evan screamed. "De Mouton always said you were willing to stand on someone's heart! OW!"

"Alaina doesn't love you!" Luc shouted.

"Hey Luc," Charlie interjected from the sidelines. "Take it easy, man."

"She never will!" The busboy continued.

"Luc, seriously," Charlie answered. "This place is starting to fill with hornets."

Evan continued shrieking as tears flowed out of the corners of his eyes. "Here come the hornets! Get off me!" The lawn boy screamed.

Luc looked up. Charlie and Evan were right. The air in the room began to shimmer on hornets' wings.

"We have to get out of here!" Charlie exclaimed.

The busboy stepped off the little lawn boy. Evan writhed on the floor of the librarium.

The haze of hornets was getting thick. Luc felt the hot sting of a hornet's poison on his arm. Another landed on his shoulder. Then his face. "Charlie!" He yelled.

Luc heard flapping. The air began to clear.

"This way!" Charlie instructed. "Follow Richard!"

"What's happening?!" Luc yelled.

"Pigeons eat hornets! Everybody knows that!" Charlie shouted as he grabbed Luc's shirt and dragged him into the stairwell.

"That can't be true!" Luc answered as his roommate pulled him.

"Well, it's either that, or Richard is just really devoted to us!"

As the two ran into the stairwell, Richard flew in front of them, picking off hornets with surprising agility. The boys tripped down several turns on the staircase behind the bird before spilling out into a side street, free and clear of tiny winged menaces. The pigeon flew off.

"Where's he going?" Luc asked, out of breath.

"Once Richard gets a taste for hornet blood, it's hard to quench the thirst, I guess," Charlie stated.

"Look," Luc said, catching his breath. "Thanks man. I appreciate you being here today."

"Stop stalling. Go get the girl, brother," Charlie answered with a smile.

"Make sure you get out of here before the police arrive," Luc urged as he ran off.

"I will."

"Hey," Luc said as he turned to Charlie one last time before leaving. "Please thank Richard for me."

"Thank him yourself when you get home tonight. I'm making dinner for you and Richard," Charlie stated, "in honor of you growing up and taking a few risks."

"You? You're making dinner?"

"Fine. I'm ordering something in."

"That's more like it."

"And I'm picking up some beers on the way home," Charlie asserted with a nod.

"Sounds good. See you then," Luc answered smiling.

* * *

Luc Martin sprinted around the corner to the front of the building. Coat-check Carl picked up splinters of the shattered front door on the sidewalk. Phyllis must have taken Dorian and Marianne out the entrance with authority.

Luc knew he needed to get to the river. He didn't know what he'd find there, but that was his only clue to Alaina's whereabouts.

But he didn't look far to find trouble. There, standing in front of 17 serious looking men, was Janet, furious, and hungry for breakup revenge.

Chapter XXI.

"Janet!" Luc gasped. "What's going on?"

"Luc Martin," Janet said as she stood in the middle of the street, panting with rage. The 17 men behind her all cracked their knuckles and loosened the muscles in their necks. They took up the entire narrow Parisian street.

"I'm here to break up with you," said the woman scorned.

Luc sighed. "Janet, I'm sorry. I don't have time for this. I have to get out of here. Did you see which way the two people on the horse went?"

"Don't change the subject. You've treated me badly since the day we started dating."

"I have not!" Luc protested.

"...and my 17 little brothers are NOT happy about it."

Luc looked at the group of men standing behind Janet. One of them pointed at him, and then pointed in his own mouth.

"Wait, *those* are your 17 little brothers?" Luc asked.

"Yep. And they are pissed," she said.

"They're not *little* at all!"

"Just because they're not older than me doesn't mean they're little."

"How is that possible, though?" Luc asked. "I mean, scientifically? They're all huge. Shouldn't the youngest be a little kid or something?"

"We're a blended family. I was my dad's only child, but when he married Nancy, her seven sons came with the deal. Then, they adopted some our age, became foster parents for some more... but it's not the point."

"Oh, I see. So, they're not all *really* your 17 little brothers," Luc said.

"Um... excuse me? Are you saying we're not family?!" Janet yelled. Almost all of the 17 brothers clenched their fists. A few huffed. One was turning so red that Luc thought he might burst.

"I wouldn't piss these guys off even more, if I were you," Janet continued. "We've got six university rugby players here, a few footballers, two amateur boxers, a handful of log throwers, and one aspiring botanist who's also a member of the Future French Minor Miners Association. He's a hard worker, but not a fighter. You should be worried about the other sixteen, though. You're a dead man."

"Janet, I'm sorry. What do you want from me?" Luc pleaded.

"I want to break up. And I want to make you pay."

"Pay for what? And we're already broken up!"

"No! We break up when I say we break up!" She exclaimed.

"Great, you've said it. So, it's done. I have to go," Luc said.

"You're not even sad?!" She screamed.

"Sure, of course I am... if that's what you want."

Janet shook her head. "Not good enough, Luc Martin. I want you to pay for being such a jerk."

Luc heard the telltale, two-tone sirens of Paris' police.

"You know what, Janet, I've got to go. And guess what? Charlie was right. Sometimes to be happy, you just have to hurt people's feelings. It's part of life. You don't have to like it. So, if that makes me a jerk, I'm sorry. Honestly, I should have made my feelings clearer early on."

Janet fumed. The boys huffed again.

"But now, since you are here to hunt me down, I have no problem saying that we're done," Luc continued. "And I'd be happy to explain why to you sometime and tell you all about how you were controlling, rude, dependent, and super crazy, but for right now, I am going to chase after this other girl that I really like, because that's what's most important to me right now."

Luc exhaled. That felt good.

"Kill him, boys," Janet whispered with tears in her eyes.

*   *   *

Luc had never run so fast in his life. Being pursued by 17 vengeful men was not something he'd ever experienced before.

"Get back here, you little bastard!" One brother shouted out.

"I'm gonna stand on your balls!" Another shouted.

"And I'm gonna keep your eyes in a jar on my nightstand!" One added.

Luc felt the air cut between each strand of hair on his head as he ran.

The busboy turned a corner and glanced down at the river. A good distance ahead, he saw a large white horse on the opposite bank next to a boat. Two people bade it farewell, and it turned and galloped off into the city. The busboy squinted and saw a girl with shining auburn hair. It had to be Alaina.

The busboy led Janet's brothers as fast as he could down a wide stone stairway to the riverfront. The boat pulled away into the water. Several police cars stop on a bridge to watch the barge start down the river.

Luc fumbled his way down the stairs to reach the banks of the Seine. He could feel the breath of the 17 men behind him. "Alaina!" He called as he ran alongside the river. "Alaina!"

Way out on the water, he saw Alaina turn and look.

"Alaina! Hey wait!"

Luc felt a hand brush the back of his clothes as he ran. Janet's brothers were on top of him. He had no choice.

The busboy leapt off the stone riverbank, using his arms and legs to churn through the air. He hit the dark water, which chilled him far more than he expected. He gasped for air and took a quick glance behind as he started to swim. Janet's brothers stopped on the quay to watch him.

"You'll never make it!" One yelled.

"We'll be waiting when you get back!" They called.

Luc saw the barge pulling farther from his reach. The cold water weakened his arms.

Before he could decide to swim further, a foam ring with a rope tied to it came hurling in his direction. He grabbed it, and noticed the writing on it: The Sir Larabee. The rope tightened as Luc was being dragged aboard.

*   *   *

Dorian and Armande pulled Luc onto the back of the boat. The busboy gulped air, being so out-of-breath from running and swimming hard.

"Luc, you're crazy, man."

The busboy looked up as Alaina looked down on him.

"I know," he gasped.

"I have to hand it to you, kid," Dorian noted, helping him to his feet. "You are a really good detective."

Luc looked around. Flova and Marianne were with them, and Luc overheard Tag telling them, "I just wish Rainbow could have gotten on the boat with us."

"I told you before," Madame Pompousselpeck answered. "I am just not sure that being on a boat with a re-venomized raccoon is the most responsible thing we could do."

"I know. I just miss her."

"We'll get you a new one. It seems Rainbow just didn't want to let go of that young man's face back there," Marianne said.

Police cars were lining up on each bank of the river. The sirens sang louder than Luc had ever heard them. The busboy turned his attention back to Alaina just as Dorian pulled her aside.

"Look, Alaina," Dorian warned with one eye on Luc. "We'll give you a minute or two here, but make this quick. Say whatever needs to be said, and if you want to bring him along, he can come. Just figure it out quickly."

Dorian looked at Luc and smiled. "Do we have you to thank for the hornets?" He asked.

"Yes." Luc swallowed to catch his breath. "I wanted to try anything."

"My many thanks," the man answered. "If you're not coming with us, make sure Charlie knows how much we appreciated his help as well."

"Yeah, he bailed me out back there," Luc managed between breaths.

Dorian looked back at Alaina. "Two minutes," he stated as he left for the quarters below. Armande did the same after a small wave and a smile for Luc. Flova, Marianne, and Tag had already gone below.

"What are you doing here, Luc?" Alaina asked.

"What's going on here? How do you all plan on escaping?" The busboy asked as water dripped on the wooden planks beneath his feet.

"We have another barge downriver to transfer to," Alaina said. "And from there, we'll disappear."

"Has that been their plan all along? Let me find the fake cup? Come back just long enough to prove they bested Cravenmoore?"

"Sounds like it. Really didn't have a choice when Tag got arrested."

"When did they recruit you?" Luc asked.

"After we saw Dorian in the park, he found me separately."

"Alaina, listen," Luc pleaded. "I just want to be with you."

"I know," she answered. "I tried to recruit you when I came to your apartment."

Luc shook from the chill of the water—and nerves. He didn't have time to stammer, let alone be romantic or poetic. "That's not what I mean. I mean that I'm in love with you."

The water seemed to be rushing by the barge faster than ever. Luc grasped the rail along the edge of the boat for stability as their speed increased.

"Pull your boat to the side of the river!" A voice called through a megaphone. Luc ignored it.

"Luc, you're not in love with me."

"Yes, I am." The busboy felt his nerves subside. He stood as straight as he could. "And until all this happened, until I met you, I would never have known how to say it."

"Luc, stop. I had a good time with you, and I'm proud of what you did on this whole thing, but we're not supposed to wind up together, you know that, right?"

"So, what?" Luc asked. "You're just going to stick it out with Dolt?"

"He's an idiot. That's over. It was one of those dumb things. He was good-looking and well-liked at the club. But the more I got to know him, the less attractive he became. I'm glad that raccoon got in a little taste of him."

"What would raccoon venom do to someone?" Luc asked.

"Tag insists he'll be fine in a few years."

"Ouch," Luc said.

"Attention rogue barge," the megaphone voice came again. "You are surrounded. I repeat, pull your vessel to the side of the river."

"So what?" Luc asked Alaina, refocusing. "Are you really going to say that you feel *nothing* for me?"

"We lead different lives, Luc."

"They're not that different Alaina. Neither of us felt like we belonged. We were both looking for something else. We were both looking for a way out. And we found it, together."

"I guess," she answered.

"Wherever you're going, I want to be there. Please say yes. Don't think about it, just do what you feel. It's simple, do you want me there or not?"

The sirens pierced the air. Alaina waited a moment in thought. Her stare was unwavering. Much to Luc's surprise, Alaina grabbed the busboy's shirt and pulled him to her.

She kissed him.

Luc's eyes closed. The energy behind her warm lips made him dizzy. It was the kind of kiss that lasts just long enough to realize it was happening in the exact moment it stops.

Luc opened his eyes in time to see Alaina lean just an inch away.

"Goodbye," she whispered. She was so close that Luc

felt her breath on his face.

Her grip on his shirt changed. Her hands drove into him, and Luc felt the railing dig into his lower back. Before he could catch himself, the busboy had toppled over the edge. He watched the wind blow Alaina's hair as the cold water wrapped itself around him again.

Seconds later, by the time his head was back above water, the barge he'd been on was an impossible distance away. There was no hope to catch it. He had surfaced just in time to see Alaina disappear below decks. She was already gone.

The busboy eyed a spot to climb onto the stone riverbank. He began swimming, only to hear a crash in the distance.

He looked over his shoulder and watched, stunned, as Alaina's barge rammed into a bridge support down river.

"Alaina!" He shouted, knowing she wouldn't hear him below decks through the din of sirens.

He watched in disbelief as the deck neared the water line of the Seine. Police swarmed on the bridge like panicking ants. Luc heard the sirens behind him getting louder as a small police boat approached him. The barge disappeared below the water line, shrinking the breath in Luc's chest as he screamed Alaina's name.

Chapter XXII.

Luc Martin stepped out of the police station. He exhaled, happy the last 24 hours were over. The busboy still wore the clothes from the tournament. His white pants were greyed with river water.

"How'd that go?" Charlie asked, leaning on the deep green wrought iron fence on the sidewalk that surrounded the building.

"How long have you been out here?"

"Not long. I've been hiding. Assumed if they didn't let you out after 24 hours, then you weren't coming out at all."

"Let's walk," Luc said. The roommates began down the tree-lined sidewalk. The warm sun forced Luc's eyes closed for a moment. Parisians passed them as they walked the tree-lined street.

"So what happened in there?" Charlie asked.

"Nothing. Just asked me a lot of questions about Dorian, Armande, Tag, and Madame Pompousselpeck. Turns out I don't really know too much about them."

"What do you mean?" Charlie asked.

"The police asked where they'd been hiding, how Dorian and Madame Pompousselpeck met, where the real trophy is. All that stuff. And I don't know those answers."

Charlie nodded.

"Once they discovered I wasn't in on their plan," Luc continued, "the police said I wouldn't be charged with anything. I get the feeling I'm not of any use to them."

Charlie placed a hand on Luc's shoulder. "Well that's good."

"I guess," Luc answered.

"Look," Charlie said. "I wanted to be here when they let you out, just so you didn't hear it from someone else, but I have some news you should hear."

"Okay," Luc said. "Should I be worried?"

"Well, everyone is fine. Your parents are okay... but the café burned down."

Luc stopped walking. "No way."

"Last night. Doesn't sound like anyone knows what happened yet."

"I know what happened," Luc said as he began walking again. "Janet."

Charlie quickened his pace to keep up. "Yeah, man. I don't think you should talk to her again."

"You think?" Luc asked.

"Your mom called to tell me. Actually, she didn't sound that unhappy. She was just glad no one was hurt. She did say something about being able to retire on the insurance money when it comes, so at least that sounds good for them."

Luc was relieved. No more being a waiter.

"What about you?" Luc asked. "Where have you been since yesterday? I take it the police never caught you?"

"After I left the club, I just had to lay low, you know? I wasn't sure if anyone saw me or anything," Charlie said.

"My guess is that you would know by now if they were looking for you," Luc answered.

"I think so too."

"Where's Richard?" Luc asked.

"I don't know."

Luc listened to the sound of their shoes on the sidewalk and worried about the bird. "How many hornets do you think he ate?" Luc asked.

"Who knows," Charlie answered. "I had to have seen him eat a thousand? Maybe ten thousand? He was going crazy."

"Is that healthy?"

"I don't know." The worry in Charlie's voice was evident too.

The roommates stopped at a crosswalk. "So, did the police keep you in a cell?"

"No. It was just constant questions. It started as soon as they pulled me out of the water." Luc pressed the pedestrian crossing button several times as small cars sped by.

"Nice pants. Good luck returning those," Charlie said with a nod at Luc's legs.

"I am going to put these in the next dumpster we pass," Luc said.

The roommates crossed the street amid a mob of walkers.

"Do you think they have any answers about the boat accident yet?" Charlie asked.

"I only know chatter from around the station. They said they didn't know what caused it yet."

"I saw a report that said no one survived," Charlie replied.

Luc sighed.

"But divers have been down to the boat," the roommate continued. "It's empty. Dorian, Alaina, everyone is gone."

Luc stepped on to the curb.

"You seem exhausted," Charlie continued.

"I am. But let's keep walking. I got to change clothes, and the farther I can get from the police station, the club, everything, the better."

"Sure. Funny about the horse though, right?" Charlie asked.

"What do you mean?"

"Well, it's missing now too."

"Yeah, I saw them turn it loose on the riverbank yesterday," Luc confirmed. "It wasn't on the boat. I saw it run off."

"I mean, give it time, right?" Charlie said. "I'm sure they'll find it out in the suburbs."

"They might," Luc said with a shrug. Then he smiled. "Or maybe not."

Charlie turned down a narrow street, but Luc stopped at another corner.

"Where are you going?" Luc asked.

"Home. Why? Aren't you?"

"I don't know."

"C'mon Luc. You have got to get out of those clothes, man. I mean... those pants are in terrible shape."

"No, I know. But this just hit me: who cares? Let's get out of here. Let's go have an adventure," Luc said.

Charlie sighed. "You want to go after her, don't you?"

"Not in the least." Luc shrugged as he gazed off at the city. "I mean, let's get on a train. I don't even care which direction it goes. Let's get drunk in some small town or something."

Charlie walked back to Luc. "What happened to you in that police station, man? You get tased a few too many times?"

Luc smiled. "You coming with me?"

Acknowledgements

Thank you, Mollie, my wife and inspiration.

Jennifer Maxson (mom), thank you for editing the first draft of this book and steering it in the right direction. Without you, it would have been pretty bad.

Jay Pendrak, thank you for reading this in its entirety, being excited about it, and quoting Cravenmoore in casual settings. Honestly, that inspired me to keep going.

Ryan Felton, your contribution was huge. Thank you for your candid feedback and enthusiasm for the project. Every writer needs another writer friend like you.

Jonny Fruits, thank you for the great cover design for this work of fiction, especially since the whole town knows you're a late-nineteenth century historical non-fiction guy.

About the Author

Pres Maxson, by the numbers:

.00114	Height, in miles
163,904	Weight, in small marshmallows
107	Age, in pony years
15¾	Preferred bow tie size
13.4	Commute to work, in songs
9	Times per day imagines self as Indiana Jones
0	Times met Paul McCartney, unfortunately
7	Number of all-time favorite Chicago Cub
39	Number of piano keys almost never played
57-68	Preferred temperature, degrees in Fahrenheit
3	Go-to dance moves at parties
x	Articles of clothing worn daily
$2-.15x$	Height per slam dunk attempt, in feet
$2x+y$	Percentage of vent power in car, where y=heavy metal songs (note the slope)
01010000 01001101 01100001 01111000	Nickname, in binary code
2	Novels written, including this one

Made in the USA
Monee, IL
24 April 2022